A World of Our Own

A Journey of Love through Autism

AILEEN McCALLAN

POOLBEG

Published 2009
by Poolbeg Books Ltd.
123 Grange Hill, Baldoyle,
Dublin 13, Ireland
Email: poolbeg@poolbeg.com

Copyright for typesetting, layout, design
© Poolbeg Books Ltd.

1 3 5 7 9 10 8 6 4 2

A catalogue record for this book is available from the British Library.

ISBN 978-1-84223-371-9

Typeset by Type Design in Caslon 10.6/15
Printed and bound by
CPI Cox & Wyman, Reading, RG1 8EX

poolbeg.com

ABOUT THE AUTHOR

Aileen McCallan was born in County Tyrone. She worked as a lecturer and counsellor before giving up her career to care for her son with autism. She is the mother of three children.

ACKNOWLEDGEMENTS

Everything begins and ends with family, so to Mum and Dad, brothers Sean, Terry and Phelim and sisters Deirdre, Jacinta and Áine, who have always encouraged me in my endeavours, for the texts even when "Thumbs" didn't text back. I am blessed to have you as my family . . . also to all my in-laws for all your support.

To Christopher, for boiling the kettle and serving treats with warm loving hugs.

To Cian, for all you have taught me, for the back massage, for pulling me away from the PC to jump on the trampoline and curl up beside you on the sofa.

To my darling Laura for polishing my nails, for "making" my hair and applying Barbie's make-up and kisses to my face while I typed.

To Eamonn, for giving me permission to share our story. For sharing the bumpy road and a few hard lessons. For loving our children. You are a wonderful father.

To Brian Langan at Poolbeg Press for accepting a mumble jumble of my thoughts and believing in me that I could deliver a more articulate version.

To Martina for telling me I could and for Chris who told me I would.

To all my helpers, especially Bebhinn, for feeding my

darlings and entertaining them while I typed.

To Mary for allowing me to work among your personal things and for trusting me to feed the fish, especially Gordo, who liked to be alone.

To Donna, to whom this book is dedicated, to her husband Declan (hugs to Luan and Mia) and Donna's family. Your kindness is imprinted on my heart.

To my many many great friends who allowed me to find my way back myself.

To Maura and Mary and everyone at the Tara Centre in Omagh for lighting the way.

To everyone at ICRfm, The Inishowen Independent and Point2Point for the support and the craic.

To all parents of children with autism – those I know who share my journey, and those I don't who send me love, light and wisdom across the cyber waves.

To relations, friends and anyone who has ever put their hand in their pocket to support children with autism.

To Geraldine, for catching the typos and for capturing the moment on the cover of this book.

To Cian's cousins – too many to name but not too many to thank.

Warm and loving thanks to all.

For Donna

PREFACE

I wanted to write a book for as long as I can remember. I shared this burning ambition with my school friends once as we lay on our backs and watched the clouds float by. At that time my muses were probably Emily and Charlotte Brontë and Harper Lee. Little did I know the inspiration for my book would come from my own child.

Thus rests in your hands my book, hardly a masterpiece or even a unique story, as autism no longer can be considered a rare condition. Families the world over have been touched by autism. Personal experiences will differ from family to family but we all have one thing in common: we struggle for services in the shadow of systems that fail them. In this book I attempt to do two things: to give you a bird's-eye view of what it is like to live and love a child with autism in among those shadows; and to shatter a mindset of a dire prognosis, born when there was little known about autism and countless other disabilities, when individuals where doomed to institutions. Today, this mindset and poor prognosis still prevails and shrouds families affected by autism in a blanket of hopelessness. I want to roll back the blanket and blow the cover on a new autism that is treatable and celebrate the effective therapies and treatments that exist with a heartfelt wish that one day they will be accessible to all regardless of how big or small the progress is, and that families affected by autism and other disabilities will receive vital support services they so desperately need to be the best they can be. As sure as the sun rises in the morning, it offers each of us a new opportunity to see autism in a different light.

Wisdom becomes knowledge when it becomes your personal experience

PROLOGUE

How vulnerable he is. That's what I am thinking as I support the whole of him from slipping under. Warm milky bubbles spill over his softness as he pushes his chubby limbs out and in, lapping the water about the edges of his bright blue bathtub. A warm misty scent of lavender and a pale glow of yellow cocoons us. I am lost in the folds of his skin, in the depths of his eyes, in the sound of gurgles, cooing with pleasure. There is no denying it. Cian loves his bath.

A drone of traffic thickens and steals through an air vent high up on the wall of the small bathroom tucked away at the back of our home in County Tyrone. I lift my head. The belly of a dark December evening has settled against the mottled glass, like a black stain between the folds of muslin, hanging like clotted cream about the window frame. There is little need to disturb the pretty seashell tiebacks; the star-patterned material would only hang like a veil and is too transparent to curb the swell of the dark. I need to get a blind. One of those bamboo types held up with string. That would be nice.

Every now and then an orange shimmer travels across the glass. Car wheels creep and stall on driveways. I can almost taste the relief as engines and working minds are switched off for the weekend. A bubble of excitement builds up inside me. We are going away. Leaning forward, my hands scoop Cian's squishy body out of the frothy water and I wrap him in a fluffy white towel.

His damp body moulds round me. I gather him to me like I will never let him go, smelling him, kissing his floppy black hair and rubbing his cute button nose against mine. Full plum lips spread into a wide toothless grin while his lake-green eyes gaze at me under the longest lashes any girl would die for. Just like my first-born, he is the nearest thing to perfection I have ever seen. Cuddling him close and humming a lullaby, I rummage around inside the hot press for a babygro, silently thanking God for another wonderful boy, our little laughing angel.

In the bedroom he cuddles and pulls at a fluffy black-and-white Dalmatian dog while I chat to him and smear hydrocortisone cream over the angry blotches of infected eczema on the backs of his arms and knees. I attempt to dab a little on his smarting red cheeks, but Cian objects and grabs at my hands.

"Okay. I don't like it either, boss."

I screw the lid back on the tube and dress him. Thinking. He will soon need a bigger babygro. Cian coughs intermittently and I place my ear on his chest, hoping he isn't coming down with something again. He has only just finished an antibiotic! The rattle of the front door interrupts my thoughts. Just as I squeeze Cian's toes into a pair of soft Santa booties, our mischievous two-year-old bursts into the bedroom, landing on top of me.

"We got diesel. We got diesel. I wanna go. I wanna go now!"

Turning my attention to Christopher, I tickle him until he is begging me to stop.

Cian gurgles and looks on while Christopher squeals and kicks.

"Daddy, DADDY, HELP!"

Eamonn appears at the bedroom door, car keys in hand.

"Everything's ready. The car's full of diesel, the whole of Mothercare is in the boot and all the bags – except this one."

He shoves the keys into his pocket, makes an eagle-swoop for Christopher and disappears down the hallway with his son hanging upside-down over his shoulder, protesting and kicking wildly.

We are going away to Donegal, to the Redcastle Hotel on the north coast, two nights' B&B with one evening meal, family room with sea view. A little pre-Christmas break. It is our first break away with the two of them. We can't wait.

We will snuggle up on crisp white sheets and watch *Postman Pat* videos instead of the news. The kids will make a mess while we make plans. We will ride on a train going nowhere and eat chips and red sauce out of brown paper bags. We will change their nappies and they will change our minds. We will build sandcastles with blue buckets and yellow spades and wish we could live by the sea. We will take them for a drive to rock them to sleep and they will take us for a pair of idiots as they look back at us in the mirror. When finally their eyelids droop we will turn the car and tuck them into bed, crash in an exhausted heap, munch on chocolate and marvel at the two of them. Sometime later when their bodies are still with sleep our bodies will surrender to each other and there we will stay until Cian stirs and Christopher bounces on top of us, wanting to know if spiders can fly.

And now the car engine is running. It is time to go. I slip on my jacket and take a last glance round me, hoping I haven't forgotten anything. My eyes fall on a faded photograph of my grandmother's wedding day. I never knew my grandfather, but it is only three years since Granny Drummond passed away. She is alive in my memory. I touch the pewter frame, admire her wedding hat again and say a prayer.

Look over us, Granny, and keep us safe on our journey.

I turn to Cian. He is gazing at me, deeply, solemnly.

"There is wisdom in those eyes," I smile.

I lift him and fix him in the curl of my arm. He answers me with a steady angelic gaze. *Like he knows.*

Something about his serenity troubles me. I suddenly pull him to me, gripped by a thought. *If anything ever happens you, I could not bear it.*

* * *

I was not to know that moment would spill over in my memory for years to come. I was not to know a cruel, unforgiving condition might have already taken hold of my innocent child. Creeping up quietly, like a thief in the night, stealing the smile from his face and the twinkle from his eyes. I was not to know it would permeate every aspect of our existence and rock the very foundations of our happy family life, challenging all that was familiar, changing our lives forever.

1

Wrenching the back door open, I take a gulp of the sobering October breeze. A moment of panic rips through my insides. We have just been celebrating Christopher's third birthday . . .

"Happy Birthday to you,"

Chirpy voices hush and the hum of adult conversation fades as everyone joins in.

"Happy Birthday to you,"

I make my way past a row of smiling faces and beam at my "big" three-year-old, jigging up and down, dwarfed by the size of the large solid pine carver chair he is standing on.

"Happy Birthday, dear Christopher,"

His mouth opens and his chunky hands clap at the sight of his birthday cake, a long green spotty caterpillar, loaded with chocolate and brightly coloured Smarties with three blue-striped candles twinkling on his back.

"Happy Birthday to you."

"HIP, HIP, HOORAY!"

Cheers fill the room.

I place the "caterpillar" at a safe distance in front of him, next to his birthday cards, all wishing him love and fun on his third birthday. Eamonn is standing on the other side of the chair, his arms outstretched, ready to catch Christopher should he fall. The sheen of the candles dances and sways, reflecting pure glee in Christopher's eyes. Eamonn cups his hand between the candle flames and his little fingers. Cameras flash and click.

"Smile!"

I quickly scan the room for Cian. It would be nice to get a photo of them together. But the cheering has started. Christopher is already pulling in his breath. Eamonn reaches behind him and wraps his arm about my shoulders. Our proud three-year-old son is standing between us, grinning from ear to ear. This is his moment.

One big puff and the candles are blown out.

"Look up."

Eamonn squeezes my neck and I smile.

Snap.

The family photo is taken. The video camcorder records the scene. Mum, Dad and Christopher. Cian is missing.

Christopher's guests bob up and down, lining both sides of the table.

"Okay, who wants a piece?"

My voice is a little forced.

"I do."

"I do."

"Me too."

"Can I have the piece with a smartie in it?"

"I want some blue icing."

"I only want icing."

Riddled with orders, I cut and paste several pieces of birthday cake onto floppy paper plates. The lights are turned back on. Conversation among aunties and uncles, grannies and granddads, neighbours and friends, rise again behind the high-backed farmhouse chairs. Christopher is still standing on top of the chair. His cheeks, forehead and chin are smeared with chocolate and cream as he munches happily on his birthday cake.

Before long, all the little ones are suitably content. Cian returns to my mind. I glance round the room.

Where is he?

"Will I make a cup of tea?" my sister Jacinta asks, quite familiar with the amnesia that takes us over at busy birthday parties.

"Of course, go ahead."

I move towards the kitchen.

Where is Cian?

"Can I have more Coke?"

A flushed face peers up at me.

"Sure, give me your cup."

Seizing a large bottle of Coke from the kitchen worktop, I twist the cap, and begin to pour the fizzy Coke into a pale red plastic beaker. I survey the kitchen and dining area again. Coke fizzles to the top, spilling and spitting over the sides, like my overloaded mind.

Eamonn is opening a birthday gift for Christopher. A new *Postman Pat* video.

"Will you put it on, Daddy?"

James tugs at my arm. "When are we going to play the

games?" Ronan needs his lace tied. Katie is crying. Liam wants a party bag. Fintan trips and cuts his knee. I look for sticky plasters and check in the toy box in the wardrobe for Cian but he is not there. A balloon bursts. Kevin blows up some more balloons. Ellen can't get the toilet door open. Party horns shriek. Megan won't give Eva her straw. Little feet, running here and there. Sticky fingers clutch cake and paper cups, and half-eaten cocktail sausages.

"Do you want tea or coffee, Aileen?" Jacinta shouts at me over the din.

"Coffee, please, thanks."

I mindfully step over the *Postman Pat* fanatics settling down to watch the new video and mutter gingerly to Eamonn.

"I can't find Cian."

Eamonn gets to his feet, scrunching a pile of disused birthday wrapping into a ball.

"He's probably in the toy box in the wardrobe. That's where he usually is."

"No, he's not there. I've already looked."

Ursula taps Eamonn's side.

"They can't hear it."

Eamonn points the remote at the television and I mutter to no one in particular.

"Have you seen Cian?"

Everyone joins in.

"Where's Cian?"

". . . Anyone seen Cian?"

"Cian?"

"CIANNNN?"

Sarah Jane and Patrick get up from the table.

"We'll look outside."

"I'll look in the bedrooms," Jemma shouts.

"He couldn't be too far away." Mammy reassures me.

A little arm pulls the end of my jumper.

"Where's my cardigan? I'm cold."

"Okay, I'll get it. What does it look like?"

My head is spinning.

"It has butterflies on it and it is green and it is mine."

The little voice sounds as anxious as me.

I reassure her in the most cheerful and calm voice I can muster.

"Okay. Don't worry. I'll find it."

Pushing the door of the utility open, I walk towards the bundle of jumpers and coats on the worktop. I can just about make out a tiny piece of mint-green, woolly material buried under a mountain of blues and reds and greys.

Retrieving the cardigan from the pile, I turn and hand it to the little girl. She skips off as a blue and yellow striped jumper plummets to the floor. I bend to pick it up and, at the same time, catch sight of the top of Cian's head behind a pile of washing. He is pulling at the threads of a cream blanket hanging out of the wash basket.

I catch my breath for a second.

"My goodness, Cian! You gave me a fright."

He doesn't look up. I reach for him, laughing with relief. He gives me a fleeting smile but displays no signs of anxiety or upset.

Gráinne pops her head round the door, radiating energy. She thanks me for the great party, apologises profusely that she has to leave because she has to pick someone up in Omagh, reassures me that Megan and Eva had a ball and

11

asks if I have seen their coats. She catches her breath and at the same time suddenly becomes aware of Cian in my arms.

"Oh! You found him!"

I nod my head as I point to the large bundle of discarded coats and jumpers.

Gráinne moves past me and begins to fumble through the piles of clothes.

"Where was he?"

"In here, playing with the dirty washing!"

She gasps.

"All on his own?"

She swings round, clutching two shocking pink duffels belonging to her twins.

"Wish my girls would go off somewhere and give my head peace for five minutes," she jokes. "You are so lucky. He is soooo good."

She touches Cian's toes and smiles at him. Cian pulls his feet away and gazes at the light hanging from the ceiling.

Tilting her head to one side, she runs a hand down his back.

"Isn't he placid and so content? My girls are so demanding. They have me running rings round them."

"Your girls are not demanding. They just know what they want."

Slowly it is dawning on me that Cian is not demanding at all.

Gráinne bursts out laughing.

"God, they know what they want all right. They have me exhausted. I could do with Cian for a while. He is therapeutic!"

She touches him and looks into his face. Cian is resting

12

his head against mine, still watching the light above my head.

How can he gaze so steady at a sixty-watt naked bulb without blinking?

"He really is *so* content. It's like . . . he's in a little world of his own."

Gráinne laughs affectionately, checks her watch, groans with frustration and tells me she really needs to be going. Clutching the coats, she walks back into the kitchen again, totally oblivious that her words have rooted me to the spot.

"Cian is found, everyone, call the search party off, he's found, and he is fine."

I hear her calling, letting everyone know that Cian is safe and well.

Others join in.

"It's okay, Cian's found."

"Where was he?"

"He's here."

"He's found."

"In the utility."

"Cian's found."

He's fine.

Everyone relaxes except me.

I am staring at Cian as though I have never seen him before. *If Cian is found why does he look so very lost?*

Leaning against the utility wall for support, I know something is not right. He should have been in the middle of everything. He should have, at least, been upset. Gráinne's words hang around me like a thick fog.

". . . in a world of his own . . ."

I have heard that phrase somewhere before, when I

13

worked in the area of special needs groups many years ago. I cannot focus. I feel nauseated. I need air. Wrenching the back door open I take a gulp of the sobering October breeze. A moment of panic rips through my insides, the first of many moments to come.

2

Moments. That's it. A series of moments held in a memory. Some so vivid, as if it happened yesterday. Some foggy and confused, like some mixed-up nightmare. It is hard to pinpoint the exact moment, the heart-stopping moment when we realised something monstrous was taking place, something that was about to flip our world.

Maybe it was when he disappeared at Christopher's birthday party; or that day when I call to see Ann, and her husband Dominic comes from outside and joins us in the kitchen.

"Is your wee lad hard of hearing?"

"No, not that I know of. Why?"

"He was standing looking at the trees in the garden. I called several times, but he never looked round."

Maybe it is the day in the park when my mother and I frantically dance and point and probe the air, willing Cian to look up at the thick line of smoke and the Boeing 747 roaring above his head. He doesn't look up.

I flop down on a bench and look all about me, everything a blur. I can sense it then. Something coming . . . something fast and furious . . . I can hear the rumble . . . the thumping in my side. I look at Mum, the strain etched in her face. She doesn't look at me.

* * *

Cian was an easy, happy baby, full of smiles and mischief.

"No," he would snigger, his finger wagging, copying me when I scolded him for going near the fire. He was a good eater and a great sleeper. He spent most of his time rummaging around toy boxes and hiding in kitchen cupboards, creating havoc wherever he went. He was a pretty active boy and had an infectious giggle. He loved the sound of music and the scrape of our front door against the tiles when Daddy came home.

"Dadada, Dadada," he would shout as he ran to meet him. He would share some new words like "zar" (star), "duck" and "a-e-po" (octopus). And we would laugh and tell him he was wonderful. And life went on, filling up our memories with scattered moments, but none of them bothered us that much. We failed to notice the signs.

The only thing that did concern us was the recurring infections that never seemed to go away. His temperature flared up almost daily and parts of his face and body broke out in an angry skin rash. Sometimes the eczema bled, causing Cian great distress. We spent a lot of time going to the doctor and returning home laden with antibiotics and hydrocortisone cream. This worried us because Christopher had never needed a doctor or antibiotics. We also felt a bit silly running to the doctor with eczema and minor illnesses that were treated as normal childhood complaints.

* * *

On a chilly November morning when Cian is fifteen months old, Eamonn bundles him up in his little woolly hat and "boiler suit" and takes him to the health centre for his MMR vaccine. He is sleeping and he doesn't stir, so Eamonn says, his voice full of regret, like it isn't right somehow. The next day Cian has a low-grade temperature and is lethargic. His ears and his eczema are bothering him again.

A few nights later, at bath-time, Cian stares intently at my lips. He is trying to say the word "duck", a word he has said many times before, but now it is barely a whisper.

Is he lip-reading? Surely I would have noticed if he did that before? Maybe he's deaf!

I share my concerns with Eamonn, who quickly dismisses the thought.

"He can't be deaf. Look!"

Eamonn punches the button of the remote control. On comes the TV and in races Cian. He loves music, funny voices and familiar jingles, like the introduction to *Coronation Street*. Nothing is strange about that; Christopher loves them too. We all breathe a sigh of relief, only catching it every now and then if he doesn't turn as quickly as we expect or doesn't look where we are pointing. Truth is, his behaviour is terribly inconsistent.

* * *

For the next few months, we sway in and out of concern. Most of the time I am very distracted, no matter where I am. I can't get Cian out of my head, even during Margaret's "hen night" in Letterkenny.

"Just because Christopher is so bright doesn't mean you are going to have two geniuses in the house," Anne laughs, making light of my concerns and no doubt trying to make me feel better. It is true. My first-born is very inquisitive and mature for his small years. He prefers to watch the Discovery Channel and nature programmes than watch cartoons but still, my insides jitter. No one seems to see what I can see.

"Cian doesn't come to his name any more and he has stopped talking," I persist, tears welling up in my eyes.

"He's only a toddler, for God's sake! I know loads of kids that don't talk until they go to school," Clare reassures me.

* * *

I am almost convinced they are right, until one evening I drop Christopher off at a birthday party and pick up Eamonn.

As I pull up, Eamonn waves and strides towards us. He strains his neck to catch sight of two chubby faces in the back seat.

"Where's Christopher?" he asks as he pulls the car door open.

"At Patrick's birthday party."

"Ah, that's right," nodding his head, remembering. "So how are you?" He smiles, leaning into the car.

"Good. I've made a curry."

"Great, I'm starving."

He turns his attention to Cian. Placing one knee on the passenger's seat, he hides his face behind the headrest, reaches down the sides of the seat towards Cian and roars in a deep loud voice. "Where's the bear . . . where's the bear? Is he over here or is he over there?" He waves frantically at the words "here" and "there", then peeks his head over the headrest and laughs out loud. "I'm coming to get you! I'm coming to get YOU! Here's the BEARRRR!"

He grabs Cian's feet and runs his fingers up Cian's legs to his stomach. Cian squirms in his seat, barely looking at him. Eamonn suddenly stops and looks at him. He throws a glance my way before turning towards Cian again.

"You not well, wee man? Is my wee soldier not fit to fight today? Oh, what's the matter? Tell Daddy all about it. Come on. Whose boy are you?"

Eamonn rubs the bare feet and pulls Cian's toes as he gazes into Cian's face. Cian does not return his gaze. Instead, his blank, vacant gaze bypasses him and stretches into the grey evening mist, beyond the car windscreen. He is still and quiet.

"Ah, come on, Cian . . . give us a song . . . what do you say? Maybe you're tired, like your ould man. Is that what's wrong? Ah, sure we can't play when we're tired."

He pats Cian's knee gently before turning round into a seated position. I do not look but stare into the grey night too.

Eamonn clicks his seatbelt into place.

"Did he sleep today?" A hint of anxiety quickens his tone.

"No, he didn't." My voice sounds small.

"He's tired then?"

I fumble with the car keys.

"Yeah, I guess he is."

The deafening silence weighs heavily in the air we share.

What is wrong with Cian? Why did he not shriek with laughter? Where are the frantic kicks of excitement? Why did he not react?

The car jolts forward as I let off the brake. My heart is thumping so hard I can't hear the car engine. I start to pray, frantically, in silence.

Sacred Heart of Jesus, I place all my trust in thee. Please God don't let there be anything wrong with Cian. Please let him be okay. Granny, please help us.

All the while, I am writing a "to-do" list in my head. It begins: *Ring health visitor first thing tomorrow morning.*

* * *

Later, when the curry is eaten and the boys are asleep, Eamonn makes tea and we talk about Cian. The kettle bubbles and clicks off. Eamonn detaches the lead and starts to pour the hot water over his tea bag in his cup.

"What do you think is wrong?"

"I don't know. I don't want to think that anything is wrong but he has been a bit quiet lately, don't you think?"

I put some dishes in the dishwasher.

"Maybe he's sick or uncomfortable or something. Maybe he is teething. Do you want a coffee?"

"Okay."

I don't want coffee but I answer out of habit. I plop down

at the dining table, suddenly feeling weary. The silence between us is broken only by the opening of a cupboard or closing of a jar. Eamonn wrestles with the wrapping of a packet of Hobnobs and I suddenly feel angry and envious all at the same time.

How can he think of eating at a time like this?

He manages to get the packet open and offers me one. I shake my head and he sets the packet down on the counter. He munches on the chocolate-coated biscuit as he completes the mundane ritual of tea-making. I watch him concentrating, wondering what he is thinking about. Three Hobnobs down and I'm thinking it must be true – nothing comes between a man and his stomach. Eamonn wipes his mouth with the back of his hand, puts the Hobnobs away and turns towards me.

"His eczema is bad again too, and that can't be too pleasant for him; and," he turns and points a spoon at me, "he had that awful throat last week."

He continues to stir his tea ferociously and pours a drop of milk into my cup.

"Well, I was thinking we should get him checked out with the health visitor."

I take the cup of coffee Eamonn is reaching out to me. It is hot and comforting. The aroma reminds me of Little Italy in a Melbourne suburb many moons ago when all I had to worry about was the price of a tram ticket.

"Well, it will do no harm." He remains standing, sipping his tea and munching furiously. "When are you thinking of contacting her?"

"Tomorrow."

"Tomorrow?" Eamonn looks up over the steam rising

from his cup. "You're on the ball. I'll not be about tomorrow. I'm working in Monaghan."

"That's okay. Sure, you don't really need to be here. She'll only have a look at him and I'll ask her what she thinks."

"Okay then, that'll do."

Eamonn takes a sip of his tea and walks into the living room and lifts the remote. The television hums and Eamonn stands in the doorway. Frank Mitchell is presenting the latest UTV weather forecast. He warns that temperatures are going to drop, to watch out for icy patches. The dry spell is over and we need to expect heavy rain in places. I look up at the sky. A huge blanket of dark cloud is draped over our home, holding its breath. I place my elbows on the table and put my head in my hands.

Frank wishes us all a very pleasant evening and the advertisments come on before the early evening news. Eamonn turns towards me.

"I'm sure he's grand though. He just isn't well, poor mite."

He turns back into the living room and settles down on the sofa to find out what's happening in the rest of the world, leaving me lost in mine. A nagging feeling somewhere deep in the pit of my stomach tells me I am not sure that Cian is grand. I am not sure at all.

3

The health visitor comes and goes in late January. Her visit is short, with no major revelations. Cian plays quietly with his toys while she observes him. He is not engaging, but her presence doesn't bother him. Every now and then he glances at *Rugrats* on the television. The health visitor moves his toys about and talks to him. He doesn't take much notice; she doesn't find that unusual.

"Many children refuse to engage with other adults when their mother is present," I am reassured. If the health visitor has any immediate concerns she doesn't show it, but she agrees to refer him for further assessment, "to be on the safe side." We talk for a short while. Before she leaves she nods in the direction of the boys.

"Is it any wonder the little man isn't talking?"

Christopher has cornered Cian in a chair. A pile of crisps are lined up on the arm of the chair while Cian happily munches his way through the savoury feast.

"That's another reason for slow speech. Older children often tend to the younger ones' needs, which prevents them fending for themselves," she offers.

More reassurance, more denial.

* * *

The letter for the assessment arrives, as does the day of the appointment, three months after the health visitor's visit. A clear blue sky yawns and delivers April sunshine. Everything is brilliant and bright. Life is good – not perfect, but good. I set out for work as usual, feeling less hurried. I had given up a full-time pastoral support role in a local secondary school for a part-time counselling position in the local college before any suspicion had arisen about Cian's development. This was a time when I had decided to put my career on hold to spend more time with the boys and with my parents. I had made the right choice. There is more time to enjoy the boys and I love the afternoons when we go swimming or visit Granny and Granddad and still have plenty of time to prepare for dinner before Daddy arrives home.

It is during this time that our worries begin to fester about Cian, but we are less concerned since the health visitor came. Cian is such a happy child and he is always humming a tune. He seems to have an ear for music and he likes nursery rhymes and books. He enjoys simple games like hide-and-seek and playing in his push-along car. Christopher is still doing loads for him, and enjoys "babying" his younger brother, so we let him be.

"They will grow up and grow away from each other soon enough," my mother assures me.

His physical condition continues to worry us, however. Even family members start to notice. Eamonn's brother-in-law makes a comment one morning when Cian is lying on the sofa, listless and pale.

"That young boy of yours is always sick."

His casual remark troubles me. Sean doesn't see Cian that often but Cian is always sick when he does. Our baby is so poorly that the endless stream of complaints almost become the norm – diarrhoea, vomiting, infected lesions, tonsillitis, head colds, pharyngitis, croup. There is no end to it, and no end to the antibiotics, Calpol and Fucidon.

* * *

As I join the slow-moving traffic worming its way into Omagh, the news on Radio Ulster filters in and out of my consciousness – the latest on the peace process, the rise in drug use. A traffic warden appears from nowhere and starts to direct traffic, speaking to each driver as they pass. I turn down the radio volume, roll down my window and wait my turn. When I reach him, he informs me of a diversion ahead.

I drive on, turn right and turn the radio up again, just catching the tail-end of an interview – something to do with Autism Week.

"AUTISM?" I spit the word out into the empty car. It takes me a while to connect.

What did she say? What week? That word. Something about that word?

I turn up the volume. The presenter is thanking the guest for her time and announcing the latest road traffic news just as I drive through the college gates.

As I walk towards my office, a young girl comes running towards me to cancel an appointment. Post is placed in my hand. Someone calls out, "Morning." I barely lift my head as I fumble with a set of keys to unlock the door. A voice calls out to me.

"Aileen, there will be a fire drill today at ten o'clock."

I turn in the direction of the voice, nod but see no one, nothing. I shove through the gaping door. The "College Counsellor" sign rattles as the door slams behind me. Everything sprawls on the floor as my body slumps in a chair. The radio announcement about Autism Awareness Week floods my mind. Autism – a condition I had read about at university. I had written an essay about it, for God's sake. But it is a rare condition – *what was it* . . . I struggle to remember the statistic . . . *one in a million? Thousands, anyway.* The special needs adults I worked with; out of the whole centre, only one of them was autistic. He was in my group. He couldn't talk and used to sit on the floor and try to look up my skirt. *Jesus!* I would scold and he would laugh, the innocence hanging out of him. *God!* He lived in a world of his own.

Isn't that how Gráinne described Cian on Christopher's birthday?

I close my eyes and try to focus on my breathing. Cian's appointment with the community paediatrician is today at two o'clock. Eamonn and I have barely talked about it. After all, I am just being OTT, comparing my first child to my second. All the little moments start to clump together and spin my head like a washing machine overdosed with detergent. I try to focus on my desk, my diary and the walls. For the first time I notice that there is no window in my room. I never missed it before. How did I not miss a window? Even a prison cell has a window. The thump in my side gets louder and louder . . . I can feel it now, the hollow in my stomach stretching, something gripping, chilling me . . . tightening the muscles in my neck . . . it's getting closer . . . the fear of it . . .

* * *

The morning sun stays around and makes for a bright warm afternoon. I collect Christopher from nursery and Cian from Margaret, our childminder. Eamonn arrives home early to accompany me to the health centre. Christopher jigs up and down beside me.

"Please, Mammy, can we have a barbecue? Please, pretty please?"

"Well, maybe, after we come back from the town." I fasten Cian's seatbelt.

"Oh goodie, I'll make a list in my head of what we need."

He runs around the front of the car and hops into the back seat beside Cian. Eamonn locks the front door and offers to help Christopher with his seatbelt. Christopher pushes his hand away and gives him a stern look.

"I can put on my seatbelt. I can do it myself!"

"Okay, Mr Independent, let me hear the click."

Christopher struggles with the belt and Eamonn and I look at each other. We could be to Omagh and back before we hear the click but we are so proud of "Mr Independent", we just wait and say nothing. On the way to the appointment, Christopher talks non-stop about the barbecue. He is so excited. He wants to know what we are going to barbecue.

"How about some pig's trotters?" Eamonn teases.

Christopher squeals and Cian pulls at his blue and yellow Winnie the Pooh socks. I can see him in the passenger mirror above my head.

He is happy, that's all that matters. I reassure myself once again that everything is just fine.

Pulling up at the health clinic, Eamonn suggests I go with Cian and he will stay with Christopher.

"Better you go, Aileen. You know more than me about these things and you could do without a few distractions." He winks at me as Christopher chips in.

"I want to go with Mummy."

Eamonn swings round.

"But we have a barbecue to organise, buster, and you are our personal assistant."

Christopher laughs and we all join in.

"Sure, we'll only be a few minutes."

I lift Cian out of his car seat and allow him to run on before me.

* * *

Inside I find myself waiting in a long narrow corridor where someone has gone mad with mouldy-coloured green paint. Cian runs up and down the corridor, over and over. Eamonn's words haunt me. Why does he think I know more about these situations than he does? I wish he was here with me now.

A door opens. A petite lady with swarthy skin and dark

eyes steps into the corridor. She is clicking a blue ballpoint pen.

"Cian McCallan?"

Cian is running towards me at high speed. I grab him, just in time, before he careers into the lady.

"This is Cian." I smile.

She looks at him briefly.

"Apologies," she offers, flashing a professional, measured smile. "We are a little behind schedule this afternoon. Come in."

Her long dark wavy hair is tied loosely at the nape of her neck. Small obstinate curls escape and dangle, gently framing her fresh face. The air plays with her silky floral top as it floats and swings behind her. She is very pretty and very pregnant.

Cian stands in the doorway taking in his surroundings. It is not a room that Cian will want to stay in for very long. It is small and boxy, and Cian takes up position at the one small window to the left of the door. I stand awkwardly, not quite sure whether to sit or remain standing. I decide to sit.

". . . health visitor?" The paediatrician is staring at me from behind a desk, thumbing some letters in a file.

"Sorry, yes. The health visitor referred him, just to be on the safe side." Her eyes study my face for a moment and roam over Cian before settling on the notes in front of her again. She asks me a few questions about Cian's development, writes down a few notes and abandons her desk again to examine Cian. With my help, she weighs and measures him. Cian wriggles and giggles as she pokes and prods, listening to his heart and checking his abdomen.

Without comment she jots down some more notes as I do my baby up again.

I try to straighten his clothes but I would have better luck dressing an eel. After washing her hands the paediatrician watches Cian knock over some blocks that are perched on top of a table. She tries to encourage him to build them. He hovers over them, momentarily, proceeding to flutter around the room like a butterfly in a garden full of flowers. He eventually settles at the small window and stares into the open space beyond the glass. I sit in the opposite corner. Sun rains down on our heads through Velux windows while the paediatrician tries to engage my baby in the most rudimentary dialogue and predetermined tasks designed to assess his speech and language development. Cian is more interested in the trees swaying outside the window. As his body sways in rhythm with the trees, the doctor's gaze becomes more intense. Her mouth turns downs and her eyebrows frown as she observes my darling boy.

I can taste it now, it's coming at me; I suck in some air and wait for her to give me a lecture for comparing my two children. She will tell me I am an over-protective mother and advise me not to expect so much from such a young child and send me home to enjoy him. Any time now she will tell me I have nothing to worry about, that my nagging concerns were unwarranted. Any time now . . . but she doesn't speak. Her gaze is blank and emotionless. She is trying to engage my son but Cian is ignoring her, walking aimlessly round the room, touching the walls, more like a small tiger pacing around a zoo enclosure than a butterfly now. The silence is deafening. She finally leaves Cian to pace and squeezes her tidy bump in behind her heavy desk again.

"Hmmm . . . I shall refer him on. It's difficult. There is a waiting list. If he's in the system . . . We'll start with hearing."

The paediatrician does not look at me but remains detached. The pretty mother-to-be is talking to the table now, something about waiting lists, the different assessments, the urgency of getting him in the queue, but I am no longer processing her words or looking at her. I am looking at Cian and his pale angelic innocent face pushed against the cool glass, oblivious to the words that hang in the air, marking his fate.

I am unable to respond, stunned, swooning like a bird after nose-diving into polished glass. I want to get out but I can't feel my limbs. A lump throbs in my throat and I swallow hard. Cian rockets towards me and nails me to the wall. I wrap my arms around him, clutching him to me to save him from this devastating fate. The silence engulfs me, the unknowing petrifies me, the helplessness breaks me, and hot, burning tears spill over the back of Cian's t-shirt, faster than I can will them to stop. I need out.

"It's you and me, kid. Let's go."

My voice is croaky, dull. The pen stops scribbling. Silence. I struggle to squeeze my toddler into a pair of Clark's shoes. The pen nib starts to scrape again, across the damning form that has Cian's name written all over it. Whatever training she got for remaining detached has stood her in good stead. I stand up and gather our things. I try to compose myself, and clear my throat. A distant shaky voice that sounds nothing like mine speaks.

31

"I would like Cian to be assessed at once. We might go private to kill the waiting time, to know for sure what . . ." My voice trails. I swallow hard. I don't know what I am talking about. I don't know where I am going to go but I know we need a name. We need a reason. We need help. "Would it be possible to have a letter or some verification?"

"Of course. I'll do something out but it will not be until the end of the week? I will leave it for you at reception, but I have to warn you, the Education Board does not accept a private assessment. They only accept their own."

She bows her head again and continues to scribble.

"Thanks, I'll collect it then." I ignore her warning. I am much too upset to comment or debate about the internal politics of Education Boards but somehow I know that hurdle number one has just been thrown at me.

I walk back down the corridor and wonder if it is ever going to end – the spinning. Cian runs alongside me, happy, free and heedless of it all.

* * *

We eventually arrive at the car. Daddy and Christopher are laughing and joking, the way we left them. They are sitting in the sunshine with an agreed list for the barbecue.

Christopher is bouncing up and down.

"Daddy said we are all going to get ice cream if I was good and Cian was good, Mammy. And I *was* good, Mammy. Wasn't I good, Daddy?"

"You were, son. You're our wee star."

Eamonn reaches for Cian and lifts him into his baby seat.

I watch him struggle to close the safety catch and look at his face.

"Mammy, was Cian a good boy?" Christopher persists but I am unable to speak.

Eamonn makes no reference to the appointment or what has taken place. I know why.

"Was he, Mammy?"

This is the way it is supposed to be.

"Mammy, was Cian a good boy, Mammy?"

Just routine. Nothing to worry about. I can't tell him. I look away and bite my lip.

"Mammy, was Cian a good boy, Mammy?"

I swallow my anxiety and hope they cannot hear it.

"Yes, yes, yes. He was Chrisy. He was."

"Goodie. We are all going to get ice-cream."

Eamonn laughs and tickles Cian's toes.

"Maybe Cian doesn't want any?"

He tickles Cian's toes and runs his hands up to his neck, leaving Cian squealing with delight.

"Daddy, Cian does want ice cream."

He snorts and folds his arms at the idea of someone not wanting ice cream.

"You're a silly billy, Daddy."

Eamonn laughs and we both climb into the front of the car.

"Can we get the ice cream now, Daddy?"

Uniformed children walk past, laughing and talking with their friends.

"I want some pink icecream."

The traffic is building up, with workers making their way home. A young mother is bending over a pram, attending to a baby smothered in baby-blue fluffy blankets.

My, how we protect them.

Shoppers and dog owners are still out walking, going about their business, enjoying the afternoon sunshine. The world has not ended after all. I just feel like it has. Everything and everyone is well and we are going to get ice cream.

I try not to look at Eamonn. He is leaning back, pulling Christopher's legs, telling him pink is only for girls. Christopher is disgusted and folds his arms. I close my eyes against the glare of the sun and the spin in my head.

No, there is no need to tell him just yet. We shall have our barbecue. He will know soon enough.

4

Not long after the pediatrician's assessment, Cian is called for a hearing test – a brain stem evoked audiogram.

It is ten o'clock in the morning. We are shown into a tiny ward, equipped with a hospital bed, a small sink and some breathing apparatus attached to a wall on the left-hand side. A faded floral curtain shields us from the rest of the hospital.

Cian must be sedated before a number of tubes are attached to his head.

Sleep doesn't come easy. For hours we try to humour a very unsettled little boy who tries to escape past the curtain a million times over. With his back against the floor, he slides and pushes himself round and round with his heels. He jumps on the bed, up and down, up and down, and turns the taps on and off, despite our protests. The heat in the hospital is exhausting. Lunchtime comes and goes and Eamonn and I are both starving and completely worn out.

Eventually we allow him to stand at the sink and let the water from a running tap spill through his fingers.

Sometime in the early afternoon a tall, sophisticated lady consultant in a slim white coat comes to check up on his progress, or rather lack of it. She arrives with noisy heels and a wide smile. Our frazzled fed-up son is lying in a twisted knotted position on top of the bed, humming "Incy-Wincy Spider". For a brief moment she towers over him, her fist on her hip and her elbow in mid-air with her head tilted to one side.

Turning her head towards me she peers over her spectacles.

"Do you think he has a hearing problem?"

Her voice is solemn and terribly posh.

"No." My answer is matter-of-fact.

"Nor do I." She shakes her head and looks at Cian. "He has perfect pitch." Bending slightly, she tousles Cian's hair. "And you are a very good boy," she adds in a slightly animated voice.

She studies Cian's face. His eyes do not return her gaze but fall on a shiny badge in the lapel of her coat. He reaches to touch it and she remains in a compromising position, allowing him to explore the smooth metal edges with his fingers. A moment later, she pats his head again and gently removes his hand.

"Good boy," she whispers. Nodding at the nurse, she steps back into the corridor and tugs the curtain back in place. The click of her heels echo down the corridor and eventually fade away. An hour later, Cian fades into a false sleep. The procedure seems futile but the test must be completed so hearing can be ruled out.

The results are normal. Cian is not deaf. It is no consolation. I had secretly hoped there was something wrong with his ears. Ears can be fixed. Deaf people can live normal lives. They do not live in a world of their own. Fear fills the empty hollow inside me. We leave the hospital after four o'clock just as the tangerine sun darkens and dips in the sky.

* * *

The next afternoon I collect the community paediatrician's letter. A flock of crows flap into the air as I walk out of the health centre clutching the letter.

Schoolgirls giggle on a pavement bench. Someone brushes past, oblivious to the turmoil reeling inside me. A bell tolls in the distance and the schoolgirls move on. My body weighs heavily as I sit and rest my back against the bench. I say a prayer and rip open the envelope.

"I would be grateful if you could see this 21-month-old boy as soon as possible."

It continues with a few details about the pregnancy, delivery, and the results of the medical examination. My eyes scan over the familiar information until the last paragraph.

"Developmentally, however, there is evidence of severe global delay . . . behaviour . . . unusual . . . didn't respond . . . even to loud clapping . . . no eye contact at all . . . impossible to engage in any activity."

Global. I glare at that one word. It grows on the page, balloons out into the space around me, behind me, above me. Everything is global these days – global warming, global

37

pollution. Now my son has global delay. The enormity of the word does not escape me. I lift my head. I hear nothing. See nothing. A white blur stupefies me.

I check the letter, the name, address and date a dozen times, in case there has been a mistake. Cian's name is on it, all over it. A name is so important. It is what defines you. Cian is short, brief and uncomplicated. It is an old Irish name meaning "ancient warrior, enduring". In legend, Cian was the son of Dian Cecht, God of Healing of the Tuatha Dé Danann. I look at his name, the name we had chosen. *The only name we had chosen.* He was destined to be a boy . . . but a boy with no name? The white blur speeds up. *Will he ever know his name?* The black print on the page becomes fuzzy and unfocused. My frozen hands fall to my knees, gripping the damning piece of paper. A howling wind tortures the corners of the letter and the leaves about my feet. Rain begins to spit but I feel nothing. I am not here.

I am feeding ducks with two little boys who are fighting over the bread. We are flying cardboard kites and baking cookies. We are wide-eyed at the moon and building snowmen. I am telling them stories and showing them photographs of tiger snakes in Australia and working elephants in Thailand. They are in awe of the glaciers lying against the New Zealand coastline. We are going to go there one day and to every other country in the world. When they get up a bit, when they get bigger, some time before Daddy teaches them to drive, definitely before they get married and leave us alone again. A siren blares behind me, smashing through my dreams and aspirations.

I slowly fold up the letter. What has happened to him? He passed all his milestones. What happened in six months?

How could a child just stop doing things? Margaret never voiced any concerns about Cian. She was looking after him every day. She gave him her undivided attention. An attentive, caring mother herself, she would have noticed. Surely I would have noticed?

I sit for a long time watching the leaves swirl angrily about my feet, my hair and back damp with mizzle. Eventually I force my body to move and head back to the car. In the driver's seat I sit, my bag still attached to my shoulder. Dropping the keys in my lap, I place my hands over my face and weep. *Maybe it was my fault. Maybe I didn't eat enough fruit. Maybe I drank too much red wine. Maybe I danced too much one night. Maybe I breathed in too much perfume.* The reasons come thick and fast and more and more obscure. I have no idea that the same overwhelming grief and guilt will crash over me, like a great big tidal wave, again and again, for many months and years to come.

5

As it turns out I do not need the letter or a private assessment but find myself two months later sitting waiting in the local child and adolescent clinic. This time both Eamonn and Christopher are with us. My eyes run rampant up the undressed windows, over the pale cream walls and high ceiling, trying not to think. Cian wanders, lifting animals and small things. Christopher hands Eamonn a toy to fix. He fiddles with the yellow and the red of it. I am glad they are with me. A consultant child psychiatrist and a consultant clinical psychologist enter the room and lead us to a larger room with a few seats in the centre and a scattering of toys in one corner.

After a few formalities they turn their attention to our twenty-three-month-old child. While one consultant asks questions about Cian and his behaviour, the other consultant observes and tries to interact with Cian. During the assessment we are ushered into a blackened lab with a one-way mirror. A technician is seated next to us. Cian cannot see us but we can see Cian. We can also see how some invisible thing is preventing him from engaging with the consultants and stopping him from coming out to play. We are unable to reach for him, to let him know we are still here, loving him. Veiled in profound sadness, I swallow my pain defiantly in case I become undone.

After a tea break, concerns are shared about what Cian can and cannot do.

"Is it autism?"

The consultants look up.

"Is it?"

The child psychiatrist's voice is quiet but direct.

"It is too early to say. He is very young. He is not displaying all the signs, but his behaviour would be suggestive of autism or PDD-NOS."

The breath leaves me. I have no recollection of Eamonn's immediate response, apart from asking, "What's that?"

"Pervasive Development Disorder – Not Otherwise Specified."

Some vague piece of knowledge lodged in my memory tells me PDD-NOS is no consolation. There are some more questions to answer and paper work to be completed. I try to speak, but the words trip and lose themselves in half-broken sentences. There is a nervous energy about me. I am led to another room, away from Eamonn and the boys. So I can break down, I suspect.

As I leave, Christopher calls out, "Mammy, I am writing my name."

"I will be back in a minute, Chrisy, just a minute," smiling at him.

The consultant leads me into a small room, apologising for the mess, and gathers up a few folders from the floor by her desk.

The rest of it is a blank. I may have sipped a glass of water. I can't be sure.

I know I rambled a bit, wanting to know, not wanting to know the truth about Cian. Because of Cian's age the consultant is reluctant to diagnose his condition formally. Her attention switches to form-filling and collecting details of our family history, medical stuff, how we cope as parents. Her lips keep moving but I can't hear anything that is relevant to the thoughts bouncing off the sides of my skull.

Why aren't we talking about Cian? How are we going to release him from this thing that has taken hold?

Words clump in my mouth, clumsy and awkward, refusing to leave. A few fall out.

"What help is there?"

The pen stops.

"Well, there are therapies, like speech and occupational therapy."

"I mean for . . ."

I clear my throat.

"I meant specific help for children with . . ." I couldn't make myself say the "A" word.

I start again.

"What help is there specifically for Cian? What treatments are there?"

"Well, for this condition, and it is only suggestive today," she smiles, "there is no specific treatment."

"But what happens now?"

"Well, we will have to wait and see."

My heart stops . . .

". . . still very young . . ."

Changes gear . . .

". . . no eye contact . . ."

Accelerates . . .

". . . is aloof and indifferent . . ."

Words speed up . . .

". . . difficulties . . . language . . . social . . . fail . . .
relationships . . ."

Coming too fast . . .

Mudding my mind . . .

". . . lack . . . independence . . . problems . . . toilet
training . . . lack . . . . social . . . aggression . . ."

Over run by the sound of the thump . . .

". . . fail . . ."

Thumping . . .

". . . difficulties . . ."

And the silent scream . . .

". . . disconnected . . ."

Inside my throat . . .

". . . in . . ."

In my mouth, . . .

". . . a . . ."

In my ears, . . .

". . . world . . ."

In my head. . . .

". . . of . . ."

The thump . . .

". . . their . . ."

In my side . . .

". . . own . . ."

Slows . . .

". . . enrol him in a nursery to be around other children
. . ."

Slows . . .

". . . a support group . . . PAPA . . . Parent and . . ."

Slooows . . .

". . . Professionals . . . for . . . Autism . . ."

". . . talk . . . other . . ."

Slooows . . .

". . . parents might help. . . ."

CRASH!

I stare blankly at the shape of things in the room. Some terrible thing is preventing our child from developing and there is no specific help? Only a group for parents possibly as bereaved as I? The shock of no services cushions me in hopelessness. What Cian has, I will get my head around it. I will accept it. He is my boy. But *how* am I supposed to accept a failing system, a system that does not meet his needs? Involuntary I feel the noise of me moving back to Eamonn and the boys. Eamonn stands up and looks at me, his eyebrows raised, looking for his cue to leave. I look at the weary child in his arms and pick up my bag. He starts to gather our things as I try to gather my thoughts, trying to order the mess in my head. Christopher is jumping up and down with glee, tugging at my wrist.

"Mammy, Mammy. Look what I did, look what I did."

He waves a piece of paper about my face.

"Look, Mammy, look."

I stare at the page, struggling to concentrate, to register the eleven letters sprawled across the page making up his name. It is a proud moment. Christopher hasn't even started nursery. My emotional intelligence searches around for "proud" and "excitement" and "love" and "delight" but there is a big hole where my emotions used to be. I must improvise. I must show my delight. My arms reach out and provide a hug instead. His blond hair leans against another hole, the hole in my heart. I make sure I do not speak. There is a hole in my throat and a hole in my voice. My voice would give it away. Instead I smile a great big cheesy grin that wrinkles my face while my mind is on Cian, my darling Cian. I steal a glance. *How can this be? How can this be happening to you?*

Outside on a busy Omagh street, we hesitate, unsure. It is mid-June. Lunchtime. The smell of fried chicken and hot coffee wafts down Campie. Not far from where *it* happened . . . the utter devastation that plunged our community into darkness. Two years ago, not even. I look at Cian and try to make sense of it all. I thought he had escaped. He was meant to be with me that day. The day I got home when others didn't; the guilt of it – for daring to give thanks for being spared – haunted me while I wept with the world for others. In the shadow of that grief, I stand now, guilty once more, this time, for feeling devastated. I look at Cian again. At least I have you. It could be worse. Much worse.

Shoppers push past us with reasons to go up and down the street. Businessmen in dark suits stall at open door cafés, checking their watches to see if they have time. Time to eat. Imagine it! I look at Cian. I have no appetite. My belly is full of nauseating news. Cars jerk and forge ahead through the busy midday traffic. No time to wait, to notice that we have been hit by a freight train. Everyone is in an awful rush. I look at Cian. He hangs out of his Dad,

watching his shadow slide across the ground. I look about
me and back at Cian. I can't stop myself from looking at
him, my beautiful innocent little boy with dark hair and
eyes that would melt an iceberg. He just looks like any
other little boy. Like there is nothing wrong. It is a silly
thought. Of course there is something wrong. Isn't there?

Eamonn hoists Cian up in his arms and touches my
elbow.

"Let's go home," he says quietly.

"Yes. We must go home."

To wait and see. I lean into him.

To wait for what?

To see what?

* * *

Eamonn shakes my arm. I am slumped in an armchair,
numb and weary. Three cups of coffee are lined up on a
table in front of me, untouched.

"Aileen, the phone. It's the clinic."

My eyes strain to focus on his face, before they fall on
the clock on the mantelpiece.

Three hours have passed since our world fell apart. A
sudden thought strikes me. They are ringing to confirm
some misunderstanding, some mix-up. I gather my legs,
willing them to the phone.

"Hello."

"Hello." It is the consultant. "I'm just phoning to see are
you okay?"

What kind of a stupid question is that?

Pause.

"I just wanted to say, if you need to talk or have any more concerns, do feel you can contact me."

Silence.

Was that it? A personal touch, I surmise. Did she have some measure of our grief?

I find my voice.

"Thanks . . . thanks . . ."

I rub the back of my hand over my brow, not knowing quite what to say. After a bit, I ask a question that I have already asked. I am just hoping it is a different answer.

"About Cian. Is he now diagnosed with . . . ?"

"No, no, not yet, he is too young and in the absence of a psychometric assessment it is not possible to make a definitive diagnosis but it is suggestive of an Autistic Spectrum Disorder. He appears to be globally delayed. We'll have to wait and see."

I don't know how long I stand with the disconnected phone buzzing in my ear, wrapped in Eamonn's arms, gathering it all up from the depths of me and pouring it out without discrimination. It dies away and leaves nothing but an empty hollow hole, a depth unimagined. *Postman Pat* is bellowing out of the boys' bedroom. I reach out and shove the kitchen door over with my elbow, frantically searching my sleeves for a tissue. Eamonn rips off a piece of kitchen roll from the small stand by the cooker and hands it to me. Blotting my face, I become aware of a blinding headache. My two eyes are swollen and Eamonn pulls up a heavy farmhouse chair from the dining area. As it scrapes along the kitchen, I tell him.

"There is no one to help him, Eamonn."

"What do you mean?"

"I mean just that. There is no help."

"What about the child and adolescent clinic?"

"Their job is to diagnose and Cian is too young. They have to wait."

"But are there no tests? Can they not treat him?"

"There are no tests for what they think he has. Some abnormality in the brain. And there is no treatment . . . Oh, God."

While my grief swells and subsides, Eamonn stands staring through the kitchen window, hands in his pockets. Lost. My eyes rest on a variegated poplar standing waving in the middle of the garden. Its candy-top leaves shimmer in the sunshine in a way I have never noticed before. How busy and blind we all are not to notice what is staring us straight in the face.

"How did we not notice?" I mutter to myself, but Eamonn answers.

"Because it wasn't there. Something has happened him."

He spits out the words, one hand latched on to the counter top, the other hand wiping his face and pulling his lips and swiping at the air.

"He used to run to me. He called me Da-Da-Da. He had some words. Where did they all go? Something has happened to him and they think he has PP . . ." He swings round. "What did she say he had?"

"PDD-NOS – it stands for Pervasive Development Disorder, Not Otherwise Specified."

Eamonn's eyes rove over my face. He turns and stares out the window again.

"In other words, they don't know?"

"It's a kind of in-between description because Cian is not displaying all the behaviours common to . . ."

"And how does it affect him . . . will he talk?"

"It is too early to say."

Eamonn looks out the window again.

"And what if he doesn't . . . "

"He will be referred to speech therapy and occupational therapy but they don't specialise in . . . what Cian has."

"I see."

"I mean, they don't offer any special treatment or anything."

Eamonn picks at a plant in the window and pours water into a tray.

"Will he grow out of it?"

"Oh, Eamonn . . . " I get up and start wandering. "It's not going to fade away like some nasty rash, if that's what you mean."

Fresh tears fall again.

Some time later I walk over to my new computer. It is shiny and new and is sitting on a small stand in the dining area. It hasn't even been switched on. I have just purchased it to prepare for some private training and coaching work. I was hoping to set up my own business one day but my own business is a million miles from my mind now. I take up position in front of it and as it hums into gear I think of Cian, the lack of treatment, the ever-increasing waiting lists, and the "wait and see" policy that comes with the territory.

Cian is too young to be diagnosed yet something has switched him off. I want to switch him back on again. Waiting and seeing doesn't seem to make much sense to me. The phone line purrs slowly as I connect to the internet: www.google.com. The search box beckons and flashes like a lighthouse on the shore. I punch in the word: A U T I S M

* * *

The coffee goes cold as I comb websites, hungry for knowledge but mostly confirmation that we all have got it wrong. I am looking for something very specific – a flashing message like *"Cian does not have autism"*. The computer offers definitions, research theories and the history of autism. Cian might not have autism at all. It has to be something else. Cian is far too friendly, too fond of hugs. *It has to be something else.* I concentrate on characteristics and symptoms, many of which do not relate to Cian. The list of behaviours goes on and on: no eye contact, rocking, head banging, rigid behaviour, inconsolable temper tantrums, antisocial, remains aloof, obsessive, aggressive, hands flapping.

Nothing I read describes Cian at all. Cian is passive, quiet, affectionate, happy and plays with toys. He has a few words – well, at least, he did have. The only thing that is unusual about him is his lack of response to his name. Everything else is pretty inconsistent. One day he will do a matching exercise, the next day he won't. He plays with the telephone and puts the receiver to his ear, so he has some imaginative play. In the psychologist's office he did not seem to notice that we had left the room. But the second time, he did, so it was not straightforward. Regardless, I want to know for sure, before we have him labelled like a billposter.

After my little stint of DIY research on the computer, I decide Cian couldn't possibly be autistic. He hardly has any of the behaviours listed.

Okay, he isn't really talking much, and he is happy in his own company, and his eye contact is a bit flitting, and he doesn't really share things, and I can only remember him pointing to say "No", but surely that wouldn't be enough to warrant a diagnosis of autism?

* * *

Initially, I go in and out of what many professionals call the "denial" phase. I tell my family. Well, I actually say Cian is having developmental difficulties, which could mean anything. *I can't take myself to say the "A" word.* The following day, I "untell" them – saying I suspect it is a mistake and hope they can't remember what I said. Truth is, I want it to be a mistake. Most of them say he will be fine. I nod my head and say, "He will surely."

Whatever my head tells me, my body isn't convinced. I am unable to sleep. When morning comes, I am unable to get up. When I do, I have no motivation to dress. I only leave the house when it is completely necessary. I have no interest in food. I am unable to get through the day without breaking down. I am inconsolable.

Autism. The word swirls round inside my head like a wailing mantra. I try to sound it out. "Aut-is-m . . . Autismm . . . Au-tismm." Whatever way I say it, it sounds clumsy and awkward – a wimpish word with a hiss in it and no backbone, separating and thinning, without a solid ending. It doesn't mean anything unless you speak Greek. A word from another language is sure to attract attention and further questions. How am I even going to explain it? It is going to be bad enough having to explain Cian's difficulties without having to dissect the name of his condition as well.

"Have you ever heard of au-tis-m? My son has it. It's a Greek word meaning 'self'."

"Sorry, Cian has some condition I can't pronounce and no one understands."

"How is he affected? Well, he doesn't come to his name. He doesn't look at us and basically he doesn't want anything to do with us."

Oh My God. My Cian.

I don't want to have to explain it. I don't want to talk about it. I just want it to go away. Deirdre, my oldest sister, pops by and finds me in the garden with my head in my hands. She put her arms around me and rocks me for ages. It is the first time in my life we have nothing to say to each other.

6

In the days that follow I vacillate between anger, sorrow, denial, pity for Cian, and profound sadness for all of us. My vision of a happy family has been shattered and putting the pieces together seems an impossible task, but life has a way of spinning threads and weaving distractions in the height of trouble. Our distraction is a family holiday that has been booked and planned for the best part of a year. Even though we are reeling from the devastating news, we make a decision to push everything about autism out of our minds and enjoy our holiday. One week after the psychological assessment, we fly to Fuerteventura.

On the first morning after breakfast, we make a beeline for the pool. It is located at the back of the hotel. As we pass the reception, Eamonn grabs an English newspaper.

"You're being a little bit optimistic, aren't you?" I joke.

Eamonn laughs. In the past we were accustomed to breaks that involved eating, reading and sleeping, not necessarily in that order. We both know that this holiday is going to be very different. We will be lucky if we get to finish a meal, let alone read! As soon as the boys spy the pool, they bubble over with excitement.

I mark our territory with beach towels and floats while Eamonn covers the boys in sky-blue sunblock. They can't wait to get into the water. Christopher runs with a brightly coloured ball and Eamonn carries Cian into the paddling pool. Just like his bath, he loves it. I wave and lift the sun cream just as the wind lifts the pages of Eamonn's paper. Grabbing the boys' sunblock, I set it on top of the paper to stop it from blowing about. At the same time, a heading in the top left-hand corner catches my eye.

"TV presenter gives up work to teach autistic son. Full story, Page 25."

Instinctively, I turn to the two-page spread.

"A TV presenter from London has given up her work to teach her child with autism. She is using a programme called Applied Behaviour Analysis or ABA because she could not find the specific help her child needed . . . ABA is an early intervention programme taught in a one-to-one situation. It is designed to teach basic learning skills by breaking them down into small steps in a simple and consistent way. A record is kept of the child's progress and positive reinforcement is used to encourage and motivate the child to learn . . ."

Despite my wanting to forget autism and everything to do with it, my denial is not strong enough to stop me from ripping out the pages and tucking them into my beach bag. Zipping it up, I reach for the sun cream again and rub some onto my skin as I watch the boys from under my shades. Christopher is already in conversation with a blond-haired boy who is showing him his shark collection. Cian is splashing and jumping in the middle of all the other children. Daddy is sitting beside him in conversation with, presumably, another father. I rest my back into the sun-lounger and tilt my head forward to watch Cian.

I am not the only one who is watching him. A little girl in a white and pink polka-dot swimsuit is trying to get his attention. She wants to play with his ball. Cian isn't actually playing with the ball. He is holding it under his arm while he watches the water from a small waterfall run through his fingers. The ball slips from his grasp but he makes no attempt to rescue it. The little girl reaches out for it. She checks his face again and with a smug swing of her head, she turns towards another playmate. All's fair in love and war.

To any unsuspecting holidaymaker, Cian looks no different than the rest. Yet as I bask in the Mediterranean sunshine, I can't help but notice that, even though he is around the other children and doing what they are doing, he is not engaging or watching other children playing. Nor is he attempting to make friends. I think back to the list of characteristics that I had downloaded from the internet. I had to be completely honest with myself. One or two descriptions did touch on Cian's behaviour. I look at Cian again, splashing the water, bobbing up and down, oblivious to all the children around him. *Cian is in a world of his own. Is that what the computer meant by "socially aloof"?* I close my eyes and concentrate on slowing my breathing, determined to arrest the surge of anxiety running rampant through my veins and quickening my heartbeat.

Keeping my thoughts to myself, the holiday passes with loads of fun and without incident, until we are about to leave. As we wait for the bus to shuttle us back to the airport, Cian disappears. We start to search frantically. I go straight to the pool area but he is not there. Eamonn goes back to the apartment. Other holidaymakers check out the soft-play areas, the restaurants, the toilets, but he is nowhere to be found. I am verging on hysteria when, suddenly, I remember the Kids' Dolphin Crèche. We had taken him there on two occasions at the beginning of the holiday.

"It's too far." Eamonn blinks, rubbing his forehead and shaking his head. "He wouldn't know how to get there, for a start."

I go anyway, running along the zigzag white-walled path, past all the apartments, which all look the same. I wonder if I am going the right way. As I turn a blind corner, I see the red-topped building before me. A man is standing inside the swinging gate shaking his head. "No, he's not mine, but he must have come in with me."

I follow his gaze and catch sight of him, running towards the swings. Cian has just gate-crashed the Day Care Centre with another family in tow. He is completely unperturbed by the fact that he is on his own and his family has a plane to catch. It is another sign, a sign of his phenomenal memory, his love for freedom, his lack of fear – his vulnerability.

At the airport we wait in a queue to go through security. Eamonn is explaining to Christopher why the men in uniform want to check our bags. I am clutching Cian in my arms, making sure he has no opportunity to escape. A child in a wheelchair becomes agitated. His father asks if he can go ahead of us. Automatically, I move to the side and the man hurries past, muttering, "Thanks. My son has autism. He doesn't understand waiting."

I stare after him, watching him, pushing past security to catch up with him.

"But why is he in a wheelchair? Autism doesn't affect a child's walking ability, does it?"

He throws me a weary look.

"Missus, if I let him out of this wheelchair he would just bolt. I would lose him in seconds. He could end up on a flight to Hong Kong." I nearly laugh but when I look in the man's face I realise he isn't joking.

"When he was as young as your lad there . . ." – he makes a gesture towards Cian – ". . . he was just like him."

I wince.

"You wouldn't think there was a thing wrong with him. He was as happy and content but as he got older, well, he's just not programmed for this world. He is eleven now."

"But you take him on holiday?"

The thought of not being able to take Cian anywhere freezes me to the bone.

"Well, yeah, we take him on holiday but *he* has the holiday. I'm exhausted. My wife's not fit to handle him any more. She is a bit . . . you know . . . it changed her . . . wrecked her. She can't cope." He shook his head. "He never stops, never sleeps, you see, and no matter who promises what, there is nothing for him."

Oh God, I heard that before.

"We have no school for him and the staff can't handle him. They don't get enough training, you see, and they don't understand autism . . ." He looks about him and takes a deep breath. "At least, they don't understand my son. In fact nobody truly understands, only parents who live with autism understand." He shrugs and turns his hands up to the sky. "So what do ye do? We can't even get respite. I had to give up my work. My wife had to give up her work a long time ago. She doesn't go out the door now. When you're caring twenty-four/seven, you're easily forgotten and it brings you down, you know. I had my work for a while but the lad is too big now for my wife to handle." His voice slows and becomes almost inaudible. "Aye, she kinda has retreated into her own world now . . . and, you know, she loved singing and dancing." For a moment his face softens.

"So, you don't get any help?"

"A young girl comes over once a fortnight for two hours. But, sure, she's not allowed to take him out, or be alone with him. We can't leave the house. It's ridiculous. The girl doesn't know what to do. We end up making her tea!"

"But don't you complain?"

"'Til 'am blue in the face, love, 'til 'am blue in the face, but it doesn't change a thing. We just live in our own mad world and nobody gives a fuck." He lifts his hand and wobbles it about. "Sorry . . . I didn't mean to . . . it gets the better of me sometimes."

"Do you have any other children?" I ask cautiously.

"Yes. I have another boy. Peter. He is two years younger than Kieran here." He gestures towards the wheelchair. "But Kieran here acts like his brother doesn't exist." His face and voice soften again. "We did have an incident on holiday, though. Peter dropped his straw and quick as a flash Kieran handed him another one," the father laughs tenderly at the memory. "I know in my heart . . . if he had got a chance and we got the right kind of help . . ." his voice fades.

The boy begins to get agitated again, making loud birdlike sounds and flapping his hands up and down.

"Ah . . . well." The man sucks in a heavy sigh and stretches out his arms. "Have to keep moving. Thanks for asking, for listening. We are invisible to most, you know."

I hesitate and look at Cian. *It would be wrong to tell him. With Cian in my arms. Listening.*

Kieran's dad waves a farewell, "All the best. Safe journey," and moves off, pushing the wheelchair in front of him, leaving many years of painful memories behind. "Bye."

"Safe journey."

I hug Cian to me, feeling sorry for the man, feeling distraught for Cian, for all of us, all the while gazing after them until they are swallowed up by the crowd.

* * *

When we return home we waste no time. We are adamant to find a way to prevent Cian from fading further and further away from us. We pull out all the stops to make Cian's world fun and full of interesting things. Everywhere we go, everything we do, Cian and Christopher are part of it. We sing silly songs and play simple games to encourage Cian to take an interest in the world around him. Eamonn transforms our garden into a mini-playground, complete with swings, slide and climbing frame, a paddling pool and a sand pit. The swing is a big hit. Cian loves it. Wrapped in his bulky anorak, he leans his lower back against the blue plastic seat and waits. Shadows slide across our son's angelic face as he watches the cloud float across the sky. He momentarily forgets that he wants a push.

"Okay, Cian, what do you want?"

Still watching the sky, he reaches out and pulls at my arm, throwing it in the direction of the rope.

"Oh, you want a push?"

Silence.

"Okay, but you are going to have to help me."

Fixing his tiny body onto the swing seat, I pull his arms gently up to tease his fingers around the rope. I let go and so do his arms. I repeat this exercise a few more times. Each time his arms flop limply to his sides.

"Okay, I'll hold you on then."

I push and pull at the swing as best as I can, trying to keep his bum on the seat and a ghost of a smile on his silent lips.

We stock up on books and puzzles and highly stimulating toys that flash and dance and make noise, hoping to motivate and to show him what a child's world is all about. We play silly games.

"Let's have a crawling competition!"

"Come on, Mummy, come on, Daddy." Christopher's chubby fingers lock round ours and try to pull us up. We groan and moan but eventually line up along the sitting-room wall on our hands and knees for the fifth time.

"Ready, steady, go!"

Christopher is way ahead. Cian is cackling with laughter. He has the most exciting and weird family around.

"Living here is like living in Butlins," Eamonn shouts.

"Wait for me, Christopher. You are just too fast for us. Come on, Cian."

I lag behind Cian to keep his little bum in the air and help his knees stay in the crawling position. We play games like Simple Simon and peek-a-boo until Cian lies down on the floor, tiring easily. He looks miserable, with dark circles under his eyes. We continue for another while because Christopher is still very keen to play but eventually the games peter out and I put on some music or start to sing and act out nursery rhymes. Music and song never fail to get Cian's attention. Cian climbs up on one knee, Christopher sits on the other. Humpty Dumpty. Incy-Wincy Spider. I make up and act out songs about animals, food and body parts to tunes like "If you're happy and you know it".

There's a spider on your tummy on your tummy.
There's a spider on your tummy on your tummy.
There's a spider on your tummy.
Now do you think it funny?
There's a spider on your tummy on your tummy.

I tickle them both until they howl with laughter.

"Again. Again." I mimic the Teletubbies.

We have races, from one end of the hallway to the other.

"Ready, Steady, GO!"

Christopher and Cian run together until they crash into me and land in a heap on the floor. We dance and sing, Christopher holding one hand, Cian holding the other, for many hours a day, because I love to hear them laugh wildly, I love their eyes glistening with devilment, but mostly because I do not want Cian to disappear. With all I have, I hold on to every piece of him to stop him from falling over into the abyss.

I find a place for him in a local crèche. He will start in January. In the meantime, family life is punctuated with appointments, assessments and reviews. I fill in endless forms and information sheets, regurgitating the same details for all the different departments.

7

On our first visit to the occupational therapy department, assessment proves difficult. Cian is very distracted by other toys stacked up on high shelves and in closed cupboards. He takes the therapist's hands and throws her arms towards the locked doors and shelves that groan with a colourful array of delights that are out of his reach. I suspect Cian thinks he is just in another toy room. Any further assessment is not possible.

The therapist apologises for the room, expressing their need for more space to store equipment, and suggests that we wait until she can book a more suitable room. Cian leaves the room reluctantly and very upset because he did not get to play with the toys. Outside I carry him, kicking and screaming, in the pouring rain. He throws himself down and rolls in the puddles, as we both get soaked to the skin. I manage to bundle him into the car but he shrieks wildly, thrusting his tormented body and mind recklessly. My attempts to wrap him up in the seat belt are futile. Arching his back, he forces himself out of his baby seat and screams blue murder on the floor of the car. The rain stings my back and legs as he kicks and lashes. Twenty-five minutes later – ten minutes more than we were in the therapy room – I finally get him fixed in his chair. He is inconsolable the whole way home.

* * *

On the next visit we are led to a different room with no toys and sparse furnishing. Cian co-operates for tabletop activities for five minutes, completing four activities. His play and hand function appear age-appropriate.

For other activities, Cian displays little interest. His interaction with the therapist is variable. At times Cian moves away from the therapist when she attempts to gain interaction. At other times Cian engages well and sometimes sits on the therapist's knee to complete a task. He also responds positively to praise.

I leave with some encouraging ideas on how to improve concentration and attention span. The first available date for the next review is in six months' time.

* * *

At Cian's first speech therapy appointment the speech therapist asks me questions about Cian's medical history, his birth, his development to date. She takes a few notes and suggests we come back in six months' time.

"Six months!"

"We have a very long waiting list."

"But I have been told Cian may have autism."

"I'm afraid our waiting list is very long."

"Cian needs help now," I insist.

"I'll see what we can do."

Cian is reviewed in five sessions from May through to November.

The therapist observes some occasional vocalisations and single words. Cian also shows signs of developing his imagination but because of his fleeting level of attention and concentration, it is impossible to ascertain his level of comprehension. Furthermore he "follows his own agenda" and interacts on his own terms. He allows someone else to play with him for a short while before he moves on to another toy. He is using some appropriate eye contact and turn-taking.

His name then nosedives to the bottom of a very long waiting list.

* * *

Individual speech therapy is not offered to Cian, but he is invited to attend a music therapy group. Because Cian enjoys music so much, I take him along.

I have not anticipated the large group – parents, carers, children with varying needs, buggies and bottles, wheelchairs and other equipment – in the room. While the rest of the group take their seats and focus on what they came for, Cian explores his surroundings with intense curiosity, roaming around the rather large activity hall, checking out cupboards and toilets and lightly touching everything in his reach. I eventually steer him into a seat but he doesn't stay there for very long.

Before I can stop him, he is out of the very large semicircle and springing towards the musicians. He plucks the strings of the guitar and bangs the keyboard. He attempts to sit on one of their knees and runs his hands up and down the sides of a pair of green corduroy trousers. The musicians are forced to stop until I move Cian away and block his path with some chairs. Everyone is listening and clapping to the music's beat but they are looking at Cian. He is pushing the "barricade" and attempting to climb over the chairs.

Suddenly he turns to a child sitting next to us and pulls a dummy out of her mouth. The mother gasps, immediately regretting her action, but she can't conceal her annoyance. Cian giggles and runs away with the dummy, laughing like a very badly behaved child. The music slows and the clapping gradually fades. I wish the ground would swallow me whole as I go to rescue the dummy and prevent Cian from climbing into a bay window. All the other children, with various disabilities, sit quietly by their parents' sides watching. I can't catch my little Pac-man. He is racing round the large room, attempting to climb on anything that he can get a foothold in. I chase after him, wishing I had stayed at home. The therapist is trying to get the group focused again.

"Okay, everybody, look this way. Listen carefully and follow my actions. This one is called 'Two Little Dickey Birds'."

I grab Cian and hoist him up on my hip. Protesting and kicking, he pulls my hair and scrabs my face as I return to our seats to give the grief-stricken child her comforter and collect our things.

"Right, everybody, look at me, are you ready . . ."

No one looks at the therapist. They are looking at Cian writhing and screaming at the top of his voice. I raise my hand to say goodbye. Some of the parents raise their hands, looking very puzzled indeed.

Cian is the only child in the room who has no outward signs of a disability to explain his behaviour. His stunning dark eyes and perfectly shaped features give nothing away. His mischievous grin doesn't help matters. I make my way to the door as the therapist demonstrates the exaggerated actions to the chosen nursery rhyme.

"Two little dickey bird sitting on a wall. One named Peter, the other named Paul."

As I exit the room, I enter a world of isolation, helplessness and panic. I have exhausted the extremely limited services offered to Cian and his antics are exhausting me. Holding on to Cian and my sanity by a thread, I have no idea who to turn to, who to talk to. Ironically, I talk to Cian and it is Cian who gives me hope.

8

Cian's new crèche is on my way to work. I wrap his chubby body up in his Bob the Builder coat and place him in his car seat. Before I have edged out the driveway, he has kicked off his shoes and is playing with his socks in his hands. Sometimes he laughs hysterically for reasons beyond my comprehension. I convince myself that angels are talking to him, but at other times I am eventually forced to stop the car as a great big tidal wave of emotion hits me. I wait until I am composed again, staring at him through the rear-view mirror and two swollen red eyes. Why isn't he curious about where he is going?

When we arrive at the crèche, he does not wave to say goodbye, nor does he seem excited to see other little boys and girls. Instead he totters on in without looking back. I never know from one day to the next what he does or how he spends his day. When I collect him, the staff nod and smile and call him "cute". It isn't long before I sense that they have their suspicions that Cian is a little different from the rest of the children chattering to each other and crying after their mammy and daddy.

On the way to and from the crèche I am met with silence. The silence oozes out of the back seat into the front and bubbles up until I cannot bear its density. So I start to talk. I name everything I see. I tell Cian about my day. I ask him about his. It doesn't matter if the conversation is only one-way. There is nothing wrong with Cian's hearing. He is listening. Cian likes music, so I play music. Pop, classical, show tunes, all sorts, always watching for a reaction. I sing nursery rhymes louder than I have ever sung before. He hums along, sounding some of the words out. "Old MacDonald" is his favourite. He can sing "E-I-E-I-O" and so I sing it the whole way to work, and the whole way back. I talk about the green grass, the green trees and the green hills, until I am green with anxiety. If I see an animal, I brake suddenly and call out, "Look, Cian, cows. Do you see the cows?"

When I spot a horse one morning peering over a gate I stop the car.

"Look, Cian. Horse. I see horse. Old MacDonald has a horse!" I start to sing, "Old MacDonald has a horse."

Twisting round in my seat, I turn his face gently towards the window. My finger points in the direction of the horse. I tap the glass beside him.

When he fails to look up, I get out of the car and gather his reluctant body across the wet grass and ragweed and head towards the gate. Hoisting him up on the gate, I point out.

"Look, Cian, the horse, do you see the horse?"

He makes a fleeting attempt to look but is more interested in licking the cold bar of the gate we are leaning on. The sandals on my feet sink deeper into the cold earth and my body grows cold and weary. Blinded by tears, I turn towards the abandoned car and put Cian safely back into his car seat again. I tell him he is beautiful and maybe we will try again tomorrow.

Sometimes there are sheep in the fields. Driving along I "baa" when I see a sheep. I talk about the colour of the sheep. I count the sheep. I sing "Baa Baa Black Sheep".

One afternoon I catch sight of a whole flock of sheep at a gate. I stall the car and swing round to Cian. Before I lift my hand to point at the sheep, Cian's eyes bore into mine.

"Baa!"

I open my mouth to speak but I can't. Instead, I break into hysterics. I race round the car to his side to haul him out of his car seat and dance him around the road, kissing and hugging him. I laugh until I cry. I have talked so much about sheep Cian must think I am nuts about them. A horn blares, letting me know that my car is in the way, but it doesn't matter. They can toot all they like. They will just have to wait. I am collecting my Oscar. I have pierced Cian's armour.

* * *

With renewed enthusiasm I scour website after website for information. I hope for interventions and ways to maximise Cian's potential.

Cian runs up and down and up and down the kitchen floor or lies staring at the ceiling, lethargic and sickly, with little gusto for life, while I make phone calls, taking notes and underlining useful information. I find little in the way of local help. I have already contacted Parents and Professionals and Autism Northern Ireland (Autism NI (PAPA)), the organisation that the child psychiatrist suggested. While Cian tears the brown envelope into a million tiny pieces, I sift through the information pack only to realise that PAPA is an information-giving and advocacy group. They do not provide or endorse any particular therapy or treatment.

I phone Colum, a parent in Dublin. There is talk of parents setting up schools in their own backyard and going to the High Court to pursue their children's basic right – an appropriate education to meet their needs. I ring Doreen in Donegal. Paddy, her husband, answers the phone. Doreen is in liaison with a local school to explore the possibility of developing autism provision. It sounds progressive and I suddenly wish I were in Donegal.

Other countries seem more advanced in their treatment and prognosis of autism but parents have to pay for most of the therapies and treatments themselves. Some therapies sound interesting. Many are verging on the extreme side of lunacy and all are ultra-expensive. I read about parents who are paying astronomical sums for just a little ray of hope from the dark world of autism. Autism, I find, is big business. Everyone has different opinions about which therapy is best. Most advocate their own therapy while condemning all of the others. The path to choose is as clear as murky water.

Despite the tremendous contradictions, providers and consultants do seem to agree on one thing: early intervention. The younger the child, the better the chance they have in learning new skills and behaviours. Panic fills me. Cian's third birthday is approaching and I still haven't found any clear direction or guidance on how to address his needs. I beat myself up for not acting sooner, for not doing enough, even though I couldn't have done any more.

The hands of time race around the clock face. Time evaporates and I feel I am doing the very thing I disagreed with the most. *Wait and see.*

I email Benita in Africa and Rickie in Australia. I phone Colleen in America and Jackie in England. No matter who I ring and what country they live in, it becomes clear to me in the thick black of the night that they all have one thing in common, apart from the autism. Parents with backbreaking determination are doing it for themselves, fighting very hard and advocating for their children's rights.

I am forced to face the truth – the awful, disturbing truth that Cian is going to get little help unless we provide it.

* * *

Days before Cian turns three, he is invited to a speech therapy group in Enniskillen. He is still under the caseload of the speech therapist in charge of language delay.

The group meeting is an hour and a half away from our home. I don't know how Cian will react when he gets there. Normally after such a long journey there is a fairground, a swimming pool or a bag of chips. This time there is only a grey-white building and a set of steps.

Cian thumps up the steps of the community centre in anticipation. We are shown into a small waiting room. There is a box of toys in the corner. Cian marches straight over to the wicker basket and kneels down. I breathe a sigh of relief. I keep an eye on him as I absent-mindedly flick through a well-thumbed magazine. Something about his behaviour makes me stop and observe him.

He is sitting by the basket, exploring a toy car with his mouth. I observe for another while and realise he is mouthing the toys like a six-month-old baby. *When does that stop? Isn't it around nine months?*

The speech therapist pops her head around the door and smiles.

Cian bolts straight past her and joins the rest of the children in another room. The speech therapist throws back her head and laughs. "That's that sorted then."

The group work lasts approximately an hour. A couple of other mums enter and their children go and join the group. We sit in silence, trying to avoid each other's eyes as we strain to hear the voices of the children in the next room. I don't hear Cian at all.

We make this weekly pilgrimage for five weeks. At the last meeting the speech therapist informs me that Cian's needs would be best met by specialists dealing with learning difficulty. His play skills are limited. Mouthing of objects is evident and listening skills are fleeting. He can "block out" the outside world but still communicate with others for activities he enjoys. His favourite activity involves music and holding hands with others in the group. He uses single words and odd phrases. He engages in brief periods of attention and concentration. The speech therapist acknowledges the difficulty of making a clear diagnosis of Cian's difficulties but suggests he has specific language impairment and recommends that he be monitored closely.

A pre-school tutor is assigned to work with Cian once a fortnight, introducing him to jigsaw puzzles, beading and basic play skills.

* * *

For Cian's third birthday we decide to go away for a short break to Rossnowlagh in County Donegal.

Every morning, breakfast is served in the dining room. It is a beautiful old Victorian building with high ceilings and detailed window dressings. The tables are endowed with white linen tablecloths and a small posy of flowers with silver cutlery. There is a cream condiment set on each table, full of milk, cream and sugar. Cian wants to play with the long thin packets of sugar. At first we allow him to play with a few packets, until the paper gets wet and he starts sucking the sugar out of the paper. Not just the little packets on our table but on everyone's table. It is impossible to keep him in his chair. He starts to cry. We confiscate the packets but Cian has got the taste and nothing will do but he wants more and more.

The second morning, we clamour down to the dining room and ritually lift all sugar bowls within reach. It isn't enough. He still manages to get sugar. Before leaving the breakfast table, we make an unusual request.

"Would it be possible for the dining room to be sugar-free tomorrow morning, at least until we leave?"

The owners are happy to oblige but it doesn't stop Cian from wandering round looking for it and watching other holidaymakers pour sugar into their tea. We are ready and waiting to pull him back each time he attempts to pounce on some poor unsuspecting guest. While we finish up and check that we haven't left anything behind, Cian grabs the opportunity and hijacks a man at the next table, swipes the sugar out of his hand and spills it over the man's shirt before the rest of it reaches his mouth. The man is shocked and disapproving and starts to rub his front frantically with a white linen napkin.

Eamonn grabs Cian and makes an attempt to apologise, mumbling something about Cian's love for sugar.

The man stops cleaning himself and glares at us. "Well, I would just say 'NO!'"

Eamonn bundles Cian up on to his shoulder and walks past me towards the door. "Now why didn't we think of that?" he mutters to me.

I lift the rest of our belongings and walk after him. It is becoming a struggle to have to explain to people what is wrong. Instead we have started to remove Cian from such situations because he is increasingly becoming more frustrated and has begun to tantrum in public, which only encourages sideways glances and comments from strangers. But what they don't realise is that even though he looks "normal", he doesn't have the same social skills or understanding as his peers. Nor can we reason with him. He is unbribable.

* * *

Eamonn carries Cian as I help Christopher with the buckets, spades and picnic rug down the steps towards the beach.

It is not long before we realise that there is no need for any of it. Christopher runs off towards the rocks with his bucket and spade while we look around to find a place to park the picnic rug. The beach is dotted with many families enjoying the July sunshine. Excited children run to and fro, skipping into the water, playing with the gushing tide lapping round their ankles. Cian has the same idea and immediately dashes to the water. Only he keeps running until he is knee-deep and there is no sign that he is coming back. Eamonn is fast on his heels and sweeps him up into the air, before walking back to where I am standing. Eamonn plops Cian down on the sand but, like a magnet, he bolts straight back into the water.

We soon learn that Cian has no sense of danger or fear of water. Eamonn can't let him go. Cian wants to be in the water and refuses to sit on the rug next to us. It is a continuous task to keep him from the water or from eating handfuls of sand. I have left my glasses and suncream in the car but I can't go back for them. I can't leave Eamonn alone, so I stand at the water's edge with my fists resting on my hips, watching Eamonn in the water for almost an hour, lifting Cian up and down, up and down. My shoulders start to smart and the glare of the sun pains my eyes. Christopher comes back and forth to show me a shell or a dead crab. Excited shrieks of other holidaymakers carry in the sea breeze. Mouthwatering smells waft from portable barbecues. Mummies are bare-shouldered and bare-legged, reading magazines. Daddies are leaning over car doors listening to football matches on the radio. Some are building sandcastles and burying their laughing children in the sand. An hour later, we still haven't managed to sit down together once.

* * *

Later that evening, while we pack the suitcases and prepare for leaving in the morning, we spill out our thoughts to each other. One thing becomes clear: language delay would not explain all of Cian's difficulties.

It certainly wouldn't explain the amount of times Cian is sick, nor would it explain some of his behaviours. We no longer doubt the diagnosis but it is not the grim reality of autism that terrifies us now. It is the no-hope prognosis and the lack of help available. *No help. No hope. Wait and see.* The words eat away at our optimism.

We talk late into the night until a feeling of sheer exhaustion comes over me and I don't want to talk any more. I tuck the pillow further under my neck and close my eyes. Eamonn rambles on.

"Cian was doing great. We had no concerns right up until last year. Maybe he's not that bad. He was playing peek-a-boo with Christopher today and came to me with his shoe. He wanted it open and wanted me to put it on. You know, I think we are worrying far too much. He'll come on great, wait 'til you see." Eamonn reaches round and turns off the bedside light.

His optimism irks me. From under the duvet I bolt upright and glare in his direction. "Eam . . . onn!" I am almost shouting. The light goes back on again. "He's not going to *come on*, on his own! He needs help, for Christ's sake! He is doing those things, but there are a whole lot of things he is not doing.

Frustration builds up inside me. I bite my lip. We are

both tired and it is the wrong end of the day to have an argument. Eamonn pulls himself up to a sitting position.

"I know, I know, I just don't know what to do. You know more about it than I do." He rubs his hand over his head, feeling the pressure of a situation he just can't fix.

"I DON'T! I just know we can't sit around and do nothing. We need to help him."

The following week my mother throws me a lifeline.

9

When the phone rings I am making aeroplane noises and funny faces in the hope that Cian will open his mouth and swallow some breakfast.

"You're saved by the bell. Listen, do you hear the phone, Cian? Look."

I reach for the handset and wave it in front of him. He looks out the window at the wind blowing the trees.

"Don't want to answer? Ah well, never mind. Probably someone wanting to sell us something anyway, Cian."

Pushing the "on" button, I speak into the receiver.

"Hello."

"Hi, Aileen."

"Mum."

I hold my breath. Mum is not in the habit of making telephone calls for idle chat.

"Are you listening to the radio?"

"No, I haven't managed to . . ."

"It's just someone was on talking about a charity called PEAT. They train parents to teach children with autism by a therapy called ABA. I have a number here if you would like it?"

"Yes, please."

I scribble down the number, thank Mum, and hang up. Later I search for the newspaper article I had stowed away in my beach bag in Fuerteventura. It is the same programme. My curiosity prompts me back in front of the PC. Googling ABA, I learn that Applied Behaviour Analysis (ABA) uses observation, repetition and positive reinforcement to teach autistic children social, language and motor skills. The theory behind ABA makes sense to me and brings back cringing memories of long nights in the library reading about Skinner and operant conditioning at university. That was all very well then; I only wanted to pass an exam. Now I want to accomplish a seemingly insurmountable task, the equivalent of performing brain surgery that would result in an enhanced quality of my son's life.

Reading on, I find that ABA therapy should start when a child is young, between the ages of two and three years to maximise his learning opportunities. I also learn that ABA principles could teach Cian new skills by breaking them into small steps, rewarding his good work and then repeating each task until he has mastered that skill. This is called discrete trial teaching (DTT for short). I would also have to ensure that he could "generalise" or use his new skills in other places and that ABA principles could help change challenging behaviours.

I can feel myself getting excited and frustrated all at the same time. *Why haven't I been told about this?* After some more

Googling I find an answer to my question. There is no ABA provision in Northern Ireland and government-funded ABA programmes are unheard of in the UK. On every site I trawl, I learn that for a home programme to be successful, forty hours of teaching a week, for at least two years, are recommended. Running a programme is, in many instances, too costly for the average family. Raising funds, recruiting, training therapists and planning lessons take time and effort. I am also warned that I will never be able to leave the house again. A mountain of paperwork will weigh me down and I will collapse exhausted each night, not knowing if I am doing the right thing.

"Well, you would have to be barking mad to contemplate such a programme anyway," I mutter at the screen when the sheer twenty-four-hours-a-day nature of ABA almost causes me to close down my computer.

But I have to know one more thing. I Google PEAT (Parents' Education as Autism Therapists), and discover that they are a relatively new parent-led charity attempting to teach and support parents in ABA principles so that they in turn can teach their children in their own home. My curiosity is piqued. Maybe I could teach Cian myself, at the start at least, and I would feel useful again.

However, before I reach for the phone to call PEAT, I have to know one more thing. If I had the skills to teach Cian, would Cian be teachable?

* * *

The next afternoon, I devise a small experiment. I want to know if ABA would work for Cian. After collecting him from the crèche, I buy five packets of jelly babies and a few packets of brightly coloured Smarties. When I get back home, I line each jelly baby along the edge of the kitchen counter and in between I place a brightly coloured Smartie. I then collect Christopher from school and, after he plays for a bit, I explain to him that we are going to play a game. I point to the ledge and his eyes follow my finger.

"When you point to the sweets and say 'sweetie', I'll give you a sweet."

Christopher stares at me for a moment, trying to work out the catch. Sweets never came this handy before. "Is that it?" he exclaims in a little high-pitched squeak, his hands turned outwards and upward and his shoulders shrugged up to his ears. His little face screws up in disbelief. He thinks I have gone soft.

"Sweetie." I point upwards, and then help myself to a red jelly baby. I don't have to do it twice.

Immediately, his little finger points upwards and he calls out, "Sweetie."

"Good boy," I laugh, giving him a sweet. He munches happily while I fetch Cian.

"This time I want Cian to play the game too."

"Okay, but he's not allowed to eat all the sweets!"

"Don't worry, there are loads for both of you. Let's see can Cian point and talk like you."

I try to hold Cian still while Christopher points and shouts, "Sweetie! Sweetie!"

Cian isn't looking anywhere near him. He hasn't even noticed the sweets. I reach up and take a sweet for Christopher, making sure Cian sees it in my hand.

He looks at it with an expressionless face and watches

Christopher munch at it happily. Christopher has another few sweets before Cian looks up at the ledge. Lots of little yellow, green and red jelly babies smile happily back. He stares in amazement as Christopher reaches out for his reward. Cian makes a grab for it. It feels cruel not giving him one, but I have to believe he will claim one for himself. I hold him tight.

"Do this." I prompt his forefinger to point upwards and hold up his arm.

Christopher is excited now. He is jumping from foot to foot, pointing and shouting, "Sweetie, Sweetie."

It looks like the easiest thing to do in the whole world, especially with a line of mouth-watering jelly babies to be eaten up, but for Cian it is a very difficult task. Christopher devours another eight sweets before Cian becomes focused and makes any attempt to "play the game". Slowly but gradually, he moves less and stands still long enough to watch Christopher, who is only too glad to perform.

Christopher is on his umpteenth reward when Cian slowly raises his arm a little and the knuckle of his little forefinger probes the air. A nervous laugh escapes me.

"Sweetie! Sweetie!" Christopher shouts louder.

A soft mumble escapes Cian's lips, but we hear it.

"Etee."

Oh my God!

I fight back the tears, knowing that Cian is teachable. We have found a way to teach him, to engage with him, to reach him.

When Eamonn arrives in from work we nearly knock him over to tell him what Cian can do. We play the game again and again and Cian's little arm gets higher and his forefinger gets longer and his voice gets louder.

"Etee, Etee."

Eamonn swoops him up in his arms and his little hand grasps a jelly baby. I laugh and cry and feel like giving him the whole shelf of sweets, but he has to work for them now.

* * *

Quietly I wonder how he is getting on at "school". The very next day I get an opportunity to find out when I receive an invitation to a parents' open night at the crèche. When I arrive, parents are sitting awkwardly on little coloured chairs. I perch myself on a blue plastic chair and, with my knees nearly touching my chin, I join the mums and dads who are chatting quietly. Parents are pointing at their children's work. I listen passively while admiring the wall displays. There are pictures drawn by Orla and Eddie and Ryan and Sean. There is a display of hand-marks belonging to Niall and Eoin and Kieran. Cathal's colourful fish is hanging from the ceiling. There are photographs of Patrick and Enda, and Patrice and Conor. Sarah, Padraig and Caoimhe's sunflowers are dressing the window. My eyes search among a host of other names for Cian's name.

"Don't you just love to see their wee drawings," a mother nudges me.

I have been caught staring.

I smile and nod and look at the parents laughing and sharing stories that children have carried home. They seem to know exactly what their children have been doing in the nursery. Their children love coming and never stop talking about it. They even get upset on Saturdays because it is closed. While I listen I become aware of the difference between their experiences and mine. I don't have the faintest idea what Cian does in the nursery or whether he likes it or dislikes it. I understand that, because of his speech delay, he can't really tell me about it, but surely I would have some indication as to whether he enjoys it or not?

A member of staff approaches with an armful of large yellow folders, bulging with work that the children have completed over the year. As the name of each child is called out, the respective parent reaches up to claim their child's precious scribbles and exaggerated brushstrokes. I wait for Cian's name but the bundle of folders disappears first. As with the wall display, Cian's name isn't on a folder.

"Did you not get a folder?" the mother leans towards me again.

"Hmm? No, it doesn't matter. I'll have a word later."

"You should," she agrees. "It's lovely to have their little bits and pieces and your wee one will be so disappointed."

I quickly excuse myself before the mother starts asking questions. She is not to know that the molten lava is smouldering again. She may as well be sitting at the mouth of a volcano. I walk back out the door empty-handed.

It is a hard lesson but a good lesson. It helps me make a very important decision. There is no doubt in my mind. We are going to have to find a way to provide ABA therapy for Cian. I will give up work and take Cian home. I will teach him myself.

10

Despite having the article about ABA tucked away in my suitcase for over a year and discovering the possibility that we could teach Cian valuable skills, it takes us ages to get started. Concerns about his health prevail. He has symptoms and behaviours that are not often listed as characteristics of autism. His eczema is itchy and bleeding. He seems to suffer from headaches and tummy pains. He has raging temperatures, infections, night sweats, red ears, dark circles underneath his eyes, constipation and diarrhoea. In truth, I guess, I am more concerned about his health than his autism. We are concerned that he may not be well enough for the intensive therapy.

It is not our only concern. To fully commit to his programme, I have no option but to give up work. Giving up work is like giving up a piece of me, leaving me insecure and unsure about the future. Leaving work would mean relying on one wage. Staying at work would mean I'd be torn between my commitments to work and to my son.

I make an appointment with Maura, my counselling supervisor a co-founder, co-director and psychotherapist of the Tara Centre of Omagh to discuss the decision. Within five minutes it becomes clear that giving up work is the least of my worries. My anxieties are mostly about Cian. Outwardly I have been trying to cope, to get on with things, but inside I am riddled with anxiety. Maura insists I need to look after myself to enable me to take care of Cian. Her wisdom is lost on me. I am on a mission to find help for Cian. Then and only then will I be able to turn my attention to me.

Still, I do not leave the Tara Centre without a further appointment. Maura agrees to see me again and arranges for Mary, her co-founder, co-director and psychotherapist, to support me while I finish up my caseload. As a voluntary organisation, Tara offers me a safe, nurturing environment where the entire ethos breathes respect. Subsequently, Maura and Mary's unrelenting encouragement and inspiration and the support of everyone at Tara becomes a steadfast anchor for me when the challenges of autism press heavily on my shoulders and when I stumble and struggle to find services for Cian and for our family. Furthermore, Tara introduces me to many therapies, including bio-energy healing and meditation, that help me slowly to accept and through time, let go and trust.

* * *

A week later, I get up early before my alarm goes off and dress quickly. Downing a glass of juice, I grab an apple and my bag and step into the cold November morning, pulling the door gently behind me. I am going to Belfast, to a discussion group run by the PEAT charity, which trains parents to use ABA principles with their child. I meet a large group of parents who are all trying to run ABA programmes. Many of them are struggling to finance the programme, as most of them like myself have been forced to give up their work. The education boards have been unwilling to recognise the validity of an ABA home programme and are not prepared to support the parents to help pay for it. I try to brush the practical issue of finance aside and gain a basic knowledge of ABA, the importance of positive reinforcement, a definition of prompts, types of prompts and how to keep a score of the child's progress.

After the meeting I make an appointment with the consultant to help me draw up a programme to teach Cian basic learning readiness skills. He pencils Cian's name into his diary and promises a home visit.

* * *

When I get back home, Eamonn meets me in the hallway, clutching Cian in his arms. His face looks pale and anxious.

"Cian followed you this morning. I haven't been well since."

"What do you mean?"

"He must have heard the car or something. He let himself out and Bridie Breen brought him back. She said he was in the middle of the road. A lorry driver got him. He was walking the white line. He was away up the road after you, no doubt. We were all still sleeping. I never heard a thing until Bridie knocked at the door."

We live right beside a dangerous part of a main road. Without saying anything, we both know we have another major decision to make. Danger is too close for comfort this time. We have to move house.

* * *

The ABA consultant, Stephen, arrives a week later. After he meets Cian and discusses his needs, he draws up an outline of a programme I can start with.

He describes how an ABA session is made up of a number of simple tasks. Each one is called a discrete trial. He begins to demonstrate what he means. He leads Cian to a small table that I have set up and encourages him to sit. With two wooden blocks and a bucket, he kneels down beside him. He places the bucket on the table with one block in front of himself and one in front of Cian.

"Do this."

Cian looks out the window.

He takes Cian's hand and places it over the block, prompting the required motion for him. Stephen drops the block into the bucket.

"Good boy!" He pops a Smartie into Cian's hand. Cian sits looking around him, happily munching. Stephen repeats his action again and again while Cian watches the pocket containing the Smarties.

Over time, the awards will be faded until Cian can intrinsically imitate. Stephen then shows me how to record data and how to monitor Cian's progress. Finally I have something concrete that I can help Cian to learn. It is enough to empower me, to enable me to feel useful again.

Waving Stephen off, I clutch the two A4 sheets, my passport to freedom. His first programmes of learning are highlighted in a fluorescent orange marker, which focus on *Attending Skills*, *Imitation Receptive*, *Language Expressive*, and *Language and Pre-academic Skills*. It is a ray of hope for me and connects me to many wonderful parents who are doing their best to provide treatment for their children in the shadow of a system that continues to fail them.

* * *

November quickly rolls into December. I am sitting on a Gothic high-back leather chair, a gin and tonic in my hand. A girls' night out. Everyone is excited, laughing, filling the air with perfume and memories of schooldays, college graduations and rucksacks. It is our annual get-together, the one night in the year I really look forward to, but tonight I feel different. Drained.

Veronica arrives in, home from Canada, distracting me. We make a fuss. I wonder what it's like in Canada. The autism services. Conversations float past me, over me, mingling with the smoke drifting from other people's tables. Glossy lips sip wine and move and laugh. I try to be myself, most of myself. I try hard to concentrate, to focus, to remember to smile, to remember names of children, to congratulate them, to commiserate with them. Ann-Marie, Margaret, Michelle, Teresa, Anne, Clare, Marian and Veronica: we have all had our fair share of trouble in the past year, but I can't shake mine off. It's in my clothes, my hair, clinging on to me, drowning with me in a cocktail of panic and fear and gin and tonic.

A waiter hands around long detailed menus. Heads bow and disappear behind them. I try to dissect the florid descriptions and give up, laying down the menu in front of me. A salad will do. I have no appetite. Arms and faces and eyes roam around me, thickening and thinning, filling in the gaps, pushing past the abstract paintings, closing in the dark red walls and creating shadows in the dim orange glow. I feel claustrophobic and rise and scan the wine bar in search of the toilets. Cutting through the crowd, tension tightens around my neck. It takes all of me to push the toilet door open. Heat and voices rush in with me and then silence as the door swings closed.

White light hurts my eyes. A Hungarian chant filters overhead. I press down on the cold tap and sigh into the warm stuffy air polluted with a sweet sickening fragrance. Water gushes over my hands. Not cold enough. In the stained mirror Cian is looking back, his dark eyes solemn and vacant like the eyes of an angel. Untouchable. A toilet flushes. The door creaks open. Someone is beside me with polished nails and jingling bangles, turning on a tap. I look up. Eyes meet in the mirror. A girl in a pink top smiles at me. I smile back. We wash and dry our hands together, looking, trying not to look. I wonder if she can tell I'm faking it, like the way she is. Her tan. I can smell it. I wonder if she can see the holes in me.

Taking my place again, familiar faces look up and smile. I smile back, the tension slipping a little. Marian asks me about Cian. I start to talk. There is a lull. Everyone is holding their breath, listening. No one is drinking. That's what the "A" word does. It stops you in your tracks. Ten minutes later, I am still talking about the "A" word.

"I've heard about this therapy that might help." I try to sound upbeat and take a sip of my drink.

"Can you help autism?"

"I don't know, but I want to try and help Cian." Cian. The thought of him fortifies me. "Oh, I know, of course . . ."

"So what is the therapy?"

"It's called ABA. Have you heard of it?"

Most of them are teachers. They are bound to have heard of it.

They all look at one another, pull a face and shake their heads.

"Well, it's a one-to-one intensive therapy programme . . ."

I tumble through explanations, tripping over my words, stumbling on the names of things, stuttering, all the while convincing myself that I am doing the right thing.

" . . . There is more to it than that; Cian gets rewarded for working well and the therapist has to keep data and stuff, but that's the gist of it."

"Who is the therapist?"

"Well, there are no therapists as such. Parents have to find their own therapists and train them up. I am going to teach him myself for a while . . ." My words are racing without pause, afraid that if I am interrupted I will lose my train of thought, my reasoning. "I will advertise in the local paper and in Omagh College maybe . . ."

I gallop on, afraid someone might undo my decision, take it apart, piece-by-piece. My friends have opinions and my best interests at heart but they do not know autism. They do not know disability, the loneliness of it. What it is like – the devastation, the desperation while the world sits back and waits.

"Hopefully I will be able to train others up with the help of a consultant. He is from a charity called PEAT that helps train parents. They are based in Belfast."

I talk as if one word from them would break the spell.

"What do you mean by intensive?"

"Forty hours a week." Eyebrows rise and mouths drop open. "But I hope to start with ten, maybe fifteen to get started."

"And is there a school or . . . where?"

Everyone is looking at me.

"No, no school. We have to teach him at home. I've already handed in my notice at work." A sound of someone sucking air. "We are moving house. Oh, did I not say? It's the road. It's too dangerous for Cian. He has been running out of the house. Anyway it is only a few miles away from where we are now but it is off the main road and it has a spare sitting room. We are going to turn it into Cian's therapy room. We just need a few shelves and things." I make it sound like I am going to do a spot of decorating, but even to my ears it sounds like mission impossible. "We will start in January."

I take a deep breath and finish my gin.

No one seems to quite know what to say.

They take the news well; that is, they don't scold, or disagree or faint or anything. They just look at me as though, this time, I have completely lost the plot.

One by one, they lift their glasses and sip on their drinks, smiling at me smiling back. Someone calls the waiter and I sink back into the red leather couch again, knowing they can see the holes in me.

11

The van is packed to the gills. I have read that transition is difficult for kids suffering from autism but Cian shows no signs of anxiety or stress as we pull out of our driveway. He is cuddled up with Christopher on top of a small sofa jammed against the rest of our furniture, humming his own version of "Jingle Bells". All that we own shakes and rattles as we gingerly make our way along a frosty moonlit road. Christopher strains to catch a glimpse of the jolly lights fussing and flashing from rooftops and Christmas trees and gardens.

"Mammy, how will Santa know we have moved?"

"Because you put your new address on your letter, silly."

"Oh. I forgot . . ." Christopher pauses. "Mammy, do you know what I asked Santa for?"

"I think you asked him for a bicycle, am I right?"

"Yes, but I asked him for something else too. I didn't show you." His voice weakens.

"What was that, darling?"

"I asked him to get Cian a voice because I can't understand why God didn't give it to him in the first place."

It is out of the blue. Eamonn and I look at each other. *Christopher knows Cian isn't talking!*

Leaning back into the van I touch his face, hoping he doesn't sense my sadness. I smile at him smiling back at me and thank God for his goodness. I straighten my body again and look up at the navy sky above me and wish upon a star that Santa Claus delivers. The unnatural silence that swells between my boys stifles me. Christmas doesn't soften the blow.

*   *   *

Despite our best efforts to make our new home look Christmassy, Cian takes little interest in anything around him, apart from the crib. We can't stop him from kidnapping baby Jesus and the donkey. All the little gold and white angels from the tree and the entourage of wise men, who are not supposed to show up until twelve days after Christmas, are pulled out from a cardboard box and become part of a complex circular pattern in the middle of the living-room floor. Cian strongly objects if anyone touches them.

"He is organising a conference," Eamonn declares.

I laugh and shake my head. It is now commonplace to find humour and reason for Cian's fascinating behaviours.

"Yeah, he's bringing all divine powers together."

"Uh huh, and a spiritual delegation is meeting to destroy all failings of society and to close down all . . ." Eamonn pretends to preach.

". . . roads that don't lead to the true meaning of

Christmas." I finish his sentence. Eamonn smirks and goes off to rummage in a cupboard for some chocolate.

"Why does Cian not play with my toys, Mammy?"

Eamonn stops munching. "Well . . . he likes playing with other things."

"But they are not toys. You said . . ."

Christopher is looking at Pikachu and I take a long sip of my wine. Eamonn looks on, not sure where this conversation is heading.

"Hmm . . . that's true. But, look – he's pretending they're toys. Now, we need to get to bed before Santa comes . . ."

Christopher stares for a moment, watching Cian make the same pattern over and over on the living-room carpet.

"Come on, let's get ready for bed." I jump up and grab my little perplexed son. "Santa's coming."

Christopher gasps and smiles again.

* * *

Early the next morning he appears at the side of our bed, all five years of him jigging up and down, proclaiming that Santa has come and Cian won't wake up. He trails his daddy out of bed and I grab the camcorder.

Christopher shakes Cian frantically and scrapes him off the mattress, too excited to notice that Cian can barely stand. He manages to stumble to the top of the stairs, plop himself down and lean his head against the banister.

"Look, Cian, Santa has come . . . Look, Santa presents." Christopher leans over him, pointing, trying to get him to look. Cian's body is non-responsive. Christopher turns to us. He is so excited he can hardly contain himself. I remove the

101

camcorder from my face and switch it off. It is quite clear. The joy and fun of Santa is meaningless to Cian. He will not be partaking in the festivities this year either.

Eamonn clasps Christopher's hand and leads him down the stairs.

"Come on, then. Let's see what he got you."

Christopher pulls the cover off a brand new bike and screams with delight. He sits on the saddle and we take some photographs. Suddenly he remembers Cian at the top of the stairs. "Come on, Cian. Look, this one is yours." He drags the sack to the bottom of the stairs. Cian looks lost and confused.

I wrap my arms around my weary three-year-old and carry him down to the bottom of the stairs. He struggles in my arms and I let him go and watch him curl up in a small pile to finger a piece of woollen thread that has unravelled from the hall carpet.

He stares at the Christmas tree lights as we all take turns to coax and cajole him into the spirit of Christmas.

"Here, Cian."

"Look, Cian."

"Open, Cian."

Christopher shakes a present in front of him and rests it on his knee. Cian looks down at the present covered in snowmen and Santa's reindeers, tied up with a big red bow. He shoves it back into Christopher's hand again. Christopher looks at his daddy and me.

"Ah, Mummy, the poor wee thing doesn't know how much fun this is."

I force a smile, hoping it doesn't crack. It is much too early for tears.

"You open it, pet."

Christopher is delighted. He has another whole new bag of presents to open. His little brother walks off and twists the shiny balls off the tree. He piles them up on the floor, feeling them, shaking them and eventually matching them with their pairs. He pulls at the tinsel until the floor is covered in gold and red sparkling threads. The tree looks beaten up and robbed. Just as my heart sinks further and further into my bed socks, Eamonn slips an envelope into my hand. I open it up and find a Christmas card, a keyring and a little note: "Chill out, honey, and get back to your swimming." The keyring boasts full membership of the Glenavon Hotel's Leisure Centre.

I am delighted with my Christmas box. When I met Eamonn, I was a keen swimmer. Since the children came along, trips to the swimming pool have been few and far between. Eamonn promises to keep house when I want to go. It is a good plan in theory, but I know that putting it into practice, tearing myself away from autism, will be much more difficult. I am finding it harder and harder to let go.

Throughout the course of the day the Santa presents are finally examined for a few short moments and then discarded. Cian returns to his old toys and, like the Christmases before, his new toys will have to wait for days, maybe weeks, before he shows any interest in them. We do not give our present. I am saving it to motivate him in the therapy room. Visitors drop by and we go visiting but it is all too much for Cian. He is found wandering outside or alone away from the crowd and noise and the over-stimulating environment. When Christmas Day ends, we are left with a very confused and unsettled child, but all is not lost.

Over the holidays we convert the extra sitting-room into Cian's new "therapy room". Cian's Christmas box – an indoor trampoline and some other "cause and effect" toys – have taken up position in the room. I spend hours pouring over the ABA manual on how to teach him. We will start with fifteen hours a week in the beginning, three hours a day, five days a week.

There is a flicker of hope in my heart. I feel useful again.

12

8.30 a.m. Cian and I pick through our breakfast. We are still in our pyjamas but I am keen to make a start and lead Cian into the therapy room. I hope to fit in three sessions before 11.30 – time enough to shower and dress then.

The new trampoline soon becomes a favourite and highly motivates him. I decide to use it for attention skills and record his responses in my head until I can complete the data sheet. Holding his hands, I give him the instruction in a clear concise voice.

"Look at me."

His look is fleeting but even the slightest movement will earn him a bounce on the trampoline. His response gets better and better and he goes higher and higher, giggling wildly. I mostly play with him. He loves rough and tumble games and I am hoping they will encourage language and eye contact. Every five minutes I go back and stand at the little table and chair.

"Come here."

I use an even tone and look directly at Cian, the way Steve and the book instructed.

No response. Cian is gazing at the patterned wallpaper.

"Come here."

This time I go to him and gently steer him to the table, immediately rewarding him.

"Good boy!"

I squeeze half a dolly mixture between his pursed lips for his efforts. He runs off munching as I record a "P" to indicate that I had manually prompted him for his second trial. A moment later I repeat the command and have to prompt him again, followed up by a reinforcer. On his data sheet I record "NR P P" for no response, prompt and prompt and go and join him for some more rough and tumble. "Aeroplane" is his favourite. I sail him through the air on my feet while he laughs. We then move on to the next task.

I place him near the chair.

"Sit down."

No response.

Eyes averted, he allows me to press him down. He takes his reward eagerly.

"Sit down."

I manually ease him onto the little wooden chair and finish the discrete trial with a reward and a cheer. For the next half hour I divide the time between teaching him and playing with him, encouraging eye contact and language at every opportunity through rough-and-tumble play, singing nursery rhymes and making up songs. We go for a break and then return to complete the process all over, again and again. By 11.30, both of us are shattered.

It doesn't take me long to realise I need more help. I place an advertisement in a local paper. *"Wanted: Reliable, energetic person to work with our fun-loving three-year-old son on a one-to-one intensive home programme. 15hr pw. Training provided."*

* * *

I have three callers one morning just after Cian's therapy session: an educational psychologist arranging a date to assess Cian, a lorry driver looking for directions – and Halle Berry.

Well, that's what I call her, with her sleek cropped hair, swarthy skin and flying jacket. She laughs and tells me her name is Adrienne, that she is the new health visitor and is wondering when it would be convenient to check Cian's hearing and eyesight. I look back at her, my mind racing. *How on earth am I going to get Cian to comply to such tests. Doesn't she know he has autism?* Beckoning her, she follows me into a very untidy kitchen, waves away my offer of tea and eases herself into a chair full of cushions, clothes and teddy bears.

"Cian has a habit of heaping cushions and clothes and all sorts into piles."

Halle rubs her back into the heap behind her.

"Hey, it's pretty cosy actually."

We both laugh. Feeling at ease, I spill out my concerns about testing his ears and eyes. I tell her about ABA and how I hope it will help him.

Halle doesn't bat an eyelid, suggesting she come back in a couple of months to "give him a chance" and "maybe we could work it out the ABA way".

Warmed by her optimism and her ability to think outside the box, I tell her to let me know when she will be calling. Walking back down the hallway, I catch sight of my face in the mirror and the slightly distorted "smiley face" that I had painted on my forehead that morning in red marker to encourage Cian to look at me. I break out in hysterics and swoop Cian up in my arms.

"They think I'm mad, Cian. Now they know I am."

* * *

A week later, I hire my first ABA therapist. Leona is a happy jovial character with a great smile and a background in child studies. She can start immediately and is willing to work with Cian five days a week but she warns me that she is actively seeking work in a school setting. I had hoped to train someone up who was prepared to stay with Cian for the length of the programme but after the poor response I was glad to hire Leona. I help her become familiar with ABA principles and the programme. Trying to teach Cian and the therapist at the same time is difficult and demanding. I am still unsure if I am carrying out the programme correctly. Leona has more questions than I have answers. I contact Steve and he makes another home visit. He is delighted to see that Cian is happy to come to his chair and work at the small table. A number of new programmes are introduced that focus on receptive and expressive language and pre-academic skills.

We need more help. I run the advert again. This time I get a better response. Callers want to see what is involved. I spend days demonstrating ABA techniques to potential "therapists". Cian remains very aloof. Some try it out and find it isn't for them. It is hard to teach a child who gives little back.

Each time I walk by Granny's photograph I ask her to find someone who would be good for Cian. One Thursday afternoon I receive a phone call from Donna.

"I am phoning regarding working one-to-one with your child. I am available in the afternoons if you still need help."

The next afternoon a shy, hesitant twenty-something stands on our front doorstep. She is dressed in a navy blue tracksuit with long sandy hair tied back in a ponytail.

"Hello, I'm Donna."

Before I can answer, Cian bounces down the stairs half-naked, roaring "AREBAREBAAAA," speeds past and leaps under a bunch of cushions in the middle of the living-room floor.

"That *was* our little Mowgli. No prizes for guessing how he earned his name." Donna's eyebrows rise up with curiosity and smiles.

Little Mowgli crawls from underneath the blankets, bounces up and proceeds to walk around the room in circles, making no attempt to look at our visitor.

I remove a multitude of cuddly toys and household items that Cian has precariously stacked on the settee.

"So, you are free in the afternoons, Donna?"

"Yes." She perches herself on the arm of the sofa next to the window. "I work in a playgroup in the mornings."

Suddenly Cian approaches Donna and examines her car keys. She has a number of little colourful trinkets attached to the metal ring. He examines them for a moment, hands them back and proceeds to climb over on top of her. Automatically, Donna holds on to him as he steadies himself on the back of the settee. She makes no attempt to engage with him, but continues to speak in a slow, deliberate voice.

"I have been looking for something in the afternoon. I prefer to work with children but most are in school at that time . . ." Her voice trails off.

Cian makes a loud crowing noise, leaps from his standing position and crashes into the bundle of toys and clothes I didn't quite manage to clear away. Unperturbed, Donna asks me about the one-to-one programme, her eyes following Cian's every move, every now and then smiling at his antics.

She is calm, mature and unassuming and can start immediately. I am delighted to have her on board, not knowing that I have just hired my "backbone" for the next number of years.

While Leona works mornings and Donna gets to know Cian every afternoon, I submerge myself in autism literature and courses and read as much as I can on the concepts of ABA. I cut and paste pictures from catalogues and magazines and stick Velcro on the back. I make up Velcro charts and data sheets and rewards. When I am not cutting and pasting and gathering material for his programmes, I oversee Leona and Donna working with Cian and teaching Cian myself.

In the evening I study his progress and consult the manual again on how to move his programmes on. I encourage Eamonn to be more proactive, more involved with reading and the learning around autism. I trail him to courses, suggesting evening tea on the way back. One way to Eamonn's heart is certainly through his stomach.

I hand him pages and pages of notes as he comes through the door or after dinner with a cup of tea and a slab of carrot cake for encouragement. He sets them aside and later I find him dozing in an armchair with the sheets sprawled on the floor. He is tired. I am full of anxiety. So is Eamonn. Of course I don't know this. He never tells me. I never tell him either. We are just tired. Somehow we muddle through, the silence saying everything.

"Cian's gonna be all right," he will say, swinging him up above his head. I secretly admire his optimism.

"He's gonna be all right only if we get him help," I answer, exasperated. I tut and he teases.

"Come on over here and tell me what you found."

I start trying to explain complicated theories and reasons I don't even understand. Researching autism is like digging in quick sand. He nods and looks interested, every now and then sneaking an odd glance at *Coronation Street*. Until he nods when he shouldn't and I know he isn't listening. I get mad all over again.

I storm out as he protests, "Ah, don't be like that. I'm just tired."

And he is. He has been working very hard, particularly since I gave up work. He thinks I should relax more. I find it impossible to relax. I can't understand the mentality of watching soaps on TV when we are living out our very own serial drama in our own house!

During one of these evenings it becomes clear to me that Eamonn is having great difficulty facing the brutal fact that Cian has autism. He hopes it will just go away, willing Cian to start talking and kicking football and answering him back.

He doesn't have the energy to take on the reality of what we are facing and tries to put it out of his mind.

I am the opposite. I think of nothing else. If I can get Cian sorted then I can get back to work and back to my two-up two-down garden out the back complete with swings and slides. Life would be good again.

* * *

Eamonn does get me to relax a little, however, by suggesting I go for a swim. I agree to go if everyone comes with me. The boys love the water. At first Cian is difficult to watch. He has no concept of danger and from the start he wants to go into the big pool. Eamonn bounces him up and down in the baby pool until one evening Cian escapes his grasp. Fearless and without armbands Cian jumps straight into the pool. While I am hyperventilating, Eamonn dives to the rescue, but there is no need. Cian starts to flap and wriggle like a tadpole. Christopher is jigging up and down.

"Mammy, Mammy, Cian is swimming. He is swimming."

We cheer and laugh and cry and cheer all over again. Christopher bursts into tears.

"Ah, pet, what's the matter?"

He gasps for breath.

"Mammy, why did God not let me be able to swim?"

"Because we learn to do different things at different times. You can talk and Cian can swim!"

He cheers up immensely.

Around this time, when Christopher has been introducing Cian to his friends he would often say: "This is Cian and he can't talk."

The next time I hear him introduce his little brother to his friends, he says: "This is Cian and he can swim."

* * *

The boys enjoy the swimming so much that we contemplate taking out family membership. We are unable to avail of the public swimming pool at the time as it is not suitable for Cian's needs. It is too crowded, too noisy, with many rules and regulations that we find Cian has great difficulty adhering to. In the quieter hotel leisure centre we can supervise him more easily without feeling under pressure from the shrill of staff whistles and public scrutiny. Both the staff and members get to know Cian and take an interest in his growth and development, which means everything to us as parents. It is more expensive but it is the one fun activity in the week that glues us together and relieves stress.

We decide to scrape up the money. When we go to pay, Paula, the manager of the hotel, wants to speak with us. She expresses her delight to hear about Cian's swimming talent and is fully aware of how invaluable our swimming trips are to the leisure centre. She wants to support Cian and us as a family and offers him full membership of the club, with no charge attached. As a parent struggling to find services and constantly facing a serious lack of understanding about the complex needs of autism, this gesture is immeasurable. Paula's insight not only welcomes Cian but also supports our family's needs and appreciates that our trips to the hotel leisure centre are not a luxury but an essential need.

* * *

In therapy, Cian is mostly happy but his attention span is extremely poor and there is an angelic dream-like quality to his gaze. When he is sick we skip therapy and I cuddle his lethargic body in a duvet and put on *Postman Pat*. I take him to the doctor again and again because of the constant high temperatures, conjunctivitis, sore throats and tonsillitis. He is on his twelfth antibiotic before I realise he isn't getting any better. He starts having outbursts as though he is in pain. Pain that fast become part of our day and most of our night.

13

The computer stops whirring and turns black. On tiptoe, I feel my way through the dark to the bedroom: 12.55 a.m. Akin to cat's eyes, the red digits glare at me as I slide under the duvet. Late again. Eamonn stirs but says nothing. He has given up giving off. I shut my eyes and sleep comes almost immediately.

My eyelids snap open. 2.35 a.m. Holding my breath, I remain still, waiting to see if Cian's traumatic outburst passes and fades back into the night. It doesn't. Another piercing scream resounds from the boys' bedroom. Eamonn stirs.

The scream turns into incontrollable sobbing.

I can barely make out Christopher's tiny voice. "Mammy, Mammy, Cian is crying."

Eamonn stirs, pushing back the duvet.

"It's okay, I'll go," I whisper.

I will the dead weight of my body to a standing position,

115

blink away sleep. Christopher appears at my side. "Mammy, Cian is crying and I can't get to sleep." His whimper is croaky and full of yawns.

"It's okay, darling, you snuggle up beside Daddy and I'll sort Cian."

I fix the duvet round him, his tiny body lost in the safety and security of our king-size bed. His eyes close immediately and I marvel at how easy it is to comfort a child without autism.

Another wailing scream speeds me down the corridor. Light escapes around the bathroom door and cuts a thin line into Cian's room. He is lying outside the blankets in the usual foetal position, sobbing. I try to soothe him with my voice.

"Poor Cian, what's the matter, what's wrong?"

I feel silly asking Cian a question he is unable to answer, but I ask anyway. I don't know what else to do. My shadow falls over him as I rest a hand gently on his head. His hair is wet with sweat. Immediately, he pounces back, arching his body away from me, kicking and screaming, twisting and turning his head, barely missing the corner of the bedside table. I reach for a pillow to cover the edge. Cian bounds upward, loses his balance, grabs the curtains, causing the curtain pole to give. Both tumble awkwardly on to the floor. The curtain pole clatters against the wooden floor and Cian scurries, spider-like, into the corner between the bedside table and the wall. For less than a second, his black eyes pierce mine. His lips are pulled tight as though trying to spit out something. He scrapes and scratches his throat, pulling at his face. He opens his mouth but his tongue won't do what he wants it to do. Throwing himself back, he writhes on the floor, crashing his head against the hard wood. A high-pitched lamenting sound escapes from his mouth. I try to read the emotion etched on his face. It could be any one of anxiety, pain, frustration or fear. It continues for some time like a wailing mantra, scraping the dimly lit silence. I try to protect his head but he will not let me near him. Instead he huddles in a lopsided pile halfway under the bed, his tiny body rising and falling with every sob.

Time passes. Hunched awkwardly against the edge of the bed in the profound loneliness of the early hours, I can only wait until he needs me, if he needs me. An aching sensation spreads from my neck to the lower part of my spine but it is nothing compared to the hollow ache inside me. I don't know how to console my child. I don't know what is wrong with my darling boy. I am his mother and I should know these things.

Some time later, I coax his spent body from its hiding place. Back in the bed he holds on to a piece of me as the dark slowly turns an inky blue. The bulge of the moon softens as streaks of crimson bleed a new dawn. Sleep doesn't come but he is restful in the crook of my arm as we share the making of a new day together. Until the next night.

Night after night he screams out like a wild cat, out of control, banging his head off the walls and throwing himself against the furniture, waking him up, screaming and shouting, switching the light on and off, jumping on Christopher.

We offer Christopher a new room but he refuses to be separated from Cian. One night as I bend to kiss them both good night, Christopher lifts his head from the pillow and whispers in my ear, "Mammy, if Cian wakens tonight I will look after him. You get some rest."

Just six years old and already succumbing to the carer's role, a role I have at times encouraged out of necessity and other times discouraged, as I want Christopher to be a child first, free of responsibility and worry about his brother.

So we keep them together and tuck Christopher in safe and warm every night where we have been lying. Either Eamonn or myself comforts him and tries to rest while the other makes an attempt to comfort Cian. When it is my turn I lean into the sharp cold of the bedroom wall, and sit in a stupor, not understanding. Not being understood. Just thinking, often cursing the condition that torments our child. I apply the new skills I have been taught in the bio-energy course and send healing light across the room to the crumpled shadow, who used to be so content and slept all night long. I send him all my love, apologising for times I have been impatient, telling him I will not give up on him. Prayers and novenas pour from my mouth. His huge eyes stare into nothing but sometimes his pupils move suddenly under a furrowed brow or his lips relax and shape like a subtle smile. It is then I think he is listening. I tell Cian Granny and all his angels will help him. I tell myself I need to keep strong. I have to hold on for all of us even though I want to fold like a pack of cards.

14

Everyday life continues but everyday activities are becoming harder. New behaviours are manifesting and changing constantly. One day Cian loves noisy books and squeaky toys; the next he is petrified of toys that talk, flash or move and they all have to be removed from the house. He takes an interest in moving objects and walks towards moving cars and buses. At shop doors he becomes petrified and refuses to walk past "ride-on" cartoon characters. His screams fade to a gasping sob just as we arrive home without the groceries we went for.

Fear spreads to other children's toys and other people's houses. Sometimes we arrive at a friend's house, but Cian refuses to go in and becomes distressed. He climbs into the car again and ignores our friends, who cajole him, thinking he is shy. Explaining why he is frightened only earns a puzzled silence, a shifting of feet. Then the coaxing starts again, but the light sprinkling of endearing words cannot magically make the complex condition of autism disappear. I have conversations in doorways until I decide it is easier to go.

* * *

At home, when he is not in the air, he is usually lying on the floor, lethargic, pale and miserable most of the time. He crawls under mats and buries himself under cushions and rugs.

At meal times he only seems to be interested in eating sugar from the sugar bowl and dry Weetabix straight out of the box. What is more alarming is that he seems to prefer non-edibles – dirt, sand, toilet cleaner, the contents of his nappy, jewellery . . . everything but food. This behaviour jogs my memory and reminds me of my father, not because of his eating habits, but because of things that he had taught me. I was reared on a farm. My dad is a man of the soil. He can predict the weather by observing the colour of the frogs. He can read the time by the shadow of the sun. He cared for his animals like a mother does her babies. He could tell by their behaviours what they needed. If a cow started to eat bark from a tree, he would say, "That cow is deficient in something." He would tend it and make it better again.

In the University of Google a cyber-parent suggests I go to Cian's doctor and get him to run a test to check how Cian is metabolising minerals. It is good advice but from my experience there is more chance of the doctor running me out of the surgery!

I read up a little more and learn about pica, the eating of non-foods, and introduce a mineral supplement – two drops in Cian's juice – without the test. Three days later, it has all stopped, so much so that I think I have imagined it and get careless with the drops. I haven't imagined it. It all starts again. The mineral supplement is like magic but it isn't magic. Cian's body is obviously deficient in minerals.

This incident causes me to become interested in what is going into Cian's mouth and wonder if food is causing some of his difficulties. His ears flare bright purple, his eczema bleeds angrily and putrid diarrhoea leaks out of his nappies, lifting the skin from his bottom and in between his thighs. I change his milk from cow's milk to goat's milk and spread raw egg over the burnt and blistering bottom. We use aromatherapy oils to induce sleep. We drive all over the country to healers and priests. We receive relics and prayers in the post. Before long, Cian's little bed is like a religious shrine.

I find an internet site supporting parents who have introduced a special diet for autism – a gluten-free, casein-free diet. I learn about two proteins, one in wheat and one in milk, that can cause havoc in the gut lining of children's stomachs. On the advice of other parents using the diet, we can either try out the diet or get Cian's urine tested for the offending peptides. A little sceptical, we decide to test. It comes back positive. I go back to the doctor who grants me a prescription for gluten-free food and a referral to a dietician.

* * *

Cian flits through the toys, discarding them just as quickly. He wanders around the room, examining the walls and the legs of the chairs, touching everything he sees. As the secretary walks into the room Cian suddenly runs slam into the Lego, causing it to come crashing down, with Elmo tumbling to the floor. Cian squeals "Umpty umpy" at the same time the secretary asks me his name.

I jump up and beam at Cian. "He said Humpty Dumpty. Did you hear it? He definitely said Humpty . . ."

This draws a complete blank from the secretary as I try to pull myself together. *Way too much information.*

"Mmm. Cian McCallan . . . for the dietician . . . 10.00 a.m." I hand her the letter and turn back towards Cian, my grin as wide as Elmo's.

The lady beckons me to follow her and behind her back I put my thumbs up at Cian.

"Good boy! Humpty Dumpty sat on a wall and you knocked him down – good boy. Now Cian, let's . . ."

"GO!"

"Yeah, good boy, nice talking."

He runs after me and I give him the thumbs-up again before turning towards the bewildered secretary standing in the door frame waiting for us. As I reach the dietician's office, I realise Cian is not following, dart back and grab his hands from his mouth before he eats the loose paint he has just peeled from the wall. I swing him and Elmo up in my arms. By the time I get to the dietician's office, the secretary has disappeared.

The dietician looks up and gestures for me to take a seat. Cian climbs onto some piece of unidentifiable apparatus sitting in the corner of the room.

"So. This is Cian."

She makes another note.

"Yes."

"And you are worried about his diet?"

I clear my throat.

"Well . . . not worried, exactly . . . Well, yes, worried about Cian, about his *symptoms*. I have heard about a diet; we would like to give it a try. It's called the gluten- and casein-free diet? We got results of a urine test back from the Autism Research Unit at Sunderland University and it shows a high level of opioid peptides in his system. Apparently Cian may not be breaking down food particles properly. We would like to try the diet and see if it helps."

The lady's face gives nothing away and I am not sure if she thinks I am being rational or ridiculous.

"Where did you get this information?"

I pull a book from my bag: *Diet Intervention and Autism – Implementing the Gluten Free and Casein Free Diet for Autistic Children and Adults: A Practical Guide for Parents* by Marilyn Le Breton and Rosemary Kessick. "This book amongst others."

She glances through the book and hands it back to me. "Well, you know more about it than I do."

I breathe a little easier. I like her honesty. She observes Cian for a moment. He is playing with Elmo again.

"It doesn't look like he is wasting away. There is no harm in trying something for a short while to see if it would help." She studies a three-day chart I had drawn up on Cian's daily intake of food. "Okay, looks like Cian's diet is pretty balanced." She imparts some advice about basic nutrition for kids and wishes me luck.

Our body language must signal to Cian that we are done because he suddenly drops dopey Elmo and bolts over towards me. With one swoop, I lift him up, shove my book back in my bag, smile in appreciation and leave the non-judgemental dietician to prepare herself for her next client.

* * *

While Donna and Leona are working with Cian I source plausible foods and bake and cook and bake some more. The books advise us to go slowly. We go cold turkey. Removing milk is easy. Removing wheat is a nightmare. It is in everything. Grocery trips to the supermarkets take hours. I lurk among shelves, examining ingredient lists that are longer than Christopher's letters to Santa and come to realise that Cian can eat very little. Wheat is in pizza, chicken nuggets, cereals, sausages, some brands of oven chips, ham, baked beans, soups, sauces – in fact, everything that he will eat for me. Choice is practically non-existent. My only answer is to swing a few pots and pans and produce them myself.

For the first few weeks, most of my efforts go to the bin. Not even the dog is interested. To introduce the new foods to Cian, I go back to the dancing and cajoling, again to no avail. We try to keep forbidden food out of reach. Anyone who drops by for a cuppa watches me stand on top of the worktop to retrieve sugar and biscuits hidden above kitchen cupboards. Sometimes these foods are pulled from the kitchen fan or the dishwasher, my wardrobe or locked in the utility room. It is completely abnormal. Cian keeps finding them until we stop buying goodies and lock the kitchen.

Cian's sugar cravings drive him crazy. He wants more and more gluten-free biscuits and banana pancakes. I find a product called Stevia over the internet to sweeten his foods.

There is a bit of an aftertaste to it and it is difficult to bake with but at least it gives Cian a choice of something sweet. I keep a food journal and swap favourite foods with gluten/casein-free foods. Out goes pizza and puddings. In go peach pancakes and fruit purees. Some nutrition, disguised in pancakes and the ever-versatile muffin, finds its way into Cian's stomach.

In the early weeks it is difficult to know if the diet is helping or not. Cian is hyper and seems to be more irritable. I go back to my book and it confirms that the child may have a reaction to the diet:

Children crave the very foods that will have to be omitted. When they don't have them, they suffer the associated withdrawal symptoms and lows. It is difficult and time-consuming to begin but it does get easier and it is worth it.

It is also suggested that when gluten and casein are removed, other intolerances may show up.

Family and friends are sceptical and think I have gone mad. Trialing foods is hard work and to the outsider difficult to understand. One day Cian can have a banana; the next day he can't. He can't have treats. This is particularly difficult for Cian's grandparents. That's what grandparents are for – sneaking treats and getting away with giving forbidden sweets. Now they are forbidden to give Cian anything. It is stressful in other people's houses, trying to keep Cian from lifting food. I am told to let him be. I am almost persuaded. The endless cooking rituals and the withdrawal symptoms are becoming unbearable.

Until one evening I walk into the hall and Cian is building a twelve-piece jigsaw puzzle all by himself. No one has told him to do it. No one is helping him. Cian builds the puzzle piece by piece. I am flabbergasted. It is the first time I have seen him do something constructive. The next morning, I check with Leona and Donna. They both comment on his alertness and reassure me that he is responding more quickly in the therapy.

It is a start. We are no longer sceptical. The books explain that it takes nine months for gluten to leave the system, so we know we have to be patient. We are in for the long haul.

Behaviours gradually settle down and Cian seems to come from behind "frosted glass". He is not as disconnected with our world and seems to be more aware of people around him. His eczema dries up and the angry rashes on his face disappear. He is calmer and happier. The manic giggling and bright red ears are gone. His tummy is not as bloated and he looks a little less pasty. The dark circles under his eyes don't seem as dark and he no longer has problems with his ears or throat.

The diet seems to have alleviated some of his symptoms but Cian continues to have problems. When he manages to get even a tiny amount of wheat, he becomes spacey and loses control of his bladder. He sobs and whines and bites and bangs his head. The wailing pain, the writhing and holding of his abdominal muscles must have something to do with his diet. I need answers.

15

In late March I learn of a conference being held in Dublin to discuss medical treatments for children with autism. I book two tickets over the internet. A few days later I get a call from an organiser of the conference. She asks me if I will go on regional television to create better awareness about the biomedical needs of children and to publicise the conference. I laugh into the receiver. "Thanks, but no thanks. I am as sleep-deprived as a navy seal, I can't remember the last time I was at the hairdresser's and I don't think I am up to becoming a public advocate on national television just yet."

The lady laughs. She probably thinks I am joking. She pleads with me that the conference is the first of its kind in Ireland and it could really help inform parents of these important issues. When my parent strings are pulled, I can't decline. After all, we are having some success with the diet. Since we eliminated wheat and milk, Cian has been sleeping better and his eczema and whole demeanour have improved. He seems to be less in a perpetual "dazed" state. He still needs full-time supervision but his behaviour is a little more manageable. The journalist is right. Other parents do need to be aware of the biomedical issues.

As luck would have it, I get a call from the BBC later that afternoon. The organiser had been put through to Shane Glynn's office. Shane is a very old friend of mine from college days. I had run into him the day I had been down to Belfast for the parents' workshop. Now he is at the other end of the phone wanting to know when he can come up.

The next morning, Leona is working with Cian when Shane and the cameraman arrive. It is really good to see Shane, which takes the stress out of doing the interview. In the kitchen we drink hot coffee and scones with melting butter and strawberry jam as we catch up on college days and family life.

While we are chatting I am oblivious to the cheers and claps coming from the other room.

"Good boy, Cian."

"That's the way."

"Well done."

"You're a star."

My inquisitive guests are not. They can't ignore the intermittent cheers of praise.

"Who's that?" Shane asks, his head on one side, listening.

"That's Leona, one of Cian's therapists."

I bite into my buttered scone.

"Oh!" he looks thoughtful. "So where is she from?"

"Just up the road." I take another bite that tastes divine.

I missed breakfast again. I also misunderstand his question.

Shane chokes on the hot coffee and bursts out laughing. "No, I mean, what organisation is she from?"

"Oh, sorry. She is not from any organisation. We have 'employed' and trained her to deliver our intensive one-to-one ABA home programme."

Shane stops chewing and looks at me in complete disbelief. "What? Let me get this – you have a child with autism who you have to teach yourself and you had to find and train someone up to work with him?"

"Two someones actually. Donna comes in the afternoon. I am looking for a third therapist at the moment."

Shane and Mark look at each other, then back at me.

"Why isn't he in school?" Shane looks thoughtful.

"Well, there are no autism-specific one-to-one programmes for Cian and all research shows that he needs one-to-one early intervention as young as possible. We can't wait any longer, so we have started to teach him at home."

Shane turns to Mark.

"We've got our story."

The inadequate educational provision for children with autism in Northern Ireland and my efforts to meet Cian's needs are broadcast on regional television that night. The biomedical needs don't get a mention, even though I am beginning to feel it is an equally important issue.

* * *

The conference is fully booked, mostly with parents and family members, a few doctors in private practice and a dusting of other professionals interested in nutrition and health.

I suspect that if I had not been so weary, laden down with worry and sorrow, maybe I could have grasped more of the concepts. It is the first time away from Cian and I can feel my body and mind zoning out. It is too much information for me. The intensity of the lectures fries my brain. I would need to have been a biochemist. Most of it goes over the top of my head, except the photographs – the "before" and "after" shots of children, scores of them, getting better from autism – and Dr Andrew Wakefield.

There is a tea break and I make a quick dash to the loo. Making my way back to the conference room, I bump straight into him. I recognise him from the newspapers. He is the academic gastroenterologist who has suggested a possible link between the MMR vaccine, bowel disease and autism in a study published in *The Lancet* in 1998. Before I know what I am doing, I introduce myself and start telling him about Cian – his night waking, his bowel movements, his screaming fits. He listens intently to what I am saying, his head bowed to the side, nodding. An official catches his arm and tells him it is time. He nods briefly and turns back to me. Politely he apologises that he has to go shortly but then he leans forward and asks, "What is your son's name?"

"Cian."

"Okay, if you remember nothing else from the conference today, remember this one thing. You have more power than me. You are Cian's mother. Print off the research papers, keep up-to-date, do what you have to do. You must go back to Cian's doctor as many times as it takes. Cian needs help. You must get him to listen. Your son needs you to never give up. You must continue to fight for him. Even if you don't fully understand, find someone who does."

He leaves me then to take my seat and listen to him deliver a presentation that explains a lot of Cian's difficulties.

At the end of the conference, photographs of children before and after autism are presented on a screen. Children in America are getting better through biomedical and ABA interventions.

* * *

Sitting opposite Cian's doctor, autism hangs in the air like a bad smell. We discuss the information I have learned from the conference.

"Hmmm. Yes, Dr Wakefield . . . I have read about him."

Wakefield had stepped outside the box and had challenged an intrinsically antagonistic medical board, the same board Cian's doctor is registered with. I may as well have been asking him to play Russian roulette.

I leave Cian's doctor that day with a bucket-load of sympathy and a warning to be careful of those who offer cures. They more than likely will only waste my time and money and lead me to a place called nowhere. I do not doubt there is concern in his voice and an element of truth in his warning. However, climbing into my car, I feel crushed between a rock and a hard place. For a moment I wonder if Cian's doctor feels the same way. Does he believe I have reason to question? I don't know. I only know that a serious lack of knowledge on my part in biochemistry, combined with a serious lack of confidence and confusion on who to believe, stops me in my tracks. The only thing I am sure about is that Cian's intestinal issues present just as Dr Wakefield describes.

* * *

When I get back home I am distracted by a number of calls from parents who saw the news feature about Cian's home programme. Some want to know about ABA. Some want to know if Cian's therapist can come and work with their child. Others want to know if they can come and see me to learn more about the programme. Most want to chat to another mother.

It is one of these calls that alerts me to the London Early Autism Project (LEAP), which offers a fully supervised ABA programme, complete with materials, training and a structured curriculum with ongoing support, based on the work of Dr Ivar Lovaas. With PEAT's limited resources stretched to capacity, the idea of a consultant overseeing our ABA programme is like manna from heaven. It is an obvious answer but one that comes at a hefty price: £30,000 per year.

I phone a few parents already employing LEAP to check out the service. I talk to Nicola, a parent of a little boy with autism who is following the programme. It has been a lifesaver. I can't believe she is taking it lying down – having to pay an astronomical fee for her son's education.

"Are you not angry that you have to fly consultants over from London and put them up in hotels to educate your son?"

"You sound like my husband, Brendan. I think you should talk to him." She laughs.

I talk to Brendan for almost two hours. In that one phone call we agree that we will try to further the accessibility of ABA to parents in Northern Ireland.

"But first you must set up your own programme."

I tell him I will have to wait for educational funding. He tells me I can't wait. He will help. So does Siobhan, another parent. On the phone she urges me to do all I can to get the programme up and running.

"You can fundraise. Get your family and friends to help. You haven't got a choice," she warns me. "Start as soon as you can. I will help you." And she does, in so many ways. Siobhan and Brendan, parents I haven't even met, fill me up with strength and hope.

* * *

We consider our options and make a decision to pursue funding from our local education board. Meanwhile family and friends fundraise to get Cian's programme up and running. Eamonn's sister Rosemary organises an event and the rest of the family put up prizes for raffles. Family and friends attend and buy things they do not need. Cian's cousin Leona fundraises in New York. Áine sends money from England. Relations from England and America, some we have never met, send generous donations. The school and college that I worked with present me with donations. We are so grateful for everyone's help but it is totally against what we believe. Cian's education should not be at the mercy of kind donations, but we have no choice. Early intervention must be just that – early.

I make a phone call to LEAP and an assessment is scheduled for late May.

16

The lobbying begins. I contact IPSEA (Independent Panel for Special Educational Assessment). They offer information and support to parents who home-school their children. They inform me that a child needs an assessment and a formal statement to get help with a home programme. I pen a letter to my local education authority:

". . . I am writing as the parent of the above-named child to request an assessment of his special educational needs under the 1996 Education Act."

It is the first of many letters. I write to different charity bodies, local councillors, Martin McGuinness (the Education Minister at that time), disability groups, anyone who I think may help me in my quest to obtain funding and support for Cian's intensive therapy programme.

There is no end to the long brown envelopes being delivered by Postman Pat.

"Look, Cian, it's Postman Pat, look, look!"

I twist his body round and point towards the door. Two fists cling on to the ends of my cardigan as I hoist him up in a standing position to steer him towards the door.

"Postman Pat. Postman Pat. Postman Pat and his black and white . . . cat!"

Postman Pat has spied us through the glass and knocks on the door loudly.

"It's Postman Pat, Cian. Let's open the door."

I clutch a sticky fist and mould it around the handle, gently pressing down until the latch snaps backwards.

"Hello, Postman Pat."

"Hello. Hello, Cian. Three letters today, Cian. Will you count them with me? Put out your hand."

I fold out his arms, turning his little palms upwards towards "Postman Pat". Cian's eyes are blank. He is not looking at his hands or at "Postman Pat" but is lost in the red of "Postman Pat's" van.

"Now, Cian . . . One . . . two . . . three. Three letters today."

Cian struggles under my grasp to escape. "Postman Pat" tosses his hair.

"You're a very handsome boy, Cian. You be good for Mammy now."

He climbs back into his van. "Postman Pat" gives me the thumbs-up, toots the horn at Cian and drives off. Cian does not look up, as though "Postman Pat" has never been.

I am grateful for the way the postman talks to Cian rather than to me, the way he takes time to count out the letters to Cian one by one. He told me once that he has a nephew called Matthew who also has autism and his understanding touches a chord, because it epitomises what I hope for when people meet my son. I want them to see my son and not a word or a condition or a disability. I would like them to speak to him even when he doesn't speak back, and see him as we see him: Cian, our little boy.

Getting the letters is fun, reading the letters is not. Cian gets the envelope to rip and I get the news that no charity supports individuals or education programmes that are the responsibility of government bodies.

* * *

A family adviser suggests I contact social services. When the social worker comes I sit across from her, barefaced and exhausted after another sleepless night. When she asks about Cian I tell her about his therapy programme, about his progress. I suggest I could do with some help. The social worker listens politely but Cian's therapy programme is not on her agenda. I answer her questions as she ticks her boxes and takes a few notes, but she warns me that the assessment does not guarantee services. Before she leaves, she looks in on Cian as Leona works and plays with him in his therapy room. I am so proud of him, proud of our efforts, even though they are exhausting. She asks me if I miss work. I tell her I haven't time to miss it. She nods sympathetically and suggests I should get back to it before I wear myself out.

The lack of support knots me into a state of frustration. There is no doubt her remark comes from a place of concern, but I find it extremely difficult to cope with unhelpful comments from well-meaning professionals who try to inject a sense of reality into my situation. With all due respect, they don't take Cian home at the end of the day for sleepovers. All I want is for Cian to be respected for the little person that he is and not limited by the textbook prognosis of autism. I simply want what any mother would want for their child: the best that I can get.

A month later, I receive a copy of the case plan and an allocation of two hours per fortnight for home help respite care, with conditions attached. The home help is not permitted to be on her own in our home or with Cian; nor is she permitted to take him in her car. Their allocation only highlights the inadequate services and confirms their lack of understanding of autism. How do they expect a child with autism to bond with someone they only see for two hours a fortnight? The father I met at Fuerteventura airport was right. I now understand his anger, his frustration, and the lack of hope that had ground him down.

* * *

I lift the phone and call Joe Byrne, a local councillor and MLA. After discussing at length my situation and the situation most parents suffer across Northern Ireland, he agrees to help and motions the issue in Stormont, paving the way for myself and a number of parents to present our case to a number of MLAs in the Long Gallery in Stormont Buildings. Inside the great walls of Stormont, MLAs move in and out between sessions as we blast from our soapbox about the lack of services and plead for support. Sadly, there are more parents in the room than government officials and while we are closing our laptops and gathering up our leaflets, a sense of apathy jades me. Disillusioned, I leave the Long Gallery as the next lobbying group arrives and lines up with their placards and protests to deliver their presentation.

Our lobbying event takes place just after a document commissioned by the Department of Education, the Task Group on Autism, is published. The report recommends that an eclectic approach is the preferred intervention, compared to a specific ABA therapy programme. This has implications for parents who have applied for funding for their ABA programme. ABA therapy finds itself hanging off a political cliff.

We, however, continue to seek funding for Cian's therapy programme from the local education authority. We are using a variety of teaching methods, including PECS, floortime, play therapy, schedule boards and speech therapy and occupational therapy recommendations, but it is the ABA structure and the one-to-one intensive stimulation that mostly contributes to his progress.

* * *

Easter arrives in the second-last week of April. Donna and Leona take a well-earned break from ABA. Instead, I prepare to toilet-train Cian. The cupboards are stocked to capacity with food. I have no intentions of going anywhere anytime soon. I am in no hurry; I don't know if we will achieve our goal but I am prepared to give Cian until next Christmas. I am hoping that he will be able to master this one thing by himself, with his dignity and independence intact.

Cian runs around naked. I let him go free, hoping that

when he feels wet he will become aware of his body. I run after him first with the potty, hoping to encourage the use of it. Cian only wants to play with it. He likes wearing it on his head, dancing in it, walking around with it, putting toys in it – anything but using it for its real purpose. So I toss the potty idea and let him roam free. It is not the time to be house-proud. On the fourth day, Cian's bladder empties onto the kitchen tiles. He stares down and watches it trickle across the tiles. He feels his chubby legs and I cry with joy. "Yes, Cian, that is coming out of you."

It is time to negotiate the bathroom. I make it the most exciting place in the house. Eamonn puts up a very high shelf. Everything that Cian wants is on that shelf – bags of sweets and his favourite toys. We play games of chase and I run to the toilet. He follows. I swirl him up in my arms and for a split second sit him on the bowl. Then up again and down, and away he runs, giggling. Sometimes I gesture towards the shelf. I sweep him up and ask him to sit on the bowl for a count to three – "1, 2, 3!" and allow him to grab his favourite thing. I do this morning, noon and evening, playing and waiting, giving him loads of water so he can have loads of practice.

At the end of the first week, Cian seeks out the toilet all by himself and we clap and cheer and jig up and down. Priceless! We are ecstatic. Two nights later, I attempt to put Cian's nappy on for bed. He holds on to my shoulders and clamps his knees shut. He is having no nappy. "Right, son, you're on your own." I put on a pair of brand new pants. He doesn't wet the bed that night, or the next, or the next. He proves the books wrong.

Everything that most people consider natural and

commonplace, we will have to show him, teach him, lead him and help him, over and over and over, to enable understanding until it becomes intrinsic in his mind. ABA has given me the tools to help me teach him. We continue to work on eye contact, language and play skills and encourage communication as much as possible in whatever way he can. The ABA principles have spilled out of the therapy room into the rest of our daily living. Christopher is keen to practise them on Cian. He is enjoying giving instructions but gets better fun handing over an "award".

Eamonn tries out a few "trials" too when Cian heaves a large multicoloured throw off the sofa and shoves the end of it onto Eamonn's knee. There is no eye contact, no language, no "Daddy".

"What do you want?" Eamonn teases him.

Silence.

One hand pulls at Daddy's hand.

"Oh, you want Daddy up?"

Daddy gets up and Cian runs around his feet, pulling the blanket after him.

"What do you want now?"

Cian grabs Eamonn's hand and throws it at the edge of the blanket.

"Oh . . . I . . . know what you want – you want a SWING!"

Cian drops the end of the blanket, sits on it and waits.

Eamonn and I look at each other. *Cian understands language.*

Christopher comes from nowhere. "I want a swing. Swing me. I want a swing."

Eamonn curls the edges of the blanket round his tight

fists and the boys take turns swinging left and right in the blanket.

"Mammy, Mammy, look at me!"

Christopher loves it and tumbles out to allow Cian to have his go. Cian clambers in, giggling with anticipation. He lies back, his whole body twitching with adrenaline, and we wait until he gives us the fleeting look that means GO! We swing him high, counting, "1, 2, 3, 4, 5 . . . wheeeee . . ." and bounce him down on the sofa as he shakes with laughter.

Christopher wants to be swung with Cian and I take one end while Eamonn takes the other. We laugh and cheer and count out loud, "1, 2, 3, 4, 5 . . . wheeeeee . . ." We swing high and dump our two rascals on the sofa, laughing and giggling with red cheeks as we collapse on the other sofa before our lower backs cave in.

* * *

One afternoon I put Cian in the car and go to the shop for some milk. The shop is only two miles away. When I stop the car engine, Cian starts to cry. In the shop he wails and kicks as I purchase the milk. When I attempt to put him back into his car seat again, he arches his back and screams blue murder. It takes all of my energy to restrain him back into his car seat again.

When it happens again, I notice that it is on another short journey or when I take a different road or drive past a place where he would like to stop. I decide to turn to the ABA strategies I have learnt to deal with challenging behaviour and take an ABC chart of his behaviour. Basically this involves looking at the antecedent – what causes the behaviour? – noting the type of behaviour and the consequence of his behaviour. I hope that applying ABA methods will teach Cian that every time he gets into the car he might not be going on a long journey or to anywhere in particular.

I put him in the car, drive down our lane and then turn and come back. He howls as if someone is stabbing him. Up and down I go, intermittently, for most of a week. Sometimes I go farther. Sometimes I take a different road. I soothe him with gentle words and reward him every time for remaining calm and seated in his little car seat.

* * *

Having the tools and the knowledge to help Cian in situations where he feels challenged empowers me, but there are situations where he does not feel challenged or frustrated, times when he seems oblivious to a little boy's world, times when he is content in his own world.

From the kitchen window, I watch him sitting on his knees by the swing, still and quiet, thumbing the petals of a buttercup or pouring sand through his fingers, over and over. Six feet away, Christopher and his cousins swing and jump and squeal with delight. They huddle, plot and scatter, rushing past Cian. He is not part of the gang. He does not run with the pack. He is left behind, lost in his own silence. I want him to jump up and rush after the rest of them. I want him to run and squeal and get into trouble, because that is what little boys do. I want to hear the teasing, the laughing, the poking of fun that goes on between brothers. Anything would be better than this nothingness.

Wringing my hands in a tea towel, I walk into the sunshine towards him. His head is tilted to one side, listening. The birdsong is sweet and cheerful and a hint of a smile puckers one side of his face. There is an incredible peace around him. I sit near him on an old railway sleeper. If I come too close, like the bird he could fly away. He does not acknowledge me but continues to stare out of the corner of his eye and listen. A few moments later, the bird flies away. Cian leans over and places his head on my shoulder, slipping his hand in mine. The silence cushions a connection between us, a connection that is only found in silence. Sometimes I encourage the children to include Cian. They lead him to the trampoline or kick a ball to him. Cian complies for a time. We organise play dates with other children and they encourage him but soon Cian blends back into the background again.

There is an emptiness in his isolation that grieves me but not more than when pain grips him and causes him to hurl himself against the floor, rocking back and forth, holding his head and stomach. Cian does not have the language or the means to tell us why he is screaming and holding his sides and his head. We find ourselves guessing. Sometimes we get it very wrong. We take him to the dentist. There is no obvious decay. Most of his bottom teeth are removed. Just in case. Cian continues to scream and I search and search for ways to help him.

* * *

At the beginning of May, Cian and I board a plane to visit a homeopathic doctor who is treating children with autism.

Áine meets us at the airport and drives us to Manchester. In a large Victorian waiting room, she waits as we have our consultation. Outside in the leafy car park I cajole Cian into eating some of his "special" food and chat a little about what the doctor had to say and the treatment. Driving back to Áine's home in Leeds, the road is thick with traffic that stops and starts our journey. We talk about home, life, dreams, ambitions; things we will probably never talk about again. She doesn't question any of the interventions I am trying out. But something about her demeanour tells me she is hoping, praying we find a way into the little forlorn boy in the back seat of her car who has yet to acknowledge his auntie.

17

A consultant from the London Early Autism Project assesses Cian in the last week of May, and a training workshop is scheduled for June. Thirty-five hours a week of daily one-to-one therapy is recommended – fifteen hours more than Cian is currently receiving. We need more help. I place another advertisement in the local paper and post some notices in local colleges and shops. Again, there is a poor response. Our home is miles from any college or university – students are either unavailable or inaccessible. Getting and keeping therapists remains an ongoing problem but after receiving an end-of-term report from the speech therapist and the home tutor I try to keep focused. Cian has failed to meet the twenty-five targets outlined in a list of objectives that had been drawn up by the home tutor. The report states that Cian's communication skills are severely delayed. He has shown little progress during the year, with no eye contact and minimal social understanding.

However, when the speech therapist reviews him again in September she is astonished at his progress. The last time she had seen him she had only heard him utter and understand one word, "*etee*" (sweet). Now he can verbalise over a hundred and demonstrate his understanding.

"Show me door."

Cian runs to the door.

"Point to cup."

Cian points to cup.

"Show me nose."

He points to his nose.

"What is it?"

"Dog."

Clever boy.

It is clear that Cian's receptive skills and expressive speech have vastly improved since introducing a more intense structure to his ABA programme.

It hasn't come easy. Leona gets the job she has been looking for in a local school and regrettably has to leave. I advertise again and spend hours and days training potential therapists, many of whom leave a short time later. It is difficult finding the "right" person to motivate and have the physical stamina to engage with Cian and make learning fun while following the principles of ABA therapy. Eventually I get another therapist. Anne is a young mother with two little girls of her own. She is hoping to pursue a career in nursing but is taking a year out. I am delighted that she has joined the team, bringing the grand total to two plus *moi*. Until I have three therapists, I realise I will have to do therapy myself. LEAP does not favour parents doing therapy but to keep the hours up I have little choice. I am practically doing it anyway as I demonstrate the principles and techniques and move forward with Cian's programmes.

At the beginning it is tough – tough on Cian, tough on me. Cian has to be taught everything most toddlers do naturally. I have to be a therapist when I want to be a mother. I want to cuddle and protect him, yet as his therapist I am not allowed to do either. Therapists have to be consistent and any emotional baggage has to be hung up at the other side of the therapy room door.

With a little tray of gluten- and casein-free edibles on a shelf above me and a box of Cian's favourite bits and pieces at my feet, I shape and prompt his responses until he masters every programme and then generalise his newly learned skills across stimuli and settings. We are working on gross motor imitation, teaching Cian to copy our movements. Imitation is such a vital part of learning. We all learn by imitation. Even as adults, if we don't know how to put money in a trolley or parking machine, we will watch someone else or ask someone to show us how to do it. I believe if we can teach Cian to imitate, it will help him learn so much. If I clap my hands or raise my arms above my head and ask Cian to copy me, he can't. He simply stares off into space without moving a muscle. I bring Cian in front of the mirror and raise his arms up high so that he can see himself. He touches the mirror and explores the reflection of his hand. He is very curious. I am not sure if he knows he is looking at himself. I spend hours stretching my arms above my head and encouraging Cian to do the same. Eventually he learns to raise his arms above his head. Now we have to teach him a new skill and help him to differentiate between the two movements.

"Do this." I clap my hands.

Cian stares at the space between the top of my head and the ceiling. I take his tiny hands in mine and show him how to clap. The minute I let go, his hands fall limp in his lap.

"Good clapping!" I hand him a little windmill he is working for. He likes to watch it go round and round. He is unable to blow so I blow for him and his face lights up. I blow a few more times and then I set it down again and continue with my discrete trial.

"Do this." I clap my hands.

Taking his tiny hands in mine, I clap them together.

"Nice clapping."

Lifting the windmill, I hand it to Cian and blow and blow and then set it aside until he has completed the trial.

"Do this." I clap my hands.

Cian presses his chubby hands together.

"Yeah! Well done. You are clapping."

It is a breakthrough. Sheer excitement causes me to swing him out of the chair and do a twirl as he giggles helplessly. Then I remember the windmill and allow him to clutch it in his little paws while I blow and blow.

Moments later, I tell him to "Go Play" as I tally up his data sheet: PPC. Now I need CCC to complete the mass trial, the term used in ABA to describe each task.

Then I will start all over again with a random trial, where I encourage Cian to copy a number of different movements. I will do the action Cian has already learnt like raising his arms above my head. I will raise my hands:

"Do this."

Cian raises his hands.

"Good boy." I give him his reward – a tickle under the arm.

Then I clap my hands. Cian goes to put his hands up and I shape them into a clap.

"Nice try." He gets a tickle.

"Do this." I clap my hands again and Cian claps his.

I tickle him until he tumbles over – tell him to go play and tally up my data sheet: CPC. I complete this discrete trial again and again before we have some floor time.

I spend days clapping my hands; stomping my feet; hopping on one foot. Over time Cian learns to clap and wave and jump and imitate everything I do.

Cian learns how to point to objects and body parts and identify pictures of familiar people. He learns to distinguish and name colours, shapes, numbers, prepositions and opposites. He learns to follow simple instructions and carry out tasks that he finds difficult like putting on his socks and shoes. Language is difficult for him. He needs to be constantly encouraged and gently prompted. Still, he makes pleasing gains in language and can answer simple questions. He learns how to play more appropriately inside and outside the therapy room. Thankfully, Cian seems to enjoy his therapy. He normally skips into the room, happy to go along and work at his desk and play with the toys that are carefully chosen for floor-play.

There are times he isn't well and he just switches off, on and off like a disappearing act. Now you see it, now you don't. His sleeping has now become more erratic. No matter what time of the night we go into his bedroom, he is wide-awake and wants to prowl the house, making it completely impossible for us to sleep. His body simply can't switch off at the end of the day and he is getting up again about 2.00 a.m. By the time Eamonn is meant to be getting up for work, Cian would be dozing off and we all would doze with him, cancelling therapy and work until we wake again.

Other mornings, I stand in the hallway with the slam of the front door ringing in my ears. Eamonn and Christopher have just left and I am alone again, trying to pull my little boy from the depths of nowhere. When I am unable to reach him I want to give up. It is the exhaustion that tests me the most, though the isolation, the loneliness is equally as bad.

When I am really organised and not too tired I actually have some fun too and really enjoy teaching Cian. A lot of the time Cian hums while he works. I would call him to the table. He would complete his trial promptly and get to play again. Sometimes he comes and hangs about my neck as I am tallying the data. When I am done, I wrestle and tickle him. He roars with pleasure and we rough and tumble around the floor until it is time for another trial. I get instant pleasure at watching how quickly he grasps the concepts and how easy it is to teach him in this way when he is alert and motivated.

* * *

When Jacqueline, an old school friend, calls with her mother one Saturday, I am delighted to see them both. We are just about to have a workshop. The consultant and all the therapists are gathered in the next room, ready to make a start. I quickly make some tea and buttered scones. Cian comes bouncing out from the room and immediately sits up on Jacqueline's knee. He plays with her hair and Jacqueline tickles him and sings nursery rhymes. One of the therapists calls out and he runs back to the therapy room. When he disappears, Jacqueline is inquisitive and I tell her I have a workshop and that Cian's therapists have arrived for training. I tell her about the ABA programme, how difficult it is to get therapists, but how Cian is making good progress. My speech is hurried, urgent. Jacqueline's mother smiles politely and Jacqueline listens and bites her lip.

"So . . ." I sit down and take a gulp of my coffee and ask about John and Justine and Fergal.

The therapists start to file out of the living room and Jacqueline nods towards the French doors. "Think they are ready to go. Where did you say the workshop was?"

I look at her and realise how abnormal my life is. "It's here, Jacqueline, in the house. The consultants come over every six weeks. I pick them up from the airport. Thank God all the therapists can come on a Saturday."

Jacqueline breathes in quickly. I have turned into a basket case since she has seen me last but I don't have to tell her that. She is able to figure that one out for herself.

"Oh, I didn't realise. I thought . . ."

"No, it's a workshop for Cian. The therapists are going to be shown what to teach him next."

"I see."

She nods, checks her watch, tips her cup to finish her tea and I wave them off and join the girls in the next room.

Later the phone rings. It is Jacqueline.

"I'll help you, Aileen. I don't know if I will be any good but I would like to help Cian. I will be a therapist."

If she had been standing beside me I would have given her the biggest hug.

* * *

Jacqueline joins the team. I train her up until she is ready to take two sessions a day. Donna works afternoons and Anne does two hours in the morning. I do an extra five hours on the weekend, which brings the total number of hours up to thirty-five. We are getting closer to our target. Therapists knock at the door at 8.50 a.m. and the last one leaves at 4.00 p.m. Sitting in our living room is like sitting in a public arena, a cross between a school, a bakery and a train station, with paperwork everywhere. When I am not discussing ABA with the therapists I am baking gluten- and casein-free food or meeting with other parents who are new to autism and want to learn about the diet or observe Cian's ABA lesson, so they can decide whether either intervention would help their own child. During this time I also travel to Belfast to meet with all the parents who are employing LEAP services to form a group called SPEAC to lobby for autism services and treatment in Northern Ireland. We are all instant friends because we never judge each other or ever have to explain how bad a day can get.

* * *

The work in and out of the therapy room is physically and mentally exhausting. We had been warned and had read many comments about the negative impact of ABA therapy, how we would have to adjust our entire lifestyle around ABA, how a three-year-old child should be playing not working. But we felt we had no choice. Our son didn't know how to play. Our life already revolved around Cian. We had watched Cian for too long, dropping the same book behind the same bookcase, over and over, staring at the ceiling lights and turning the knobs of the washing machine until we dragged him away. He used to spend his day climbing over the furniture and jumping off or pacing up and down the kitchen floor for ages, spinning around and around without falling down. Other times he would lie on the edge of the sofa or over the coffee table in a peculiar position, lethargic and pale with no gusto for life. At least now there is a little structure to his day and he is being stimulated and having fun.

He is learning concepts and appropriate behaviours to help him function in our world with his autism. He does not develop rigid behaviours. He learns to wait, and to drink out of any cup or glass. He does not become obsessed with keeping everything the same. He can now cope with short trips and long trips and all sorts of environments. There are some concepts that are hard to teach – abstract concepts like safety and time and body language and Cian still remains socially aloof, but there are days when Cian meets our eyes and smiles, when he answers a question, days when he immediately turns when you call him. There are many moments, precious moments I can hardly explain, when he seems to "wake up", to come alive, to suddenly become aware of us. Days when he goes to Eamonn and takes his hand and looks up at us with his face bright and alive with happiness. On such days, we lift him up and hug him and his eyes move between us, smiling and conveying a great sense of happiness. No words are spoken, but the message is clear. Cian knows his mammy and daddy. These are precious spiritual moments we can hardly comprehend, but for a moment there is a connection and Cian becomes totally in the present, his whole being radiating love and contentment. On those days, all of it is worth it.

18

It's raining and Henry won't come out of the dark tunnel. So some workmen close the tunnel and he is left all alone. One day, Gordon breaks down near Henry's tunnel. Now who will pull the express? The Fat Controller has an idea. "Henry, will you help Edward pull the express?"

"Good for the Fat Controller!"

A high-pitched squeal amplifies from behind the rusty red material. I tilt my neck to look behind me. Cian stands in a crucified position in the middle of the window. His tight fists clutch and tug at the edges of the curtains. His tiny frame is ablaze with an aura of light boldly escaping from the outside world into our living room.

I am sitting on the rounded arm of our mottled coloured settee. A greyish white phone sits precariously on the arm of the sofa, the message ringing in my ears. Two of the therapists are unable to make it in this morning.

My tired eyes dart around the room, missing the detail. I

feel a dead weight clamping my shoulders. A sensation of numbed plasticity stretches the skin on my face. I wonder how I am going to get through the morning without help and teach Cian all the things he needs to be taught. My left hand is pressing against my right temple, trying to rub away a blinding headache.

The workmen let Henry out of the tunnel. He feels much better. "Peep, peep! I'm ready," says Edward.

"So am I," whistles Henry. Together, they pull Gordon's train.

Thomas the Tank Engine theme music toots out and I brace myself. Cian leaps from the windowsill behind me onto the arm of the settee. He thumps into my back, noosing his arms around my neck and swings like an orang-utan into the mountain of cushions on the floor. Unravelling his body at lightning speed, he bolts towards the front of the television set, flapping his wrists and jumping up and down. He has beaten the reel of videotape once again. When the music ends he does a treble run around the room, crashes into the cushions and swoons in a roar of hysterical giggling. His little fingers come up to his eyes and make a bizarre pattern, spotlighted by a shaft of light escaping through the gap in the curtains.

Is there any way out of Cian's autistic *"tunnel"* before I have *"a break down"*? And if I do, *"who will pull the express?"*

I need help and impulsively reach for the phone again but before I place my hand on the receiver, I know I have no one to call. Family and friends are working. I would not ring my mother in this state and there is no one else. I drop the phone and cradle my face as the sobs rise faster and faster in my throat. Derailed, my body slides into the grey covered wooden seat of the settee, minus its cushions, trying to salvage what could have been. I could have been a great mother. I could have enjoyed rearing my children. Cian would have known how much we wanted him. Loved him. He would know his name. Had it been different, we would not have all this stress. I would not be beside myself with worry every time he runs and runs. He would be able to tidy up like his big brother and Christopher would not get upset with all the mess. I would not have to search for answers, dragging myself to futile appointments. I would not have to endure comments that were meant to comfort me.

"God fits the back to the burden."

"To be a mother of a special needs child you must be very special."

"Cian is lucky to have a mother like you."

What? I am about to take a nervous breakdown and Cian is lucky?

Anger surges through my veins like water from a burst pipe.

The reality is, there is no practical help available. No respite. No proper educational facility. No medical support. They see autism. I see Cian: sweet, angelic, happy, Cian. Christopher's brother, our child, and our life. My child's future is in the hands of a few dedicated twenty-something-year-olds, a wheat- and milk-free diet and scant pieces of information I have extracted from Yahoo autism groups.

Helplessness rocks me in a sea of grief. It fills my gullet like vomit, choking and heaving, up the throat, watching my precious son locked steadfast in a labyrinth of complex dark tunnels, offering me no understanding, no connection, no reassurance. The ache power-washes through my head, trashing and threatening, gnawing my insides that sob and fold, creating my own blackened tunnel.

I plead with myself not to crash. Not today. Not for the next eight hours. Not when I am on my own. When I must be all things to this child in front of me.

Suddenly, I get a poke in the face. A chubby clammy fist touches my hair. I lift my swollen eyes and just about make out the fuzzy outline of my three-year-old son. He cups his hands about my neck and pulls. I stand up. Cold. Pins and needles. Cursing my breakdown. Cian pulls me more urgently now and leads me to the hallway. He does a little run around and heads towards the stairs, reaching out to me. He wants me to follow him. I go with him, heavy and burdened. Cian skips up the stairs, humming a tune. It is in perfect pitch. He adds harmony. *How does he do that?* Maybe his tunnel has the odd peephole where he can bathe in a pool of white light when his pain leaves and all about him is safe. Again I curse my weakness. How could I cry in front of him? I need to get a grip.

I go towards his bedroom but he pulls me away. He is walking towards mine. He has duped me now. What is he up to? As we enter my bedroom, he runs towards the bed and grovels at the duvet. It is too clumsy but he manages to pull part of it down. He turns towards me. I am looking at him. It is only 9.00 a.m. He couldn't possibly want to go to bed but, against my better judgement, I go to lift him.

"Okay."

He shrugs my hands off and reaches for my wrists. Taking a side step, he forces his small body against mine and with all his might pushes me down on the bed. I lie awkwardly, my feet dangling over the edge. He goes to lift my feet and I suddenly realise he wants to put *me* to bed! Keen to show him I understand, I lift my feet and stick them under the duvet, plump up the pillow and snuggle in under the cover. His plum-red lips curl faintly upwards and I am rewarded with a flitting sideways glance. With the deed done, he moves across to the window and turns into the light. I study his tiny frame, one bare foot resting over the other, his elbows stretched along the window sill and the back of his hair shiny and black.

All the books I have managed to digest, all the literature I have picked up from all the internet sites I have visited tell me autistic children have difficulties understanding emotions. They don't understand feelings. If that is the case, then why has my three-year-old son suddenly torn himself away from his beloved *Thomas the Tank Engine* video and put me to bed? At that moment, as though he can read my mind, he turns his head and meets my gaze. It is probably a second but it feels like forever as I am swallowed up in the fullness of his depth. Casually, he turns towards the window again and I close my eyes to prevent the swollen dam of grief bursting again. Instead, I stuff the duvet up against my throat and enjoy a glimpse of the caring little boy behind the frosted glass who came out when I least expected, and I reflect on how miraculous it is to receive help and, even more miraculous when it comes, where it actually comes from.

19

In September Eamonn and I meet with Martin McGuinness, the then Minister for Education in Northern Ireland. Some of the SPEAC parents have been permitted to join me and we discuss the importance of intensive early intervention programmes for our children, outlining our own children's progress and our concerns about our children's future and the lack of autism-specific education and services. He listens carefully and is empathic to our needs, informing us of a Centre of Excellence that he hopes will open in County Armagh in the near future. A short time later the doors of Stormont close on local power. The issue of autism is shelved and becomes inconsequential in the controversy over Northern Ireland's Good Friday Agreement, along with every other social and economic issue. Six years later, the Centre of Excellence has yet to open.

In the shadow of political unrest, our own battle with our

local education authority, the Western Education and Library Board (WELB), to fund Cian's early intervention programme is ongoing. We have attended meetings and advocated for him for most of a year while trying to hold everything together. The clock ticks mercilessly away as we try to make every second count so Cian's learning is optimised. Cian has made so much progress on his ABA programme and I can't bear the thought of him not receiving the opportunity. In an updated report, the speech therapist verifies that Cian is making steady and encouraging progress since commencing ABA.

"Cian's vocabulary now extends to approximately two hundred words and his understanding of action words has increased significantly in the last two months. He can point to body parts. Although his eye contact remains minimal, Cian's social awareness has shown steady progress. Cian is a happy child whose progress has been remarkable in the last year. He appears to have been responsive to the intensive ABA programme."

Halle Berry calls and performs hearing and sight tests "the ABA way". She stands in the hall by our front door, holding up letters. Eamonn sits beside Cian, who points at what he sees and hears. The health visitor is thrilled to see Cian attending and being able to focus on the task in hand. We are thrilled that she lets him focus and attend in a way that he can.

With our updated reports and information on Cian's progress, the WELB agree to part-fund Cian's ABA therapy programme. It does not alleviate the paperwork, as weekly time sheets have to be filled in and invoices written up, but it does alleviate the financial worry and acknowledges Cian's need for early intervention.

We receive a formal letter outlining the terms and conditions and a copy of Cian's statement of educational needs. In Part 3 of the statement, Speech and Language Therapy have been omitted, which indicates that the WELB are not taking responsibility for providing this particular therapy. Back we go to the battlefield again, to fight for the most basic provision for our child. I contact IPSEA who inform me that when a child has a statement of educational needs and SaLT is outlined in part 3 (Educational Provision), then the ultimate responsibility falls with the local education authority; they therefore have a legal duty to supply what is outlined within that.

After several meetings and correspondence with our local WELB, they agree to include SaLT in Part 3 of our statement. However, the service will not begin until Cian's name is at the top of the waiting list. In light of this, I contact the Department of Education and the Secretary of State, which proves fruitless. They do not provide independent speech therapists! Other than the fact that no one will take responsibility for speech and language services in the UK and Ireland, they remain totally inadequate and seriously under-funded. With reliable estimates now stating that the prevalence of autism is 1 in 100 in the UK and Ireland, it is frankly startling that parents continue to fight for core essential services.

* * *

Around this time I get a phone call one morning informing me that I have been nominated for a millennium award to attend a week-long training course in Africa to help share

165

my knowledge with other families. I have the option to take Cian with me to receive one-to-one therapy from highly experienced tutors. I am excited about the award but worried about travelling with Cian on my own. My family suggests we should all go, not only for the week's training but also for a holiday. The thought of a holiday excites me but we are apprehensive about the cost of the trip and the long flight. How will Cian cope? Some people are more persuasive than others. Áine phones me up when she hears the news.

"Aileen, I heard you weren't sure about the trip so I'm putting a little something in an envelope and I want you to see it as a gift from me to Cian. It's a chance in a lifetime, so you need to make the most of it. Okay?"

Eamonn's sister Helena visits to celebrate my achievement.

"It's fantastic news. It is such an opportunity; you can't miss it and I want to help." She slips an envelope into my pocket and gives me a big hug.

When my friend Clare hears the news she is ecstatic. "Since you're going that far you should take the boys on safari or something. They would love it." Her sister Anita wants to make a donation out of money she raised for her chosen charities. Nothing would please her more if I would take it.

And so it is decided that we will all go to Africa. Eamonn enrols on the course with me. Christopher is enrolled in a summer school and Cian is enrolled for a full week of therapy. For the extra week in Africa, as the girls suggest, we decide we will take the boys on safari. Our trip is scheduled for just before Christmas.

20

Cian sleeps most of the way to Cape Town, only waking up an hour before landing. He perches behind Christopher's back and watches unfamiliar cartoons until he loses interest. He looks for fun in Daddy's arms and demands tickles and rascality.

On the edge of the "mother city", we disembark at an airport that is not much bigger than a shoebox, much to Christopher's amusement. The drive from the airport is lined with poignant reminders of the injustices of the apartheid era. Shabby townships with rusty tin shacks and plastic sheets for roofs sprawl at the feet of a sugar-coated landscape. Tabletop Mountain, lying smack in the middle of the city, has a certain mystical presence about it. The vibrancy of the city, with its countless beaches and up-hill down-dale sway of traffic, reminds me of Sydney. I am so glad we have come.

Our hotel is completely fenced-in, so Cian cannot stray

too far. There is a small pool, fenced and gated, in the back courtyard. The early African summer sun has yet to warm the freezing cold water, but the boys don't seem to mind. Every morning after breakfast, a hostess presents us with a basket of brown paper bags with handles. She ushers us towards the buffet table and gives us permission to stock up for lunch. We stock up on fresh fruit muffins and other mouth-watering delights before driving across the city to drop Christopher off in a South African summer school. He makes friends with Mica, whom he talks about to this day.

Cian's ABA therapy begins at 8.30. In the same building, our training starts at 9.00. All the delegates are parents, mostly from Cape Town, Nigeria and all over Africa. Each break time, we sit with Cian and his South African therapists in the shade among the purple and pink blossoms. Sometimes the other parents and children join us. Sometimes Sarah, the tutor, joins us. She is blonde and petite with pale skin. Her soft African accent is easy on the ear. She is excited about everything, always laughing and very articulate. Cian's therapists marvel at his knowledge and at the speed with which he learns.

* * *

After a few days, we notice a change in Cian. Everything about the trip seems to tune him in. He becomes more alert, more responsive. Every part of it is an education for him. In the late afternoon, when our training is over, we collect Christopher and take in the sites. Holding on to the boys, we wander round the Victoria and Alfred (V&A) Waterfront and look out towards Robben Island, where political prisoners including Nelson Mandela were detained in the days of apartheid. Eamonn and I would love to go on the three-hour tour of the prison but opt for a trip that will stimulate Christopher's and Cian's senses. We head to the Two Oceans Aquarium.

"And if you run riot inside, me lad, we will buy you a one-way ticket to Robben Island and they can keep ye." Eamonn wags his finger at Cian.

Inside, Cian is too much in awe to run anywhere. The meeting of the Indian and Atlantic Oceans behind the thick glass throws up sea life that we never knew existed. Christopher and Cian stand hypnotised as they press their noses against the glass, watching all sorts of wonderful sea life swim by. The thrill of the touch pool and the ragged-toothed sharks prove popular with our two boys. Cian loves to touch. We have taken him to the right place.

Every inch of Cape Town proves an aesthetic pleasure. We glide up Table Mountain in a cable-car, drenched in the glare of the blinding sun reflecting off the glass, and walk the many paths, spotting baby lizards and many other creatures asleep in the dead heat. Keen to visit the southernmost point of Africa, we drive to the tip of Cape Peninsula, battling our way through the baboon-infested park and giving our afternoon meal up to their scavenging ways. On a twenty-five-minute hike up a steep cliff to a lighthouse, we learn that we are not at the southernmost point of Africa after all, an honour that belongs to Cape Agulhas, farther up the coast. It is a most common mistake made by travellers to South Africa, but for us, there is no mistake. High above the ferocious roar of the Atlantic Ocean and False Bay, where the surging waters meet the vibration, the raging vastness of it causes a sharp intake of breath and Christopher's "Awesome" drifts on the African breeze, invigorating us and awakening our souls.

Heading back, Christopher pulls Cian close. "We wouldn't be here if it wasn't for Cian's autism." He turns his head and hugs Cian's neck. "Thanks, Cian."

Eamonn and I exchange a smile and I try to focus on the vast landscape, but it is all a blur – a happy blur.

* * *

On the way back, we visit Benita, whom I have connected with on the internet. When we arrive, evening tea is served underneath some shady trees as Cian and Christopher swing on a rope and tyre. Her own son does not join us but stays in his room, locked in his autism.

Another day, we meet Benita again. She is keen for the boys to visit Boulder's Beach, where an amazing colony of endangered African penguins has taken up residence. The beach has a surreal quality to it, with huge boulders forming little coves. Cian and Christopher swim next to the passive penguins. Benita marvels at Cian's ability to travel and I secretly thank God for simple things.

At the end of the week our course ends and Eamonn and I know all that we need to know about ABA therapy. We are ready for a new adventure, to fill up our senses with new experiences, which seem to teach our boys more than any teaching programme ever could.

* * *

I contact Mark, our agent, to check out our travel arrangements from Johannesburg to the safari. He informs me that he is in Johannesburg and offers to escort us out of the city until we are on the road that will take us to the Safari. He thinks it would be advisable. He is right. We never would have got out alive. Mark meets us at the airport and helps us locate our hired car. Driving out of Johannesburg, the roads resemble a mess of spaghetti and one-way systems. Trucks and cars speed past in lanes galore, dashing left and right and flashing lights. While Eamonn leans forward, frowning and concentrating on the red tail-lights of Mark's Mercedes Sports Coupe, skyscrapers and grim office buildings shy away from me as we leave the city. Large mounds of yellow earth pile up on the edges of the barren landscape, pockmarked and scoured from the gold mining era that created Johannesburg. Black men, women and children in dusty overalls line the route out of town, weary and bent, selling things.

Soon we are on a wide-open road that leads to a dusty crimson track, as wide as a football pitch, with no end. Eamonn and I shake our heads at our gullibility, but lose ourselves in the adventure of it all, laughing and singing, with the boys standing up on the back seat. They have their heads stuck out of the top of the jeep, singing "Jingle Bells" to burnt, deserted plains. Time passes without our knowledge. The tick and the tock, the hectic rhythm of what we are used to is drowned out by the silent barren land. Another rhythm evolves – one with more pauses and more appreciation for the sacredness of nature. The children hush and stop to listen.

We are in a world of our own, but we are not alone in this

place of visual magnificence and spiritual peace. Every now and then we pass a man or woman, who stops and waves and smiles, brilliantly bathed in a sultry red glow. We all wave back until the person has become a minute dot in our vision. Later we learn that people we met along the way have been walking for days, with no shoes on their feet and no bag on their back, and will walk back again after visiting members of their family with nothing but the hauntingly beautiful landscape and the fruits of its wildness to nourish their souls.

Darkness falls as suddenly as switching off a light. The heat is still in the late evening and, long after the sun goes down, the boys doze. It is 7.30 before we realise that we have been driving for hours. According to the mileage on our directions, we have obviously taken a wrong turn. Strangely we are not bothered. We'll get there.

An hour later, a million insects swarm around our headlights as we slow down in front of a sign that has the name of our destination on it – Jaci's Safari Lodge. It points to the right and we follow a winding dirt track grown over with foliage. A large wooden gate appears out of the darkness and a red light flashes in our direction. Eamonn winds the window down and switches off the engine. The hissing sound of insects, a walkie-talkie bleeping and talking and the crunch of gravel under feet fills the silence as the light staggers towards us. A man in a khaki uniform shines a red light in our faces.

"Documentation."

Scanning the paperwork, he reaches for his walkie-talkie. "They are here; they have arrived," he barks. I fail to place his accent. A click and a muffled voice answers him. Taking the apparatus from his face, he flashes a candid smile.

"We were worried. You were supposed to arrive hours ago. You were lost?"

"A little bit." Eamonn nods and waits until the security guard opens the wooden wired structure. As we pull up at the lodge, rangers in uniforms scatter around our jeep and rush to help us. A tall man wearing long shorts and a hat introduces himself as Jan. He has an English accent and is clearly relieved we have arrived safely. I am relieved that I didn't know we were lost for most of the journey. Our bags and our sleeping boys are carried into Jaci's Safari Lodge; the boys are laid down on two small beds below a massive four-poster canopy, all tastefully decorated in white linen, and purple and gold cushions and throws. The resting places are cool and clean-looking with elegant décor and creatively veiled with mosquito nets.

"Hurry now. Your food is waiting. You must be very hungry."

Eamonn and I look at our sleeping boys and back at the owner. As though reading our thoughts, his eyes slide past us and nod at someone standing behind us.

"Helena will watch the little boys until you come back."

I startle and swing round, stupidly expecting Helena, Eamonn's sister, to pounce out with a "Surprise", but the lady looking back is nothing like Helena. She is dark-skinned and has her hands clasped in front of her roly-poly shape with a *gélé* tied round her jet-black hair. She is wrapped in green and orange African attire and her eyes and teeth are huge and white and perfect. She smiles and nods and nods and smiles until my facial expression relaxes. Hunger and tiredness dull my anxieties and somehow I am

173

reassured that the children will be in safe hands with a stranger who has the same name as my sister-in-law. Eamonn relaxes as well and Jan stretches out his arms to guide us down a curved path edged with lanterns and across a rope-bridge over water glistening and sparkling in the flickering light of the lodge. Elephants trumpet in the distance, bathing and drinking in the night. Jan laughs softly.

"You must not worry now. You are both tired. We will take care of you and Helena will wait until you come. She is a mother too. She has ten of her own."

I turn to look at him and almost trip over my own feet, surprised at myself. I hadn't seen a mother. I had just seen a stranger in a skin that was a different shade to mine.

In a clearing, in the light and heat of flaming coals and sparks escaping from a hot furnace, we are led to a table set for three. Jan welcomes us to a bush "braai". While we order some food, he speaks to someone by the fire and a waiter called Mattie pours red wine into a very generous glass. Jan joins us, removes his hat and takes a seat.

"Now . . . thank heavens you are here. We were very worried. The road you travelled is the main road to the casinos in Sun City. There are many hijacks. I phoned your agent. He told me you had arrived in Africa. You spoke to him from Cape Town. He had arranged your transport and saw you out of Johannesburg. After that, we didn't know!" He shakes his head and holds his hands up in the air.

Eamonn and I both sit with our mouths open. We didn't really know what all the fuss was about. We could have driven forever in the freedom of it all, the adventure, the staggering natural beauty, which had cast off any worries we ever had. They did not belong to this sacred place. Food arrives for all three of us, a delicious casserole with salad and sautéed potatoes. I take a sip of the full-bodied red and immerse my senses in the sounds and smells of the African wilderness underneath the stars. While we eat, Jan shares a little of his history with us.

"I am originally from the UK but left the rat-race many years ago for the wilder side of life." His laugh is low and croaky but his love for Africa is full of passion and charm. He talks about how he came to be in Africa, his dreams for the lodge and what we could expect in the next couple of days. Handing me a woven basket full of bread, he assures us that he received our concerns and requests. Unsure of Cian's reaction to the bush and to the animals, we had requested family game drives on our own. He has it all arranged and waves at the guy he had been speaking to by the fire.

"This is Shimba. Shimba is our lodge manager. He will take you on all your drives. He will look after you and look after your little boys. You must not worry. He will knock you up at 3.30 to go out to see the animals before the sun gets too hot. You will then go out in the evening before the sun goes down."

Shimba tips his hat and tells us he will see us in the morning. His bulk fades into the dark as the waiter pours more wine and stokes the fire. Jan dabs his stew with some bread and asks about our "little autistic boy". He listens very carefully as we talk about Cian and how we have set up our intensive home programme to teach him, why we are in Africa and how Cian likes to run away from us. He nods quietly and finishes his meal. The bowl scrapes along the table as he pushes it away from him. He turns his body around to face us.

"Helena is very good. You must rest when you are here. You must not worry about Cian. Helena will understand. Take a good rest now during the day when you can. The boys can swim in the little rock pool outside your room. It is very safe. I hope you have a good stay and anything else I can help you with, let me know."

Rising from his chair, he wipes his mouth on a white linen napkin and claps Eamonn on the back. "Mattie will walk you back to your room. It is safer that way." Jan winks at me and tips his cap. "It's good to have you here. Enjoy your stay."

When Mattie walks us back to our room we find Helena where we had left her, in a quiet meditative state. She gently rises, bows and leaves. Eamonn and I feel like the King and Queen of Sheba. We have never experienced attention like it and marvel at the treatment.

Later, we learn that Jan has an autistic teenage daughter.

* * *

An unfamiliar voice slips into my dream.

"Morning." My eyelids flicker. Something's tapping. The same voice again . . . "Morning."

"Morning." Eamonn's voice shocks me into a half-wakened state.

"I'll wait at reception for you, okay?" the unfamiliar voice calls out.

"Great. Thanks." Eamonn shouts back.

I perch on one elbow and wipe the sleep from my eyes.

Where on earth am I? I can see a blanket of sky. Stone and canvas walls and a shaggy thatched roof surround me. Through a netted veil, I see Christopher and Cian looking back at me. I flop back on the bed as the boys crawl under our net. We all remember at once.

"Game drive."

Into the open-plan bathroom with its hand-built "rock" bath and outdoor "safari" shower. We wash and dress quickly. Except Cian, who loves the gush of the shower, so we try to hurry him along. The lodge has a "tented" feel to it. It is 3.30 in the morning. The sun is not awake yet. We are all very excited, including Cian – our very first game drive.

We are not disappointed and every game drive, morning and evening, is magical.

Shimba is the perfect guide and on our drives we see giraffe, lions and leopards, wild dog and springbok. We get up close and personal with a victorious bull rhino. Shimba is very impressed with Christopher's knowledge of the "big five". His obsession with David Attenborough is paying off.

One morning a leopard tortoise lumbers along inside his spotted shell in the middle of our path. Christopher begs Shimba to allow him to lift it to safety. Shimba says no at first but slows down and scans the territory. He checks his watch. 4.50 a.m. Christopher is in luck. The animals may not have moved yet. We are in a clearing and Shimba's vision is pretty good. He switches off his engine and the dead heat settles around us. The gentle breath of Africa wafts about our faces and the sounds of nature magically transport me to another reality, like how it was in the beginning – so many aeons ago. I absorb every smell, sound,

177

sight and image that I hope will remain imprinted on my memory forever.

The sun is well up in the morning sky now. We have discarded our blankets, replacing them with sunglasses and hats to protect us from the burning yellow glare. Shimba turns to Christopher.

"You know about shell-spotted tortoise?"

Christopher rhymes off a half a dozen facts about his chosen subject and Shimba is suitably impressed.

Shimba scans the territory again, pushes his cowboy hat back from his forehead and prepares his rifle.

"We got to be quick. In the bush, Christopher, you take no chances, right?"

Christopher grins and Shimba wraps a solid, weather-beaten arm around Christopher's middle, swinging him out of the six-wheel drive.

"Okay. First we allow Cian to touch it." Shimba surprises us and reaches out for Cian. "It's okay," he reassures me.

Shimba holds on to Cian as he strokes the tortoise and I take a few snaps before Christopher picks up the tortoise and carries it to safety. Just as he finds a resting place, the tortoise pees over his shoe. We all laugh and Christopher scolds.

"It isn't funny. The tortoise is terrified. You would pee too if something came along and picked you up out of the blue."

Shimba is blown away by Christopher's concern for the tortoise and tells him he will make a great ranger some day. Any concerns I have about Cian slide into the way blue yonder. He is so completely in awe of everything he hears and sees that we think he has forgotten to be autistic. It is Cian who spots the elephants.

"Elephant." He jumps up and stands behind Shimba. Shimba slows, then abruptly stops and turns off the engine. A herd of elephant slowly trundles its way through the bush to a watering hole, taking the path right in front of our jeep. Thank God I have it on film – not so much to see the elephants but to see Cian's face. As we make our way back to the lodge, Cian gets cheeky and leans down to Shimba, stealing his cowboy hat. Cian drops it on his head and plops back on the seat, looking like a proper ranger.

Between the early morning and evening game drives, Christopher and Cian swim in the rock pool overlooking the Groot Marico River. Eamonn and I lounge in the hammocks amid the birds, the butterflies and the beasts, a silent reel inside my head slowly archiving our incredible and memorable African safari experience. We sit on a private wooden viewing deck at the entrance of the lodge overlooking a small stream. Animals and birds come to drink. Cian is intrigued by the sound of an owl and other birds, which he mimics perfectly. On the viewing deck over the river, he is still and gazes at a family of baboons playing or warthogs bathing, but it is the three giraffes that he asks for the most. They come to drink at the watering hole just outside the lodge.

At sundown, the purple sunsets, streaked with candy pink and gold, shimmer as delicious gourmet dinners are served in the lantern-lit boma. My mind stops thinking. It is submerged in an inner stillness. I forget yesterday and tomorrow. I have begun to see with a fresh pair of eyes completely in the now, with three precious people in my life. Eamonn would love more time to stay. I know what he means. This euphoric state could easily become addictive. Our most difficult decision is whether to listen to the lions call or watch the incredible sunset – moments of Africa I want to preserve in the sealed urn of my mind. Many people, including myself, feel that they have a spiritual experience in Africa and that is what keeps them returning again and again to the so-called "Dark Continent". I leave Africa wanting to return with a large slice of it etched on my soul.

* * *

The trip to South Africa opens up Cian's world and our minds to limitless possibilities. One of Cian's greatest loves now is travel. He has a particular interest in aeroplanes. He loves new environments and exploring different places and is usually at his best when he is about to embark on an adventure and we do not dread a long journey or trip overseas. We do find it difficult finding suitable accommodation to ensure Cian's safety – quite often suitable accommodation is more expensive and it is sometimes difficult to find a range of activities and diet choices to suit his needs, but holidays are normally something to look forward to.

21

Ironically we are only home a week when we lose Cian. Brendan, Eoin's Dad, has organised a Christmas party in Belfast and has invited all the SPEAC parents and children along.

I keep one eye on the door and the other on Cian's red GAP t-shirt walking over a rope bridge, tumbling down slides into a bath of coloured balls. Siobhan, one of Eoin's therapists comes over to me to say "Hello". She has a lot of experience in ABA and knows I struggle with getting therapists. She offers to come on Mondays to oversee the therapists and update my programmes if I am interested. I am delighted. It will set the programme on the right track for each week.

Christopher waves to me through an aeroplane window and runs to push Cian on the swing rope.

A woman in a green top holding half a dozen coats and bags sidles up to me. "They are so fast in these places and so noisy. I hate them, ye know."

I turn my head to her and nod politely.

"Wouldn't you think they would supply more chairs for us that have to stand here and listen to this din?"

Glancing at the bags and coats she is clutching, I smile in agreement and turn my attention back to Cian. He is not on the swing. I wait for him to pop out of one of the colourful tubes.

"I can't see him," I mutter to myself. Wandering up and down, I strain to catch a glimpse of him. "Where is he? Where on earth did he go to?"

Talking to myself I almost bump into the bag lady.

"Have you lost somebody, luv?"

"My son. I don't know . . . I can't see him."

"Sure ye wouldn't see 'em for dust in here and he wouldn't want ya to see him either. But ye can fairly hear 'em . . . HA HA HA. What a din. I need a smoke. He'll be here in a minute, luv, an the cheeks flyin' af 'im."

The woman edges her way back and perches herself on something that looks like a loudspeaker, unconcerned as the flowers in May.

Catching Eamonn coming out of the toilets with Christopher, I rush up to him. "I haven't seen Cian in the last two minutes."

"He has got to be still in there. He was at the bottom of the blue slide. I only went to check on Christopher."

Overhearing my concern, Christopher grabs his friends. "RED ALERT . . . Young suspect . . . by the name of Cian . . . missin'. You – to the bottom . . . you – to the top. I will search the slides and chutes. Report back here immediately. Get ready, plan for attack . . . Attackkkkkkk!"

I grin but feel sick and head straight to a young assistant

standing by the swinging doors leading out into a huge multi-complex and shopping arena.

"Did a little boy in a red t-shirt come this way?"

She looks at the children coming in and out, looks back at me and shrugs her shoulders.

Right. There is no time to ask for the management. If Cian has left the play area he could be anywhere. Eamonn rushes up to me.

"They can't see him. He must have got out."

Other dads rush out the swinging doors and split to comb the complex. Eamonn goes to find customer services to raise the alarm as the sheer size of the place gapes back at me. On the floors below there are at least three exits, all leading out to busy roads and streets in Belfast. He could be anywhere by now.

Out of the corner of my eye, something is moving. It is the top of the escalator. I bend down to Cian's height. I see a lot more of the escalator making its way down to the bottom floor. *Of course. The escalator. He would go for the escalator.*

Eamonn and the rest of the fathers are out of sight. I haven't time to tell them, so I rush out and tumble down the escalator. *What if he got to the bottom and went back up?* Eamonn is up there. He will find him. A pair of sliding doors comes into view. If he had come this far, he would have gone through the sliding doors. Doors that Cian is no longer frightened of.

(In the therapy room the consultant introduced a "surprise box" on the table in front of Cian. At the beginning we put favourite toys and sweets in the box and very gradually introduced him to new stimuli, building it up to the toys and books that Cian was terrified of. He eventually stopped running from the room but he never played with those toys. Donna had the idea that if she tapped the animated toy or book with a stick, Cian did not seem to be as frightened. She then slowly encouraged him to use the stick to tap the item and eventually he did. The long slow process led to Cian playing with animated toys and gradually being able to cope with other people's houses and walking in and out of shops, past animated characters and through sliding doors.)

Out in the huge car park, traffic filters on and off the M2. Cars are reversing and pulling out and pulling in. Shoppers are walking and pushing trolleys. Children are running into the complex. I try to remember what Cian is wearing.

Sacred Heart of Jesus.

Fear and panic fill my throat. I am unable to scream, to speak, to holler that my wee boy is missing. Just then, I see a yellow coat in the distance manoeuvring between buildings, going out of sight and then back into view. He is too far away but I know he is a security guard.

Sacred Heart, please let him have Cian.

Running in his direction, I think he is carrying something, but I can't be sure. I am still watching the cars moving in and out, braking and tooting horns. The security guard is more visible now and he *is* holding something. I keep running, my heart thumping in my chest. My voice comes back.

"Have you my son?" I force the words out as loud as I can.

He comes closer, panting and out of breath. It is Cian. He has found Cian.

I go to pieces as the tall bearded man hands over my baby.

"You're all right, luv. I gat him. I gat him."

He places a solid hand on my back.

"I am doin' the door at Dunnes Stores. He ran straight past me. Quick as a flash he was. I noticed he had no shoes so I followed him. I called out to him but he kept on running."

I nodded, unable to speak.

"No one came after him so I figured with no shoes and all I had a little escapist on my hands from the ball pool."

"Thank you, thank you, thank you," I sob, wiping fresh tears on Cian's t-shirt.

"I held him for a while but he is a mighty strong one. He didn't like me holding on and he wouldn't tell me his name."

"He has autism."

The word registers and his gaze lingers on mine before he continues. "Well, he was very good, took a liking to my beard here, was probably wondering why I had so much on my chin and none on my head. "You'll be all right, luv, it's just the shock. I better get back. Watch him now, he's fast. He could try it again."

And he does. Again and again and again, sometimes up to twice a day.

* * *

When Cian isn't stimulated in a constructive way, his behaviours are as unpredictable as Dennis the Menace's dog. The constant supervision of him blasts all home-

185

making activities to the side. Washing spews from the half-loaded washing machine. Meat shrivels up while the belated potatoes and vegetables cook. Dishes block up the sink and food items grow beards in the back of the fridge until I fear they will walk out by themselves. I can't take my eyes off little Mowgli.

Eamonn takes him into the garden but five minutes later he appears at the back door, our nonchalant son dangling and dripping in his outstretched arms. Stripping him down, I prompt him to turn on and off the tap, to rub soap on his hands, to wash his face and teeth, mundane tasks that toddlers usually relish to do for themselves, but Cian only goes through the motions and clenches the top of the toothbrush, preferring to suck the toothpaste off the brush.

His clothes and drawers are labelled so he can find his clothes easily. T-shirts, trousers, jumpers all have their own drawer so as not to confuse him. In front of a full-length mirror, I coax him to pay attention and name each item, pointing out the label at the back and the zip at the front. We work our way from pants to shoes, painfully slowly as Cian plays with my hair and stares out the window at the trees blowing in the breeze. In Cian's world, dressing is an unnecessary inconvenience.

Downstairs again, he turns and twists the knobs of the washing machine while I load up a wash and sort out some ironing. When I lift my head again, he is eating washing powder and pouring fabric softener all over his clean clothes, his head, the floor. Resisting the ferocious scream that is ripping up from my throat, I abandon what I am doing, shove the ironing in a corner, clean him up again and slip him into a pair of pyjamas I find on the airing rack. On the floor of the living room I try to remain calm and engage him in his toys. He co-operates for a time, as if to amuse me, but eventually he turns his attention to piling his favourite things in elaborate patterns on the floor. When I am distracted he is peeling the wallpaper off the walls or poking the soil from colourful plants my mother brings to cheer me up. It doesn't take much to cause a distraction. Things have to be done – rubbish put in the bin, clothes hung out on the line, a woman at the door looking for directions, a wrong number. A second – that's all he needs – and all I need is a dead moment, an eerie silence, to know he is gone.

Granny Bridie prays and panics in the porch, while neighbours scour the road, the fields and ditches for Cian. Cian is found, sometimes stark naked and soaking wet because he has removed clothing or because he has escaped from his bath. Uncle Peter would stay with me and make me a milky coffee and try to calm me down.

"Now, don't be going upsetting yourself. He's found now. You're all right. Everything's all right."

Over time, I learn to take his advice and trust the angels to take Cian back to me or guide me to him. I have met many angels. Strangers. Fraught mothers trailing three of their own after them. Motorists. Young lads clutching Cian's small hand. Shocked to have found him. Amazed he can't talk. Shopkeepers who keep him occupied until I come. Security men in yellow coats.

Mowgli's need to run and his lack of danger and social boundaries has a huge impact on our stress levels, inside and outside the home, which begins to strain underneath the surface, wearing holes in the fabric that makes up family life.

22

I insist on taking Cian everywhere. Leaving him behind is unbearable. I want our family to remain intact. I want life to go on, even if it means trailing Cian off the ground to encourage him to walk, dressing him as quickly as he undresses, taking him out of shop windows and racing after him when he breaks free. Eamonn wants the same but he is much more rational.

As I am getting ready to attend a family occasion he casually remarks that he thinks it would be best if he were to stay at home with Cian. He is right, of course, but I want Cian to be exposed to the outside world as much as possible. Other people staring doesn't bother me, though I have to admit that Cian's mannerisms and unpredictable meltdowns are becoming difficult to handle. A child like Cian knows no boundaries and is indifferent to social rules and regulations. Left to his own devices, he prefers to go barefoot, climb on walls, skim the edges of roofs, jump in puddles and roll in sand. He can't resist lifting stones and gravel and putting it in his mouth, but most of all he loves to run.

Exhaustion gets the better of us. We look at each other, hoping the other will "go" this time, to retrieve him from eating someone's chips or from running into a lake. Eamonn wants to go home. I want to stay, to sit it out, especially as I become aware that our stress is less about Cian's behaviours and more about the behaviours of others – the stares, the snide remarks, the scolding. Someone pokes me in the back and tells me to take him out. A father shoves Cian in the head one day and tells him to get to the back of the queue. When I tell him he has no right to touch my child, that he has autism, he says it is no excuse and that I should teach him some manners. Cian's condition blots the human character like litmus paper. Strengths and weaknesses are exposed before our eyes.

There are times I just haven't the energy to keep up with him and someone launches an attack on me first before I can reach Cian. I am told that if I cannot control my child, I should keep him at home. Parents stand cross-armed, glaring at the undisciplined child who has just gone berserk, and stare at me, disgusted at my parenting techniques. I blubber out some apology, with reservation. I shouldn't have to apologise for my son – his condition upsets everyone else's idea of normality.

At the swimming pool one evening Cian is sitting on the edge of the jacuzzi, following the line of bubbles foaming in the middle and melting into a runny fizz towards the edge. He is completely engrossed, trying to stop them from disappearing. When a woman with a rather generous bosom settles into the frothy bubbles, her body becomes a kind of dam, blocking the bubbles from disappearing into the little slits at the edge of the jacuzzi. The bubbles start to pile up under her arms and around her generous chest. Closing her eyes, she stretches her arms and holds on to the sides. I tilt my head back and relax my mind as much as I can. Suddenly I am jerked out of my reverie by a spluttering, rasping breath. I open my eyes, struggling to sit up straight against the power of the water, and think that the lady is having a heart attack. She is flummoxing around in the water, trying to stand up, holding on to the side. "Could you please control your child?" she barks at me. Her sharp high-pitched tone shocks me and frightens the living daylights out of little Mowgli, who bolts straight over the side of the jacuzzi and bombs into the deep end of the pool. (At this stage, Cian is nearly five and a bit of a tadpole in water.) I look at the woman as the full realisation of what has happened sinks in. She is glaring at Cian in the water now like he is some sort of prehistoric creature, complete with horns and a very long tail. *Cian must have poked the bubbles from between her chest or maybe grabbed her chain.*

I hurl out the "A" word with no fear or hesitation, giving it precedence over everything else. "My son has autism and you have frightened the life out of him. If you had any insight at all you wouldn't have reacted as you did." *You silly self-consumed woman. How dare you sneer at my son with that screwed-up disapproving look on your face?*

Suddenly I realise how full of love I am for Cian – how he is teaching me. Because of his intolerance of certain things, we have to become more tolerant. Because he is being misunderstood, we have to strive to understand.

Because he needs us to be patient, we have to practice patience. Because we know he has little control over his behaviours, we forgive him over and over, drawing strength from his innocence.

* * *

I am still not strong enough, however, to explain Cian's behaviours, or assertive enough to tell those who object or stare to go to hell. His sensory issues prompt a need to touch everything – the walls, the ground, ornaments, the TV screen, people's heads, spectacles, shiny belts, pointy-toed shoes, jewellery, hairy chests belonging to strangers. Cian just can't resist getting a closer look. We try to steer him away from other people's belongings, but children with autism have no social filters, no sense of what's acceptable in social interaction. Most strangers smile at me, knowingly. Children do the oddest things. A child can be forgiven when he is one or two or three. But as he gets older and continues to rummage through their personal belongings, this kind of behaviour is invasive and downright rude, causing hysterical reactions.

At times I feel the power of a wild beast raging inside me – not rage with Cian, though some of his behaviours irritate me to the depths of distraction, but with others around me who stare and fuss and offer advice with little understanding and who are more uncomfortable with it than I am. It is my own vulnerability that causes me to retreat and eventually agree with Eamonn. Not only is Cian better at home, we are all better at home, where we are not judged or fixed or pitied or where Cian is not treated as a problem.

Gradually we are forced to let go of a life that was. Interests are dropped. Celebrations become meaningless. Cian's birthday is celebrated in a swimming pool, where he is happy without a birthday party that would only cause him to retreat to the quietness of his bedroom. A cake is out of the question, even if it is gluten-free, because it would be mostly full of sugar, sugar that makes him sick and unable to sleep.

As we become isolated from ordinary everyday family activities and celebrations, we start to come apart, like fragile links in a chain, loosening, becoming separate bits with key pieces missing. Christopher is invited to a birthday party or over to play. The single name on the invitation breaks me. Like I have only one son. At Halloween, Christopher goes trick-or-treating with a friend while we wrap his brother up in a blanket and drive uptown to see the fireworks display. He stares into the strange night, full of startling noises and strange faces, still and silent. Christmas comes and goes with no meaning for Cian.

As time passes by we partake in less and less. We have stopped doing things that other families enjoy doing together – shopping, church, visiting family, eating out in a restaurant, going to a football match, going to the beach, going for a walk, all of which have become an enormous struggle. It is just too difficult to cope. Eamonn and I take turns to stay at home, allowing the other to attend weddings, wakes and funerals. Eventually, autism permeates every aspect of family life. We just stay home. Staying at home is no consolation.

At home we do what we can. Sitting still is an issue. Cian is unable to sit even for a second and has difficulty holding his body in a sitting position. Mowgli tends to lounge over chairs and sofas, stand on his head or lie under cushions and rugs. We spoon-feed him lying down. He crashes his body into walls, head-butts furniture and escapes out of windows and through our double-locked front door at every opportunity. We now have to remove and hide the keys. Despite our efforts to eliminate them, many other behaviours increase rather than diminish in intensity.

Concerns for his safety force us to drench him with holy water and lock every door and window in the house so we can keep him with us at all times. We remain constantly on RED ALERT mode. When visitors or workmen come, a bunch of keys is produced to lock them in or out. It is a terrible inconvenience. Keys go missing. There are days when we are locked in the kitchen because Cian manages to turn the key at the other side of the door. There are nights we don't get to sleep in our own bedroom because we have mislaid the key, but at least we have some control on Cian's safety.

23

We try to teach Cian about safety and strangers and holding hands, but he does not have a natural sense of danger. To our detriment, we have also found that traditional methods of discipline do not work with Cian.

One day, leading him out of the house to an occupational therapy appointment, I hover at the door, remembering that I haven't lifted my keys from the worktop. I look at him for a moment, wondering if I should take him back in with me. He is running his two hands over the pebbledash on the outside of the house. He is enthralled by its texture. I decide to leave him and race back in again, grab the keys, turn off the light above the hob and lift a musical toy which Cian might like to play with on the way. Seconds later, I return to find Cian looking like something out of *Lord of the Flies*.

He is sitting at the side of the garden in a filthy puddle. His cute shorts and shirt are black with dirt as he calmly swipes muck, tribal-style, over his face and down his t-shirt. I immediately pounce on him, haul him up by the shoulders, smack him on the legs and rant at him. "Cian, NO! NO, NO, NO! Sacred Heart, have you no sense?"

Hoisting him up on my hip, the thick muck drips down my clothes, over my shoes and leaves a trail as I bounce him into the house. Plopping him down on a chair in the utility room, I glare at him. He shows no fear and laughs into the air. I want to swing for him. Instead, I run out the back door, drum the hard plastic top of the black bin with my two fists and release a barbaric scream, cursing autism and yelling at God and everybody belonging to him to the highest heavens. *How am I supposed to stay sane? How am I supposed to help him when I am driven to distraction? Help me, for Christ's sake, because I am losing it!*

I remember Mowgli. All of me stops shaking and blubbering. Speeding back to where I left him, I curse inwardly. *For feck's sake, I don't even have fecking time to cry!*

Cian is dripping on the floor, like blotches of brown on canvas. His arms have streaked and smeared the white of the washing machine as he turns the knobs round and round, lost in the click of each turn, predictable and easy. I close my eyes against the simplicity of him and beg for strength. I am being tested. I struggle with his wet things and my wet face, dabbing my eyes as I haul his shorts down over his ankles.

He stops turning the knobs and reaches for my two hands, pressing them on his legs, giggling. He does it again. Appalled, I recoil and pull my hands away. Slipping on the wet floor I fall awkwardly against the washing machine, breaking the fall with my elbow against the hard tiles. I am stunned by the sharp pain shooting up my arm, but the realisation than my son wants me to smack him hurts me more. *He must like the pressure of the hard contact against his skin.*

"God, child, you don't understand."

Cian does a little jig, flaps his arms and giggles helplessly. He does it again, lifting my hands, pushing them on his skin. The innocence of him, smiling, shames me into a sickening guilt that nauseates every part of me.

In the bath, the organic bubbles froth and fizz like my insides. Leaning over him, I carefully wash him down. Tears flow freely and mingle with the warm mist mopping my face. My child doesn't know it is a bad thing to get smacked.

* * *

"Time out" doesn't work either, not for Cian, but it works for me. It is I who banish myself to "time out" many times, putting distance between little Mowgli and me, running away from it all in case I crack under the strain, in case I end up shaking him to bits.

* * *

The day the letter comes from the doctor, I am elbow-deep in gluten-free flour and watching Cian through the French doors leading into the sitting room. He is lying under a heap of pillows and cushions, lethargic and sickly. Therapy is cancelled.

"Postman Pat" opens the door and calls out to my crumpled boy.

"Hello, Cian. What's happening today?"

Cian throws him one of his Garfield looks.

"Oh dear. We are not well today." He winks at me, holds the letters up and leaves them in the hallway.

"Bye, Cian," he shouts.

"Bye, Postman Pat." I give him a floury wave.

Rubbing my hands on a towel, I walk past Cian into the hallway and pick up the letters, just as the phone starts ringing. The portable handset is upstairs. I take the stairs two at a time, but it stops before I can answer it. Taking the handset with me, I walk back into the stairway while opening the letter in my hand. It is terribly apologetic but the long and short of it is that patients are only allowed prescriptions for gluten-free food if they have been diagnosed with coeliac disease. I need to get Cian tested before he is allowed any more prescriptions. My research has taught me that Cian's intolerances and coeliac disease are two very different conditions. Cian is more than likely not coeliac. Further to this, to get him tested, I would have to put him back on wheat and milk. This is unthinkable. Resting on the corner of the banister, thoughts scramble and separate like ingredients in a mixing bowl. What person in their right mind would want to eat gluten-free food if they didn't have to? What are they thinking? No one has ever contacted me to find out how the diet was helping Cian. By the same token, no one has visited our house at 3.00 a.m. when Cian is reeling with pain, screaming and kicking, banging his head on the floor; nor do they clean up the mess in the bathroom when Cian manages to help himself to some wheat and milk.

I look about me, knowing I have no energy left to battle

with a medical system that dismisses the gluten/casein-free diet with full-blown scepticism. A clatter of something tinny snaps me out of my thinking. The breath leaves me. I take the stairs two at a time but it has already snowed in the kitchen. A thick dusty shaft of sun illuminates a lone snowman silently swaying in the middle of it all. Cian has managed to pull the two-week supply of gluten-free flour around him. The breakfast cupboards are lying open. Porridge and muesli covers the floor tiles. Everything is white and Cian sits down in the middle of his mess, dazed by the floury dust powdering the air. I want to grab him by the shoulders and shake the living daylights out of him until he begs for mercy.

I rush at him, straight past him, out the back door, pull it behind me, run into a field and scream until the monstrous storm rampaging inside me subsides. Mindful that I am unable to leave Cian alone, I run back, check in on him through the window and slump on the back doorstep, breathless. I wish somebody would come and take him away. Immediately I am riddled with guilt. *NO. I wish someone would take* me *away. How much more of this can I put up with?* Cian is doing so well, but when he is not in therapy his behaviours cause major disruption and a whole lot of mess.

Leaning in through the window to check him again, I see little Mowgli sitting naked and still, oblivious to kitchen rules and his mad mother peering in at him. His only wish is to catch the sunbeam shimmering above his head – alive with the dusty particles he is throwing up in the air and running through his hands. The sight of him tames the rage in me like a Zen training process, usually accomplished by meditating on the Bull pictures, a series of ten paintings by the fifteenth-century Japanese Zen monk Shubun. Standing with a pane of glass between little Mowgli and me, I come face-to-face with the wild undisciplined aspect of my heart, the white shape of my son and the thin line between what I am and what I could be. In my stillness the sight of him fills me with a childish innocence, bringing me back to when I wished I could catch a sunbeam or a falling star or be the one to find the pot of gold at the end of the rainbow.

Tentatively I press down the door handle and feel my way towards the place I fear to be. The smooth particles under my bare feet squish and spread, caressing my toes, making the ground slippy and all of me white as I take my place next to him and run the dusty mixture through my fingers, throwing it high in the air, allowing it to fall over our heads and into our ears and onto our mouths, which are open wide, laughing and laughing as we try to catch the sunbeam.

24

We have had many sunbeam days, days that invite me to flirt with the darker side of reality, exposing not only Cian's vulnerability but my own.

Like the day I fill up the car with diesel and reach into the car for my purse, only to find tiny bits of ten and twenty-pound notes floating in the air, falling down around my happy boy as I helplessly look on. Cian had released his belt and torn up everything in my bag.

Or the day a man raps my door and informs me that a young lad is on the top of our roof.

There are the days that I find him in the bathroom, pouring everything down the sink and smearing my make-up (and, God knows, much worse than that) over the walls and the sides of the bath. Or in the early morning I find him in the sitting room with everything covered in ashes and Mowgli as black as soot. Boisterous and unpredictable behaviours put holes in the furniture and walls, break household objects, electronics and toys, and stain clothing and coverings, carpets and walls, causing extra expense, washing and cleaning.

One weekend Cian starts to draw like he has suddenly found a use for his hands. We can't carry paper and pens and painting material quick enough. He doesn't stop to eat or to fetch more paper. Sporadic lines and complicated shapes appear over walls and counters and tables and floors. We scold and encourage him to use only paper, not knowing he will never choose freely to draw again. In this instance, "No" means he is not allowed to draw. Guilt stagnates in my mind as I blame myself for killing his creativity, blaming autism for killing mine.

Sunbeam days change my world, consuming me, making me unavailable for functions and celebrations. Friendships become harder to sustain. Who wants a friend who bangs on about autism and little else; who hasn't the time or the freedom any more to visit or return phone calls and birthday cards; who agrees to meet and then forgets that she did; who needs to hang up just when you need her to listen; who can't fully empathise with anyone else's life because she is drowning in her own? I become complicated, drained and dazed, zapping energy, impelling friends away. I talk. They listen. I cry. They encourage. I am unavailable. I am forgiven.

Some weather the storm. Out of the blue, I would get a phone call or a text or a little card from friends I haven't contacted in ages. Olive is thinking about me. Yvonne drops by. Assumpta and Clare call up. They sit in on a session, but it is not Cian they are watching. Cian is doing just fine. Their eyes slide over me when they think I don't notice.

The smiles they arrive with quietly fade as they try to make sense of it, wondering how it is all going to end. They are full of discretion and keep their thoughts to themselves.

Paula rings – Paula, who travelled to New Zealand and back with me. I am having a bad day and put down the phone. She rings me back again, telling me to hang in, that I am doing my best. Clare and Anne call, joking and jesting, trying to make me laugh, sending my head in a spin. I have nothing to talk about but autism. I want to tell them I miss them, catching up, calling round, doing things. I want to tell them I miss the reasons why I gave up full-time work. I miss movies and eating out, sleeping in and reading and writing. I miss having the bathroom to myself. I miss having five minutes' peace to blow-dry my hair. I miss the children I work with. I miss my paycheck. What I really miss is just thinking about anything without having a black cloud hanging around in my mind. Autism. I wake up and go to sleep thinking about it, and everywhere in between. I want to tell my friends I don't even know who I am anymore.

I tell this to a dental assistant once in a packed waiting room. People come and go. I am happy to wait. All I have to do is sit. No one needs me. I don't reach for the glossy pages of last year's *OK* magazine, nor do I encourage conversation from the lady beside me. I just want to be left alone to empty my mind. I am still sitting an hour later when I glance casually at my appointment card. I am a week late. As I am about to make a quick exit, the dental assistant approaches me, looking at her list.

"Excuse me. Who are you again?"

I look up at her. She has two faces, a more defined one and a fuzzy one. I feel dizzy. I manage to pull myself up to her level. With deadened eyes, I try to focus on her face but it keeps moving. A hush falls in the room. I answer her truthfully.

"I don't know who I am."

A hush follows me down the corridor until the door bangs shut.

If I were to tell Anne and Clare that, they would die laughing and tease me some more. But I don't tell them. I don't tell them I miss anything and hope they do not see the cracks in my world.

My life has become immersed in my son and his autism and therapies and treatment and more. I have lost weight. I isolate myself. I become the patient when I attend appointments I have made for Cian. I ignore the suggestions that I may need "something" to take the edge off things. I refuse to take anti-depressants. Any depression I have is relative. I need a different kind of help, practical help, help with obtaining services for my son so I can get on with my own life, but no one is listening.

* * *

Christopher arrives home one day and says he has to write about his Mum. I ask him what he has written but he says he just drew a picture. It is a picture of a stick-like figure bent over a computer. That picture breaks my heart. My idea of motherhood is going for walks in parks, pointing out birds and flowers, climbing mountains, going for bicycle rides and having picnics. In his young life, we don't get to do any of these things without being on red alert for fear that Cian poisons himself with something inedible or runs into the nearest pond or decides to walk the "white line". Somehow, Christopher's needs come second.

There are days I almost forget about Christopher coming off the school bus. I grab my coat and rush down the lane to meet my eldest son, who is not quite six years old and already halfway up the lane. He is examining butterflies or prodding the ditches looking for all sorts of wildlife or patting the head of a neighbour's dog. He lifts his head and his arm and waves away my anxiety. We meet, I take his bag and we walk hand-in-hand up the lane. For five stolen minutes, I submerge myself in his beautiful, carefree world, the colours of the butterfly or the length of a worm – and his longing for a puppy. I tell him, "Sometime soon, when I have time to feed it."

He laughs and looks up at me and knows. His mammy has no time for anything these days.

One day I get caught up in the mess of things when he bursts through the door, shaking the rain from his coat and pulling off his wet things.

"Christopher!"

My eyes immediately dart to the clock and back to him again. My mouth parts at the sight of him. A rush of guilt and regret floods my insides, flushing my face, muddying up my mind and slowing my movements as I move towards him. He lifts his head and regards me for a moment, as though he has caught me doing something I shouldn't. Something in his look stops me from touching him. I want to hold him and have him rest his head on my shoulder. I take a step towards him but his pale mottled body has already gone. A bundle of soaking wet clothes and a damp schoolbag slump at my feet. His light footsteps climb the stairs. A door slams shut.

Before Cian was born, we had done everything together. Christopher was reared in the back seat of my car. He came everywhere with me. I had kept him close to me in the folds of my undivided attention. We spent hours laughing and playing and singing silly songs. He was a curious, carefree child, happy and interesting. He rolled in to our bedroom at five in the morning, tripping over our heads, demanding to know what number came after three. Questions poured out of him, demanding rhymes and reasons to his world.

"Mammy, where does rain come from?"

"The clouds in the sky."

"Where do the clouds come from?"

"Well, the rain makes the clouds."

"Mammy, where did the world come from?"

"God made the world."

"And where did God come from?"

"Ask your Daddy when he comes home."

Our togetherness, the joy of him, filled me up, but I couldn't get enough of him.

Now I have momentarily forgotten his existence, his need. How could I have done that?

I bite my lip and lift the sodden clothes. Through it all, I have snatched precious moments with Christopher when someone else's attention was fixed on Cian, when I have made a conscious effort to clock into his world, wanting to take up space, to be a part of him again. We would go for pizza and I would gasp at all the new Pokémon names while his eyes would roam, studying the paintings and the faces of part-time waitresses. I want to hear who he is sitting beside at school and whether he likes his teacher or not. I want to know what he had for lunch and what he drew in art. He loves art and is always drawing and being creative at home. He tells me how many lizards there are on the whole planet and about the dinosaur bones someone found in a faraway place I can't spell. No one can share this with me but my Chrisy. How can I convey to him how much I want to be with him when I can't even remember to fetch him off the bus? How do I explain that I am torn between his needs and the needs of his brother?

Snapping the washing machine shut, I thank God for swimming pools. At least we can all flap about together. I snigger to myself as a door opens, arresting my thoughts. Footsteps creak on the stairs above my head. I hold my breath and wait to hear him knock on the therapy room door, like he does every other evening. His knock, a light tap, is barely audible through the utility wall. The door opens and Donna greets him with a big "Hello". She is in the middle of her second session. In my mind's eye I can see her waving him in, touching his shoulder lightly and telling Cian to say hello. Christopher will find his way to Cian and give him a high-five and take over the role of "teacher". They will all take turns completing the little tasks set for Cian and Christopher will tell Cian he is really good today and give him another high-five. I bow my head and try to accept it all but I can't help wishing they were out in the garden playing Cowboys and Indians and looking for slugs. Only Cian doesn't know how to play Cowboys and Indians and he usually eats the slugs. I smile through my tears at the reality of it and reach for the washing powder before the smile fades quietly again.

Filling up the machine, I remind myself that Cian is progressing. The data sheets show it every night when I go to tidy up and prepare the room for the next morning. Just last night, the data sheets told me that Cian has mastered his colours, his prepositions and can count to five. He knows the names for each room in the house and can identify objects that belong in each room. He can name all the familiar people in his life, identifying each person by their photograph, and can identify familiar sounds from an audiotape. He understands well over two hundred nouns and knows his phonics. His articulation is improving and he is using the phrase "I want" and naming his needs. It isn't all spontaneous but he is being stimulated for most of the day. Nothing else really matters.

And in my heart I know that Christopher is happy too, for most of it. I have made a blunder and make a mental note never to make it again. Christopher will forgive me. I need to forgive myself. I cannot dwell on times I fail. I can only give what I can give.

The washing machine starts to whirl and water runs into the pocket of the machine tumbling down through the pipe over Chrisy's uniform. I will have them nice and clean for him. They will be dry and ironed and he will find them folded and ready to go when he wakes up in the morning. His happiness is all that matters. I must not feel cheated and bitter because Cian's needs take me away from him. He is a clever boy. He will make out and when I can I will make it up to him. I will get him back again. Until then, other families can borrow him and take him into their back yards. Patrick and Liam will continue to come and stay and build tree huts and look for insects and sneak treats. I am glad there is closeness between them. They may be his cousins, but they are just like brothers. Christopher says so. He needs them. Autism has stolen his. It is our loss, our terrible loss.

25

One Friday Anne emerges from the therapy room full of regret. She tells me she isn't available anymore and this will be her last week. I make tea and listen to her plans to go into nursing. I thank her for her time, for all she has done. She says goodbye to Cian, kissing his forehead and leaves us with no idea how much I will miss her. Anyone who has ever attempted to teach Cian takes up a special place in my heart. I celebrate with them when they report that Cian has mastered a task but when they have to move on I panic at the thought of having to train someone new.

The old familiar feeling of exhaustion washes over me. All of a sudden, things come racing towards my eyes, moving towards me at light speed, running forward, running back, creating commotion in my head, faces I do not recognise, my mother's voice telling me not to take too much out of myself. I long to lie down but I can't get up from the chair. Cian is sitting quietly for once, watching a new *Thomas* video. A restlessness nudges me into thinking I should be somewhere else. I glance at the clock and startle at the time. Elizabeth!

Elizabeth is an international pianist who hails from Germany. I met her in December 2001 at the Tara Centre in Omagh, when President Mary McAleese paid an eloquent tribute to the significance of the Centre in the peace-building movement in Northern Ireland. Elizabeth had played the harp beautifully at the event and before I left I stopped to congratulate her. Unsurprisingly, the conversation came around to Cian. I shared with her Cian's love for music and Elizabeth shared how she would like to help. Shortly after our meeting, Cian started to attend a "music therapy" session with Elizabeth once a week. He likes the music but he loves her earrings, her elaborate jewellery and her children's guinea pigs more. They are all part of his "sensory" experience and Elizabeth allows him to hold the guinea pigs at the end of the class. The whole experience is so rewarding for him.

Now he is due at Elizabeth's in ten minutes. I am never going to make it on time. I am hopelessly shattered. I reach for the phone to cancel.

Minutes later, Elizabeth calls me back. "Aileen, tell me, are you okay?" Elizabeth has a degree in intuition.

"I am okay. I'm just tired."

It wouldn't be very appropriate to disclose that I am about to have a nervous breakdown. After all, I barely know the lady.

"Have you help?"

"Not today. Donna will come soon to teach Cian. I need to tidy the house."

"Right, I have two hours. Tell me where you live? I will come. I am sure there is something I can do." Her voice is matter-of-fact. Words flow in that no-nonsense European way that is hard to argue with. I don't try. I would have only wasted her time apologising. Fifteen minutes later, Elizabeth is standing at my back door with an apron, a pair of yellow marigold gloves and a smile. She takes a long look at me and tilts her head.

"You are so very tired. You must rest while I work. I will clean your floors and surfaces. No one can think straight if the environment is not in order. Show me where I can find the cleaning equipment and then pretend I am not here."

Not long after, Donna arrives. I am still sitting in the same position. I must look a sight. When I tell her that another therapist is leaving, I break down. I don't know how I am going to manage or find the enthusiasm to start teaching Cian again. I am truly burnt out. Donna listens in her calm, unassuming way. Some time later, when I have composed myself again, she gets up from the chair and speaks.

"Aileen, I am going to pack the boys' clothes. Can you get me some food for Cian? I will wait for Christopher and I will take the boys for the weekend so you can rest."

At that, she turns and walks towards the hall calmly. She walks up the stairs as if it is just another part of an ordinary day. Giving. To Donna it is.

* * *

While Donna has the boys away, I receive an email from Helen. Sarah, the ABA tutor in Africa, had put us in touch with each other as Helen is Irish but lives in Africa. We have been emailing each other since I got back from our trip and our friendship has deepened over the cyber-waves. She told me about her little boy Conor, who has autism, and about the rest of her family. Her email informs me that her family is coming for Easter and they would like us to join them. A break sounds like a good idea. It is the first of many rendezvous.

Christopher makes a friend in Frank Jr and Cian and Conor wander and explore together. Helen and I have a lot in common besides our boys. We share the same birth date and the same sense of humour. We both slap around in jeans and bare faces. We could talk for days, swapping notes and sharing snippets of our dreams for our boys. Helen is as driven as me when it comes to helping her son reach his potential. We continue to research and live at the cutting-edge of autism treatments. Helen and I take Cian and Conor for walks and they put their arms around each other or hold their hands in tender moments, sharing the world of autism.

But Helen is also different from me in some ways. Helen is suffering from rheumatoid arthritis and is slowly recovering from this debilitating condition. She never complains. She sips dandelion tea while I drink gallons of coffee. I am a pent-up jabbering wreck and she is easy, chilled. She has that African stillness about her. She teaches me how to climb back into my own skin and see the bigger picture. Over the week, she brings me back to me.

On the last evening of our visit, Helen rests and Eamonn keeps the kids while Frank and I wander down to the local pub. He enjoys a good Guinness and success in life. Both Frank and Helen are movers and shakers. Frank is a director of a highly successful business empire. Helen is a talented music teacher but spends much of her time voluntarily overseeing a variety of innovative projects sponsored by her husband to help create a better quality of life for the disadvantaged of South Africa.

That night, Frank's eyes dance as he shares stories of Africa, building his business and his plans to develop other economically viable areas. He is full of engaging stories. As we finish up our last drink, I ask him what the secret of his success is. He tosses down the last of his Guinness and, with an air of finality, sets down the glass. For a short while, he watches the creamy froth slide down to the bottom of his glass before turning towards me, avoiding my gaze.

"Success? I will only be successful when Conor calls me Daddy."

* * *

Back home, I am sticking pieces of Velcro on the back of a visual schedule board and thinking how major challenges in life can fine-tune an outlook when Nicola, Eoin's mum, calls me up. Her therapists will be finishing off at college soon and can do more hours.

"Why don't you come down over the summer and we could rotate the therapists?"

Despite the fact that it is a 120-mile round trip from my home to Nicola's in Belfast, I consider the idea. Siobhan has been coming faithfully every Monday to oversee Cian's programme and sometimes Emma or Ben would come when I needed sessions covered. Jacqueline and Mary will not be able to work when their children are off for the summer and Donna will need a holiday.

Furthermore, Cian would get out of the house and he could have social dates with other children at Nicola's. Christopher could come with me and play with Eoin's brothers Ruairí and Conall. Nicola would be good company and I would not feel so isolated.

Besides, I had contacted social services again to ask for help. Another assessment is carried out and another form filled in as Donna teaches Cian. I get no follow-up call or respite services. Instead, they follow up Donna, wondering if she would be interested in offering respite to a child on their caseload. His name is not Cian.

And so for three mornings a week during the summer months we get up early and arrive at Nicola's just in time for the first session. Therapists rotate between Cian and Eoin. Their siblings play in the garden while Nicola and I swap notes and whine and reassure each other. Sometimes we treat ourselves to breakfast and eat none of it and talk about autism. We talk about our boys, about what ought to be and what ought not to be. Our whole conversation rarely breaks from the world of autism. We could talk about autism forever. We never get bored, because it is our life and nobody else wants to talk about it. She is wearing my moccasins and I am wearing hers. In a way, we carry each other.

While in Belfast I learn that there are a number of PhD students in the psychology department of the University of Ulster who are interested in gaining experience with children with autism. At the beginning of the semester I drive to the university and bag Cian three potential therapists. The only problem is, I live so far away. There is only one solution. If we can't get therapists to come to us, we need to go to the therapists. I make plans to take Cian to Belfast while Eamonn makes plans to run the New York Marathon with other SPEAC parents to help set up a school in Belfast specifically for the needs of children with autism, including ABA therapy. There are some fun nights meeting celebrities who are supporting us and helping fundraise for the school but all the glitz and glamour does not melt away the worries I have for Cian's future.

* * *

"Postman Pat" raps at the window. The keys are high up and out of sight on a shelf in the sitting room. Sifting through the jingling bunch, I retrieve the front door key and snap back the door handle.

"Wait, I'll get him," I turn to fetch Cian, at the same time noticing that "Postman Pat" has no post and no smile. He removes his hat and gestures as though to ask permission to come in. I beckon him as he ducks under the door frame. He is a tall man. Today there is an edginess about him. He looks tall and small at the same time. With his hat in his hands, he tells me he has not been around for a while. He was covering another district but he just thought he would drop by to let me know. His nephew, Matthew, passed away in his sleep some time ago. I offer him a seat. Across the kitchen table, "Postman Pat" – David – talks about Matthew. It seems strange sitting opposite a postman in uniform delivering news that is not mine personally but that touches me deeply. For weeks I mourn for the parents of Matthew and for Matthew like he was my own.

26

In hindsight, I must have been completely insane the night we left for Belfast. I thought nothing of wrapping my five-year-old son in a duvet and taking him out into the night, away from all that he knew, to an anonymous city. At best it could be compared to a spell in Alcatraz.

Eamonn and Christopher visit on Wednesdays and stay overnight. I travel home with Cian at the weekends and back to Belfast on Monday morning. Tuesday is the only day I don't see them – until I get a phone call one month later.

"Mammy, do you mind if I don't come down this evening? I want to stay with Tiger."

"Who's Tiger?" I bite the inside of my lip.

"My new puppy."

My heart does a double-flip and falls into my socks. I have been replaced.

* * *

The psychology students start immediately and soon Cian has a full one-to-one home programme with six therapists. The first therapist arrives at eight in the morning and the last one leaves at four in the afternoon. I update the files, move programmes on and train them in the techniques. My whole living exists around ABA therapy. There is hardly any time to eat. Time in the kitchen is spent cooking and baking for Cian.

Donna comes down one evening a week. She arrives about four and stays until late. Both Cian and I love to see her coming through the door. She does some therapy with Cian and then takes him for a drive.

Most evenings Cian and I go for a walk. We walk hand-in-hand, with our heads down against the wind, past cosy cafés that look warm and inviting. One evening I pause to read a notice in a window, letting go of Cian's hand for a moment to fix my hat. A lady is sitting in a window-seat talking to a waiter, who has just placed a mug of coffee and a dessert accompanied by a generous dollop of fresh cream in front of her. The waiter moves away and the lady folds up her paper, just as Little Mowgli appears from nowhere, grabs a lump of pie and attempts to swallow it whole. Only Cian doesn't get to swallow it whole. The woman comes flailing in on top of him, grabs the food from his mouth and throws it back on the plate.

Jesus Christ.

By the time I reach Cian, the lady is clutching her pie and giving Cian a piece of her mind. "What on earth are you doing? You cheeky, cheeky boy. How dare you!" She glares down her nose at him.

He doesn't hear her or see her. He only has eyes for the pie.

I am behind him now, wrestling with his arms.

"Can you not control this child? I have never seen such behaviour." She turns back to Cian. "Do you expect me to eat it now? How dare you interrupt my meal like this?"

She is shaking and full of rage but I do not react. I hold Cian close, struggling with one hand to pull a purse from my pocket. The lady takes a deep breath and runs a hand over her forehead. My small but contained voice informs her that my son has autism. He has little concept of social skills and other people's belongings. He has intolerance to wheat and milk and is not allowed foods like apple pie. I nod towards the table.

"It doesn't stop him from wanting it, though. We are sorry to have spoilt your food."

I reach down and set some money on the table before I guide Cian towards the door and head back to a house that is not our home wondering what we will have for tea. What the lady does after we leave, I have no idea. I do not look back. I have never looked back.

She doesn't run after me. Some people do, embarrassment and humiliation showing in their faces, forcing me to put my money back into my pocket, apologising. Voices mumble and stutter. "I should have realised."

"Yes, you should," I want to say, but I don't. You can't help yourselves. You live in world where everything goes like clockwork. Tick-tock, tick-tock, not tock-tick. You couldn't possibly know what it is like to live with tock-tick.

Some of you do, though, when Mowgli appears out of nowhere and sticks his hand in your dinner and you say nothing. You let him eat away, smile at your companions, who can't believe what they are seeing and take in the scene in slow motion, realising there is something not quite the norm here. You watch me snatch his hands away and listen carefully as I apologise profusely and explain why my son is behaving in such a way. You lift your napkin and clean your mouth and smile and say something like, "It is okay. No worries."

Sometimes you find it amusing and you laugh at the idea of it. When Cian was a toddler, I laughed too. I have stopped laughing now, as he has got older. It doesn't bother me if you laugh; it must seem quite amusing, I guess, if you are not the child's mother or father or carer.

Sometimes you watch me practically handcuffing my son, leading him away from your table and your plate, and our eyes meet, just for a second. I know you are shocked. I leave you thinking how tough it must be. Maybe you know someone like him, like me. Maybe you wonder how on earth you would cope if you were me. Maybe you thank God you are not me, but from that moment my son has touched you, changed you. I hope you can learn from him. I hope you will give thanks for simple things the way I thank God for you – sometimes – when you go out of your way to help me. When you weigh up the situation. When you notice how difficult it is for the child to wait in a queue or wait for his food in a restaurant. You allow him to go before you, smiling at me, letting me know it's okay. Or, when he makes a grab for your chips and you bring some to our table on a small side-plate. He settles down nicely and I am both relieved and grateful that you are the person we sat next too. Your kindness wraps around me, as comforting as a duck-down duvet.

Sometimes you see me struggling, trying to restrain my

child from leaving his seat, from clambering into windows, rescuing cutlery from under tables. Without saying a word, you send your child for more cutlery, for napkins, for a waiter to clean the spill and nod at my grateful smile. When we pass by your table on our way out, I bend down to give your child a coin, a gesture of my appreciation, but before it leaves my hand, you block my arm. "No, we helped you because you needed help, not to get paid. What kind of a world is it if we can't help without being paid?" I stare back at you and give thanks for your decency, surprised and saddened that I don't meet more like you.

* * *

A city is a lonely place on your own with a special needs child who is totally dependent on my care. Cian's diet and his need to run away from me leave me nervous and reluctant to take him anywhere. I am terrified I could lose him or that something would happen to him. But the evenings are long and the nights are longer.

One evening I pick up the courage and decide to go to the cinema. *Finding Nemo* is showing and Cian will enjoy the fish and the colours. It is a misty dark November evening. I snuggle Cian into his hat and coat and we walk together from the car park to the bright lights of the movie house. Cian is skipping beside me. He knows this evening is different and an air of anticipation lights up his face.

Cian is surprisingly good in the cinema. He is happy to sit and watch the film and laugh at a few funny parts. Cian's wicked sense of humour is only beginning to reveal itself. It makes my night to see him so happy and content and knowing the appropriate times to laugh. When we leave, the yellow haze from the streetlights curls around us. I ask a passer-by for the time. Ten past nine. I don't feel like going back to the house, to an empty "school". Cian looks happy and content to be out, so I decide to walk.

"Maybe we'll get some chips in McDonald's, Cian."

"Chips." Cian echoes the word in agreement.

"Okay, boss, you said it. McDonald's it is." We turn towards the city centre.

I love Belfast. I lived in Belfast in the eighties while I was at university and, despite all the troubles, I have a strong affinity with it. It is small and compact and my head is full of positive experiences. Tonight it is like a stranger to me. The streets I walked as a carefree student seem somehow threatening. Ironic that, considering there is a ceasefire. Politically, things have changed – we dare to dream of peace. Personally I have changed. I am a different person now, holding the hand of a child who doesn't quite fit into the frame of city living. Men in long coats clutching briefcases walk briskly. Taxi drivers whiz by. Partygoers traipse past in high heels and expensive perfume. Couples snuggle close and students laugh and howl and tease each other. Cian splashes in the puddles glimmering in the dim-lit street, his hand warm and safe in mine.

The bright fluorescent lights of McDonald's are unforgiving and contrast sharply with the shadows in the streets. A group of workmen with yellow coats sit in one corner and look up as we come in. Two young couples sit and glance in our direction, their eyes lingering on Cian. A man in a suit with a briefcase at his feet tries to read a paper as he gnaws at an overloaded burger. Cian makes a grab for his chips. The man leans back in his seat as I swiftly turn Cian towards the counter. With my hands on both his shoulders, I keep him in front of me while he fidgets from foot to foot. I place our order, thinking that most children would be tucked up in bed hours ago. At the table I hand Cian his chips and while I sip coffee I feel like I have kidnapped him. Cian munches on his chips, examining each one – glad of the freedom, glad of the chips.

What odds if he should be in bed? What odds what everyone else thinks? They don't know we are two prisoners out for the evening making the most of our freedom.

* * *

Cian seems to enjoy the therapy sessions, and everything goes well, until the night-waking starts and the dreaded early morning phone calls from a therapist informing me that they can't make it. On those mornings we go to the park. Cian never sleeps during the day, even if he has been up the whole night.

The damp tarmac glistens in the tepid sunshine. I slump down on a freezing cold park bench. Soon the damp patches of last night's rain will evaporate. *Like my life.* Hunched up, with one leg folded over the other, I stuff my hands in the pockets of my coat but fail to keep out the raw biting cold creeping under my skin. In a stupor I think of the night before – how little Mowgli had prowled up and down the stairs most of the night, switching on lights, taps and televisions; how he jumped from the headboard onto his bed, yelling "AREEBAREEBAAAA" over and over until almost every wooden slat in the bed had collapsed to the floor; how he fell asleep in the well of the mattress, until he awoke again, sobbing uncontrollably.

The perimeter of the park is lined with oak trees. Little Mowgli is still and gazing into the sway of them, his head tilted slightly to one side. An unzipped anorak slips from his shoulders. He shrugs indifferently, allowing it to fall at his feet. For a long time we are alone until a group of mothers and toddlers arrive. A powder-pink coat and hat, complete with mittens, whiz in and out around him, studying him attentively. Mowgli takes no notice of the child clad in designer frills but continues to stare at the trees. Looking about me, I swallow anger and unchartered tears. Cian suddenly turns around and mounts the seesaw backwards. His weight forces the seat to the ground. In a hypnotic state, he begins to pour gravel through his fingers, over and over. I move towards the other side of the seesaw to sit on it, but he jumps up and dashes past me towards a wooden climbing frame. *I am invisible*. He lies against the ropes and bangs his head off the wood. I try to stop him and notice a four-letter word hacked in the wood above his head: H E L P.

A hollow empty space swells inside me.

I am barely aware of the other children in the park, but I can hear them calling.

"I want to go on that swing."

"Mummy, look at me."

"Push me higher."

Besotted mums push higher and higher until their precious ones squeal with delight. Faster and faster until they have butterflies in their tummies. Up and down the slide until their legs tire.

A deep longing curdles my thinking and I find myself

wishing a child's voice would call out to me. *His voice.*

A toddler stares at a little girl tumbling down the slide. Their eyes meet and they share the thrill with an open grin. Instinctively they run together, finding the steps of the slide again, watching each other with fierce curiosity.

The boy with no coat is on the climbing frame. He is climbing higher and higher, cautiously negotiating the thin rounded bars. Other children gather at the bottom to watch. The boy is much bigger than them. They do not dare to follow him – it is too high, too dangerous for little folk who are shy of three years old. He continues to climb. He does not look down at his mammy.

Christ! Don't let him fall!

"Mummy, look!"

The girl in the pink fluffy duffel gasps. All the mums turn and stare at the stick-like silhouette against the grey white sky. Mums share sideways glances. My eyes remain on the boy. I imagine angels above him, before him and behind him, shielding him in a veil of gold. He unravels his body methodically, stretching his arms out in a crucified position until he is standing straight. A ghost of a smile cracks the serious, expressionless face.

"AREEBA REBAAAAAAAAAAAA."

The adults look anxiously at each other. Other mums whisper, moving their children away from the bottom of the climbing frame. They pull their children's coats tighter to them. Maybe they glance at me. I can't be sure, for my eyes are locked on my precious boy's frame. I wait in the emptiness that engulfs me now with every fresh gulp of air. I am inside a vacuum and the vacuum is inside me. It is nothing but a gaping extension of space filled with silence.

Eventually Mowgli descends the climbing frame in silence. He leaps onto the ground from the second rung. I reach for him but he dodges my arms, turning quickly, shrugging me off and darting towards the roundabout. *I am nobody*. Plopping down on a damp seat, the boy snatches the rusty orange bar of the roundabout.

"AREEBA REBAAAA"

He grins to no one in particular and waits. A little girl joins him. The little girl with the fluffy pink coat. She scrutinises him from the tip of his head to the point of his shoes. She sits down beside him, watching him, but says nothing. Neither does he. Her mummy begins to push faster and faster.

"No school today?" she asks the boy. The boy doesn't answer but stares straight ahead. Looking in my direction, she acknowledges me. I nod back.

She steals a few glances, pretending not to look, trying to work out why he seems different, why he is the same. She pushes some more and looks up at me again.

"They all love the park."

The mother *wants to know* why he isn't in school. She wants me to tell her what is different about him – what can be done – questions I am unable to answer. She wants to know but she doesn't know how to ask so she tells me that all children love the park.

The merry-go-round is flying now and the boy lifts his head. Slowly he turns sideways towards the girl. I can hardly bear to watch the fuzzy moving shape but I hold on until their eyes lock as the rush of adrenaline excites their tiny bodies. Their mouths break open in wide smiles, connecting with each other, holding on for dear life. The moment is precious and I store it in my mind so I can feed off it, again and again, when despair comes to revisit.

All too soon the roundabout begins to slow, the moment fades and so does the boy's smile. The little girl steadies herself and stands up, making her way towards him. She has just found a playmate.

"Will you come on the seesaw with me?" She jigs up and down.

He does not look up but stares into the fabric of her coat. Bending her head slightly, she examines his face. He does not share the excitement of the toddler at the bottom of the slide. Instead, he reaches out and touches the delicate pink fur. Stroking it up and down, up and down. He loses himself in its softness until, without warning, the little girl vanishes in front of him. The boy does not turn his head to wonder where she went. Stretching her neck over her mother's shoulder, the girl strains to look back at the boy.

"But I want him to go on the seesaw with me," she protests.

"Maybe another day. We need to go home now." The girl is bundled into a car. Away from the roundabout. Away from the strange child who should be in school. And then they are gone.

I could have explained. I could have told her, but I am too vulnerable today, too wrecked. Today I am unable to say autism and my son's name in the same sentence. I do not want to hear regret in my quivering voice. I do not want a stranger to say "It's okay" when clearly it isn't. I do not want a mother to see me drown in my grief – everything floating. I don't want her to see the holes in me.

A mother should be proud of her child. Not apologetic.

Denouncing autism is like denying Cian. To accept Cian I have to accept his autism. I have a long way to go.

Little Mowgli is still sitting and waiting. The park is empty now. I move closer and place my hands on the metal frame of the roundabout. A steel chill rushes through my nerve endings to a place that is already frozen. I lean towards him as though to push, but I pause. *I want to hear his voice*. My ears strain in the silence. Time stands still. Battered hope stretches out defiantly between us. The oak trees seem to hush just as I catch the faintest whisper:

"Push."

I jump up and down and cheer and laugh and cry. It is one whole word in its fullness. It is pure and meaningful and he said it all by himself. It is the words I yearn for. *His words*. The communication of knowing what and how and why.

"Good boy!" I shout in an over-animated voice.

It is enough for now. We can build on it. The sun breaks through from behind a heavy cloud and splashes over the play park. His word sparks a flint-like connection inside, kicking me back into life. Little Mowgli jiggles with anticipation. As I bend forward, he stretches out his arms and yells, "AREEBA REBAAAA," like some ancient warrior.

I push with all my might. His broad smile warms me again. I am his mother. He is my son.

* * *

It has taken me a long time to talk to the mother in the park – to unveil the truth – to open up and disclose to her the reasons why my child is the same and different. How hard it is for me to reveal how tough it is to watch her child do what my child can't – that some days my grief is more conspicuous than my love.

It has taken me even longer to understand that the mother in the park has more in common with me than I once thought. Beyond the "them and us", I come to realise that her curiosity is a mother's desire to understand a child, my son, who happens to be different. Her nervousness is a fear of something unfamiliar but as I gain courage to share and help her understand my child's difference, she may in turn be able to understand mothers like me who could be her sister, her friend or her neighbour. Through time I have tried to close the gap between "them and us" and confront my own prejudices to help the mother in the park develop an understanding that in turn will help her child, who also loves the park, to understand, to embrace and to accept what makes us all different and all the same.

27

When it is raining we stay inside the tiny two-bedroom house. If I have enough energy and Cian is in good form, I teach him myself. We "pretend" all sorts of events, acting out birthdays, picnics, Halloween, trips to the hospital and to the dentist. I show him videos of the different events. We practise blowing candles and singing "Happy Birthday" and opening parcels and pretty paper, teaching him the words associated with each.

Painstakingly, I teach him tasks like putting on his shoes, opening and closing buttons and fastening and unfastening zips. The tasks are difficult for him and I make a mental note to contact the occupational therapist.

When the therapists finish we sometimes go "shopping" or "banking" or to the post office, to work on areas such as waiting and how to pay for an item, to familiarise Cian with the different types of shops and to generalise what he has learnt in the therapy room – counting, the colours and shapes of things.

"Cian, get me two bananas."

"How many?"

"Push the trolley."

"What is it?"

I do not do a week's grocery shopping but keep the shopping trips short and focused with purpose. I hold Cian's hand tight or put him in the trolley to stop him from running away. I only concentrate on the lessons I am trying to teach Cian.

There are times when the challenge is too great. It is during one of these shopping trips, in Marks and Spencer, that I nearly give him away. We have not been shopping in Marks and Spencer but are making our way back to the car when Mowgli wrenches his hand from mine and dashes straight in through the automatic doors.

When I manage to catch up with him he throws himself down, kicking and howling in front of the meat counter. I tell him he can walk around the store but he must hold my hand. Pushing himself along the ground with his feet, he tries to escape. Bending over him, I try to haul him up. He grabs my tracksuit bottoms. My undies and derrière are exposed to everyone on the meat counter and trolley-pushers coming at me from all directions. I am mortified. I want to kill him! With sheer determination I hoist him up in my arms and disappear down an aisle, as far away from the meat department as I can.

Passing the refrigeration area, I remember I need milk. I might as well get some while I am here. Another opportunity for Cian to learn. It is the way my mind is programmed now. No matter what calamity is going on, I never miss an opportunity to teach Cian. I plop him down in front of the milk and guard his body between my outstretched frame and the cooler.

"Show me milk." I ask in the same way as I work with him in his therapy room.

Cian points at the milk.

"Clever boy."

I take a big jar and smaller jar and set them next to each other.

"Show me little."

Cian points at the small jar.

"Give me little milk."

His small hands grasp the handle of the smaller jar and shove it against me.

"Good boy. That is little milk. You are a super star. Well done."

Over the top of Cian's head I become aware of a young assistant staring at us. He has become distracted from what he is doing and looks like he is about to keel over into the fridge. I smile sweetly and toss my head back.

"That's my boy. Isn't he fecking amazing?"

I don't care how strange it looks. I am so proud. Cian got every answer right.

Little Mowgli carries the milk to the checkout. It is a decoy. It is to slow him down. He walks awkwardly with the extra weigh clutched at his side. There are three people at the checkout waiting their turn and for a moment I want to forget about the milk and run. Waiting is extremely difficult for Cian but it is something we try to work on, so I decide to join the queue and encourage Cian to wait.

Cian waits nicely for the first person in line to purchase his goods. He is still standing quietly as the next person is served. Holding on to Cian and my purse, I am encouraging him the whole time.

"Nice waiting, Cian."

"Not long now, Cian."

"You are very good. Well done."

The assistant leaves the till. She needs to get a price. The lady in front of me examines her purchases and stands waiting. We are at the top of the queue but it is not moving. We are just standing. Nothing is happening. Cian wants to move on out past the lady waiting in front of us. He pulls and pulls at my arm, pushing and pulling, falling awkwardly against the lady waiting for the assistant to return. She is none too pleased. Cian's foot knocks against her Burberry umbrella. It falls to the floor. I clamber after it, holding on to Cian. The woman thanks me with a scowl and readjusts her Burberry shawl around her shoulder – impatience radiating from every part of her. I try to rein Cian in around my body as he stamps his feet and drops the milk. It knocks against a shelf holding batteries and other small things, causing them to tumble to the floor. Simultaneously he attempts to bite my wrist. I push my fist gently against his teeth to prevent a break in the skin. With my other hand, I let go to lift the milk in case it is leaking and Cian falls to the ground.

Everyone is staring now. The assistant has returned and the woman in the Burberry shawl is packing her items into a Burberry bag but her beady eyes are on the wild undisciplined child by her feet – his difficulties illuminated by those who have no difficulty disapproving. Bending down, I touch his face and give him a hug.

"It's okay. It's our turn next."

I tussle to lift Cian's limp body struggling against mine,

screaming and shouting, until I hear another voice, a soft, kind voice floating overhead.

"Will I take you home?"

I close my eyes and in one crazy moment I wish the owner of the voice would do just that – take him, for a couple of hours at least. I immediately feel guilty. *What a horrible thought. How could I give my own child away to a total stranger in a supermarket?* Unwelcome emotion wells up inside me.

Someone edges closer, emitting an aroma of a delicate perfume. A hand rests on my back as an elegant lady with a light dusting of powder blush on her cheeks to match her pale pink lips bends down over me to speak to my screaming child. A few wispy strands of silvery hair escape from the multi-faceted clasp that catches her hair in the middle of her head. The edges of her long green coat lie on the ground and a beige polo-neck jumper protrudes from its lapels. Her eyes are soft, her voice gentle and soothing.

"Will you come home with me? I know a little boy like you." *So she knows.* Not that it isn't obvious or anything, but most people assume that Cian is a very badly behaved child. "And he is just as beautiful as you too."

She takes his hand without fear. I am terrified he will harm her but she waves me away. Cian stares at every contour of her face. A piece of jewellery escapes from inside her coat and swings over Cian. He runs the solid gold chain through his fingers again and again, examining the three coloured stones set in the three-sided bar. She lifts it off her neck and lets him have it, waving away my protests.

"He'll not break that thing. It's been around longer than I have."

I smile through my tears as she gestures for me to pay for

the milk while she entertains my son. After she pays for her items she walks me to the car, holding on to Cian's hand, smiling and nodding, all the while talking to him, reassuring him, while I quell the emotion choking me up.

We reach the car and I strap him into his car seat.

"Can I give him something, a chocolate perhaps?"

"I'm sorry, he is on a special diet . . . but," I reach into the front of the car and retrieve a little box, "you could swap your chain for a gluten-free biscuit."

"That doesn't seem a fair exchange. Tell you what." She unlatches the delicate diamond-shaped fastener of her bottle-green handbag and pulls out a set of two little cars, unopened in their plastic wrapper.

"I bought them for my grandchild. He will not mind – he doesn't play with toys but I buy them anyway. Maybe your little boy will."

With that, she offers the cars and the biscuit to Cian. He drops the chain immediately into her hand and I thank her once again for helping me. She snaps her bag closed and hangs it on her arm.

"My grandchild rarely leaves the house. It is too difficult for him and much too difficult for my daughter. He hasn't even got a school. They are fighting constantly for him but no one seems to care."

She flashes one last smile at Cian. "He is truly beautiful. It is not easy. I saw you in the aisle. You are doing your best." Just as her voice breaks she squeezes my hand, turns and walks away, leaving me wondering about her grandchild and if she had seen my knickers.

* * *

As Christmas approaches I become increasingly unsettled in Belfast and hold my breath for the holidays. I talk to Cian about baby Jesus, about Santa and presents. I make a decision. We will take a complete break from ABA therapy. Helen and Frank are coming home and we will go and visit them.

One afternoon on our daily walk Cian and I mount the steps of the bank. The tiniest flakes of snow are beginning to fall and popular Christmas tunes filter from the speakers above the doorway. At the top of the steps I pause to allow Cian time to notice the coloured lights that sparkle and stream down both sides of the Lisburn Road. He examines his shoes. Five years old and he has yet to show the remotest interest in the madness and magic that abides at Christmas time. I sigh heavily as we enter the intimidating high-roofed building and join a queue. The bank is packed. I am lost in thought, reliving five Christmas days in my head – the baby lying on a new soft play mat; slipping away by his second Christmas, but still he shook and rattled his toys. On his third Christmas he stole baby Jesus out of the crib and lined up the angels and the animals and wise men.

The queue moves forward. Cian is wrapping and unwrapping his small wrist in the rope marking the queue area. Muddled images of an ABA Christmas last year flood my thoughts. I try to block them out of my mind but they keep spilling back in. Cian is straining at my wrist. He is pulling against me. I grip his hand tighter. Looking down I see the little lost boy sitting at the top of the stairs on Christmas morning. Listless. Unmotivated. Staring into nothing. An unopened Santa sack at the bottom of the stairs. The silence.

A man stands to the side of me, hesitantly joining our queue, arranging and rearranging paperwork, pulling his wallet from the inside of his overcoat. Something drops and the man leans forward. I turn to get out of his way, to allow him to retrieve it. Cian's lucky moment. I am distracted. His hand slips from mine. Cian's agile movements weave quickly through the people lined up in different queues. I twist and nudge my way after him. At the top of the queue he gazes at a beautifully decorated Christmas tree with its frosted leaves, silver bows and purple ribbons and an inviting collection of glittering parcels underneath.

I reach out to pull him back but he reaches out first to touch a small glass figurine hanging from the tree. The Christmas lights blink and shimmer, lighting up his face as he examines it. All at once he jumps the rope, falls to his knees and tears strips of glittering wrapping paper off a parcel. I wish Christopher and Eamonn could be here to see it. I am stunned at his reaction.

Just then a uniformed member of staff comes running and clambers over the rope, shouting, "Excuse me, please leave the tree alone. No! No, don't do that!" The tone is abrupt and unforgiving. She is approaching him now, towering over him. I leap over the rope and she turns to me, scolding.

"It took ages decorating it. Please get him away from it." She is becoming hysterical and bends towards Cian. "Please leave the parcels alone!"

Cian is sitting back on his calves, examining the "gift" he has just opened. An empty shoebox. The lady taps his shoulder. He freezes, not quite knowing what to do. It all becomes too much. The shoebox. The spangling Christmas tree. The lady who spent ages decorating it. While she makes disapproving sounds I gather Cian in my arms, all of us blinded. Cian blinded with the disappointment of the present. I am blinded with tears of joy and sadness. The lady blinded by the bling of Christmas. Had she known how long it took me to see the magic of Christmas reflect in my child's eyes, she might have reacted differently.

* * *

That Christmas is our first and best Christmas with Cian taking part and showing much more reaction than he did other years. When he climbs out of bed with Christopher there is curiosity in his eyes. They take the stairs two at a time. There is no waiting, no hesitation. They both tear into their presents, checking each other's out, Cian pulling at Christopher to open his first, Christopher giddy with this new experience. "But I want to open mine, Cian . . ." Christopher laughs gleefully into the camcorder. I smile back, this time fighting back tears of joy. "Okay, okay. I'll open yours." It doesn't take much to persuade him.

He isn't the only one more relaxed. mammy and daddy are too. We have learnt by our mistakes and now we spend Christmas home alone. We advise our families who may have expected us that we can no longer visit, as it is too stressful for Cian and for the family. Everyone understands. It is the best decision we made.

We have no schedule to work to and have all day to cook dinner that suits everyone's diet. Somehow, when we eventually sit down around the table, it is the tastiest Christmas dinner I have ever had. Christmas time is now much more relaxed and Cian has progressed to a stage where he can share the magic of Christmas with Christopher.

Two days after Christmas we drive south to visit Helen and Frank and Frank Jr and Conor. Helen gets up from the kitchen table to hug me. She is pregnant. She laughs at my shocked expression. She never told me. Having one autistic child can increase the possibility of another child with autism. I say nothing, because I know Helen already knows this. I hug her to me and wish I had her courage. I tell her so. She encourages. I hanker after the idea. I would love another baby but the fear of not being able to cope overwhelms me and I toss the thought to the back of my mind.

* * *

In January we return to Belfast but the third-year students have exams and dissertations and are becoming less and less available. In February I make a decision to move back home and with Donna and Jacqueline's help we continue Cian's ABA therapy, but in a more generalised way. We introduce play dates with other children and turn our attention to Cian's sensory issues. Cian can't sit on a swing and push. He has difficulty with holding on and with posture and control. He can't blow or suck or bite certain textures in his mouth. He makes an attempt at brushing his teeth but he can't tie his shoelaces and tends to engage in high-risk behaviour that is fast and dangerous.

I am still in contact with Cian's occupational therapist. We discuss his need for specialised sensory integration work but it is extremely difficult to find an occupational therapist who is trained in SI (sensory integration). I learn of a chartered physiotherapist who has specialised knowledge in SI.

In late February, we travel to Tipperary. The private assessment lasts two days. Cian displays a number of weak areas that need a lot of work. The therapist demonstrates how we can work with Cian. During the assessment, to our delight Cian learns how to push himself and hold on to the swing. We arrive back home with a Home Play Therapy Programme and a list of exercises to integrate with Cian's ABA therapy programme to develop his mouth function, speech and postural control and to decrease sensory-seeking behaviour. All I need is specialist equipment that is ultra-expensive, a specialised therapist with postgraduate training in Sensory Integration and a multi-sensory gym!

My brother, Terry, arrives one day as I am examining our ceiling. I want to put up an indoor swing. Cian's body isn't functioning the way it should be, and he needs a lot of sensory stimulation. Terry listens and tactfully tells me that Cian may very well need sensory stimulation but the ceiling is too low. His eyes tell me I have stepped over the edge of reason.

I never do get my gym, nor do I get the specialised therapist.

Instead I become ill. One morning I awake to find my body locked in the position I have been lying in. Eamonn calls the doctor, who makes a home visit. He is very concerned, suggesting that my body is either in the first stage of arthritis or under immense stress. "In your circumstances, Aileen, and taking into consideration all you

are doing for Cian, I would tend to think it is the latter."
Before he leaves he tells me I need to get plenty of rest and
consider taking a break or two. "You need to take care of
yourself, Aileen, or you will be unable to help Cian or
anyone else."

I lean my head back and think of Maura at the Tara
Centre. Her words and thoughts have come back to haunt
me. I would love to take their advice, to take a break, to get
a rest, but we have no respite services or support for Cian.

A week later, I collapse without warning during one of
the rare occasions I take time to relax on my own.

28

Voices and muffled noise sound way off in the distance. Shadows fall over me, touching me, talking to me. I try to get up but my legs refuse to move. Pain shoots up into my hip and hammers every inch of my head. The ground is damp and chilling.

Paramedics arrive and ask me a string of questions. No, I am not on any medication. No, no one is with me. Yes, I can feel your hand. No, I can't feel your hand. Yes, I can move my arm. No, I can't move my leg. I feel cold. They are going to take me to the hospital. Is there any way they can contact home? I am being lifted onto a stretcher, covered with blankets and pushed into the back of an ambulance.

As it trundles the ten-mile stretch of road to the hospital I feel ridiculous. Eamonn had warned me I would drop in a heap one day. *Least he can't say I wasn't relaxing*, I scoff as I am wheeled down a winding corridor and squint under the full glare of the unforgiving fluorescent tubes embedded in the hospital ceiling. In a small cubicle a doctor examines and interrogates me.

No, I can't remember falling. Yes, I have lost weight. Stressed? Yes, I suppose you could say that. Blood pressure low. Bloods are taken. Right ankle badly bruised and fractured. It needs support and crutches. No, I don't think I could be pregnant. It is the "don't think" that prompts the nurse to wheel me to the nearest bathroom for a "small sample".

Back in the cubicle, pulling the blue gown tighter, I await the results and Eamonn's arrival. Peering around the small makeshift cubicle, he throws me a look that says "told you so" but makes a half-attempt at a joke.

"A&E, huh? Aileen and Eamonn, right?'

I close my eyes and shake my head. I know he is trying to amuse me but I don't feel like laughing.

The doctor returns, whips the mottled blue curtain back and greets us with a gummy grin. He glances at Eamonn and back at me, raising his eyebrows.

"Your husband, Mrs McCallan?"

"Yes . . . do you want him to leave?"

"No, I want to CONGRATULATE you both. Mrs McCallan, you are six weeks pregnant!" Our mouths fall open. The doctor's smile is still pinned to his face but there is confusion in his eyes. Unsure whether he has given us good news or bad news, he bows politely and quickly continues.

"Okay . . . so . . . the leg needs attention, some painkillers perhaps, and then you must go home and rest it . . . yeah?"

His eyes dart from Eamonn to me and back again. We are still staring at him. Shaking myself out of my half-comatose state, I hastily thank him and look at Eamonn, who is running his hand up and down the back of his head.

"Yes, thanks very much. Thank you."

"Okay."

The doctor takes one last look, nods, flashes a smile and disappears behind the curtain.

Silence swells between us. *How are we going to cope?* Eamonn turns and looks at me. "So . . ." It kind of hangs in the air, mingling with the uncertainty of our reality, but I cannot deny the well of emotions slowly filling up inside me – surprise, anticipation, excitement, joy, happiness, dulling my pain and calming my mind.

I rest back on the pillow and close my eyes. We had wanted another baby and had talked many times but never got the courage to make a fully fledged decision. Now that decision has been taken out of our hands. We are having a baby! I think of Helen. Her little baby will soon be born. I can almost see the delight on her face. Helen and Frank will cope, and so will we!

That moment changes everything that comes after. Propped up, nursing my gammy leg, swollen arm and unborn baby I am forced to surrender to the fact that I am not wholly responsible for Cian's destiny, permitting myself to let go. I pray no longer for an answer but for strength to live with the questions, trusting in the energy that gives life.

* * *

Over the next few months I become Mammy again, leaving it to Donna and Jacqueline and Siobhan to teach and work with Cian. We do things together about the house. He develops an interest in baking and helps me prepare homemade gluten- and casein-free pancakes. By the time we are finished, Cian's clothes, arms and face are covered in flour but he counts out the eggs, smashes the shells and stirs and fetches a bowl, a knife, a spoon.

My time with him now is filled with fun and learning, but in a less structured way. I can't wait to see him in the mornings. I feel like he has just been born too.

One morning I am dressing when Cian enters my bedroom, watches me for a moment, then walks towards me. He lifts my t-shirt and places his head next to my skin, holding the sides of my tummy and kissing my belly. I am not showing any outward signs of pregnancy, but there is no doubt in my mind. Cian is the first to know.

At first I think it is my imagination until it happens again and again. One day my friend Róisín calls. Minutes after she walks into the kitchen, Cian dashes down the stairs and appears in the door frame looking around him. He is just about to leave when he slowly turns, walks towards Róisín and places his head against her tummy. As he kisses her side, I know he has found what he has been looking for – a baby. Róisín is pregnant and moved to tears by Cian's reaction.

* * *

We tell Donna our news shortly after, as she is in the house every day and I feel it is only right to explain my sudden absences to keep antenatal appointments. She has something to tell us too and when she asks to speak to both Eamonn and me, I sit down and prepare myself for the worst. The only thing she could want to talk about is her leaving. Eamonn and I stare at her expectantly. She quietly smiles and jokes that we look frightened. We are. We couldn't bear the thought of Donna leaving, but that is not what she tells us.

She is getting married and wants Cian to be her pageboy. I am speechless and filled up. Cian has never been invited to anything before, let alone having the honour to be so important. Before we have time to catch our breath, she adds, "and I want Christopher to be a pageboy too". A double whammy! How wonderful for Christopher to be part of it all. My eyes fill up at her beautiful gift to our family, the ultimate inclusion.

Donna doesn't know what I am fussing about and jumps up to get Cian ready for a social date with kids his own age. Donna takes him out twice a week. Cian waits for her by the hall window. When he sees her car coming up the lane, he jumps up and down and shouts "Donna". When she arrives, he opens the door and brushes past her into the car. Donna jokes about him being more excited to see the car than her.

"Hello."

Cian puts on his seat belt.

"Hello," Donna says again.

"'ello."

Donna opens the car door and kneels down beside him.

"What do you want?"

"I . . . . want . . . ca."

"Okay. I better take you in the car then. Where do you want to go?"

Donna speaks slowly and deliberately.

"Swimm' poo'."

"Okay." Noticing he has no shoes she points down at his feet. "Where are your shoes?"

Cian looks, rips the seatbelt off, runs at high speed back into the house, grabs the shoes and drops them beside Donna before climbing into the car again.

"Okay, Cian. Put on your shoes."

Cian looks at Donna, then at the shoes and knows that Donna isn't going to put them on for him. Donna knows Cian would let you breathe for him if you let him. He reaches for his shoes and shoves them onto his feet.

Jigging up and down, he pushes Donna to move away from the door and shouts, "Let's go." He pulls the door closed and waits.

As they drive off, Cian lifts his little hand and shakes it, mouthing "Mammy" out the window.

* * *

Around this time Cian takes a little interest in gardening . . . well, his type of gardening. He becomes fascinated with a very large forgotten plant pot in the back garden, squishing and kneading the soil in it like dough. A muddy trail begins to form from the plant pot to our patio door, through the kitchen to the sink. He carries buckets of water to and fro and pours the water from the bucket into the mucky plant stand. His trains race around the edges of the pot and crash into the muddy mess he has created. He is covered from head to toe in mud. There is water and muck oozing out of every crack between the cobbles and it is impossible to keep the kitchen floor clean. Eamonn wants to move the pot but I don't want it touched.

"It'll put him off, Eamonn. He is learning so much from it. It is great for his sensory needs and his hand–eye co-ordination, and carrying the water will strengthen his upper body muscles."

Eamonn shakes his head and gives me a long look, the look that tells me I am being a little OTT. "For God's sake, Aileen, can the child not play just for pleasure, for fun, for no reason at all? Does he always have to be learning something? Does there always have to be a bloody outcome?"

I sniff at the air and fold my arms. I don't answer. I continue to watch Cian turn on the tap, lift the bucket, steady it, fill it more than halfway, set it down, turn off the tap and walk slowly across the cobbles, with the odd splash of water heaving over the edge.

Good boy. Great dynamic balance, perfect eye control and good motor planning.

I can't help myself. I measure every slice of progress, every little detail, reminding myself that I have to keep fighting for Cian because he is in a better place from where he was a year before. It is repetitive, it is limited and he is still socially aloof to the outside world, but to me he has an intelligence about him I can't ignore. Cian's progress, though slow, is a little flickering candle leading the way.

Eamonn doesn't move the plant. Regardless of what he says, I know he is very proud of Cian's achievements, even though he may not always agree on the lengths to which I go to create learning opportunities for Cian. I don't want one stone left unturned. I want him to avail of all of them because I believe there is so much I do not know about Cian's world and there is still so much he has difficulty with in mine.

Any new treatment I hear anything positive about, I give it a go. With my mother's help, I take him to England for auditory integration treatment. We stay at a friend's house and Cian receives the treatment every day. There are a few gains, a few more words added to his vocabulary and some quality time spent exploring northwest England with his grandmother, my mother. Cian enjoys the travel and the new environment. Christopher and Eamonn join us for the weekend and I catch up with Uncle Peter and cousins I have never met before but who had sent me money for Cian's programme.

When we get back it is difficult to curb the worry niggling underneath my skin about Cian's future. I know that in my heart I am unable and unavailable to home-school him. I have to find a school for him. One morning I am watering a few daffodils, bright symbols of hope sitting in the kitchen window, when I am suddenly struck with an idea.

I make a phone call and Eamonn arrives just as I put down the receiver.

"Eamonn, I am going up to the school."

"Why? Is something wrong with Christopher?"

"No, I am meeting Mr Cush. It's about Cian."

"Cian?"

"I am going to ask him if he will support an autism class in the school."

"What?"

"Grab your coat, you're coming too!"

Mr Cush considers the idea. It will be a challenge but he is willing to support it. Another meeting is arranged with the school. Mary Begley, the leader of a local community group, Camowen Rural Partnership Group, and a number of other parents attend. Many of the parents are members of IMPACT (Improving the Lives of Autistic Children Today), a local charity that is already involved in fundraising for early intervention home programmes for preschoolers. Mr Cush and Mary Begley agree to help support us in setting up an autism-specific centre in the school. It is also agreed to call it the Impact Centre.

Sadly, despite the endless support from Mr Cush, Mary Begley and her staff, funding from the government and the Education Department isn't forthcoming. Our only option is to raise the funds for the Impact Centre ourselves. The fundraising begins with generous support from the community and private businesses; without their support the Impact Centre would never have opened.

* * *

In the weeks leading up to Donna's wedding, we show Cian wedding photographs and pictures of Donna and Declan and take him to the church where Donna is getting married. It is not clear whether he fully understands but we feel it will prepare him a little bit. Donna takes great delight in bringing them for their little pageboy outfits. Both boys at this stage know Donna's fiancé and family very well. They are both involved in the rehearsals. When we go to Donna's house with the wedding present, everyone knows Cian and Christopher. Cian is in his element, running in and out of Donna's brothers' arms and Donna's grandmother tells me he is a very special little boy. It is clear where Donna got her unassuming, kind and patient nature from. Donna's family, whom I have never met before, adore both my boys equally.

It doesn't matter that one has a diagnosis of autism. Apart from keeping him away from forbidden food and danger, Cian is treated just like any other little boy. I am so proud.

On the morning of Donna's wedding, the phone rings around 9.30. We are getting ready to deliver the two pageboys. It is Donna.

"Aileen, my aunt is making a snack for Cian after the service. I told her he likes chips but she might not have the oil you use. Could you take some oil with you?"

Donna is getting married at 11.00 a.m. Even on her wedding day, she is thinking of Cian.

"Donna, the last thing that should be on your mind this morning is chips and sunflower oil!"

"I know, but I want Cian to get his snack. Make sure you take some."

A few tears fall when Cian leads Christopher and Donna's sister Siobhan up the aisle. He carries the wedding rings on a small cushion – "something borrowed", the same cushion that carried our own wedding rings. I feel especially proud that Cian is able to give Donna something precious for all the beautiful kind things she has done for him. To our delight, Cian walks up the aisle beautifully. He is almost at the altar rails when his trousers start to fall down. Apparently the wrong size of trousers had come for him and Donna was vexed. However, without getting annoyed, he organises his hips to walk a bit like John Wayne before Siobhan comes to the rescue. Pride and joy fill my heart as I watch him and Christopher sitting in their suits and ties, so quiet and attentive. As the priest performs the major part of the ceremony, Cian begins to hum and sing. It is like he is cashing in on Donna's happiness and everyone enjoys him.

At the reception, Christopher reads a poem to Donna, one that he and I had penned together. He has a scroll in his hands with the words printed on it, but he doesn't need the words. He is watching Donna's face for most of it and, as he reads, grown men cry.

To Donna
My name is Christopher, I am not yet seven
And I have always thought that angels live in heaven.
But now I know that isn't true,
'Cause I've heard Mammy and Daddy say
That Donna is an angel
And she sure looks like one today.
My brother Cian is five years old
He can swim and he can sing,
And for Donna he will do
Just almost anything.
There are many gifts that people give.
We are not impartial to new toys.
But Donna's gifts
Are extra special
To us two boys.
She has given us the gift of time
And talks and plays with me
And gives Cian encouragement
To help him learn, you see.
So we would like to thank you, Donna,
We are glad you heard Mum's call
And for giving us so much love
The greatest gift of all.
Now Donna has other jobs
And now that she's a wife
We just hope that she'll have time

For the three boys in her life.

When Christopher finishes, Cian sings the *Barney* song, "I Love You", loud and clear into the microphone, and presents Donna with the poem, framed and decorated with photos and memories of the wonderful time she has dedicated to our two precious boys.

* * *

One afternoon, I walk into the kitchen to find Cian sitting on his knees in front of the patio door, waiting for dusk to fall and envelop him in the twilight. His face appears to withhold some hidden intelligence, incomprehensible to a mere mortal like me. What is it that keeps his face characteristically angelic? Maybe it's the absence of disfiguring human emotions, I think, as Cian knows no malice or greed or vanity.

I sit down beside him, Mohican style, and share the sunset spilling into a blood-red mass flooding the horizon. The serenity in his face and his eyes gives the impression of looking through and beyond to something out of reach.

He has just turned six, as precious as when I held him in my arms when he was just a few months old. A calmness settles around me and I realise I am slowly coming to terms with the "A" word, but with that comes the realisation that his needs are greater than ever. As he leans against me, I promise him I will never give up hope, I will never stop loving him or searching for ways to make his journey easier through a world that is difficult for him to understand. He turns his face toward me as though he can read my thoughts and hangs his arms about my neck.

Just then, Eamonn appears on the other side of the patio door. He is looking at something out of my field of vision and turns suddenly, rushing towards the patio door. All at once he spots us sitting behind the glass. He beckons me to open the door and points. "Look at Cian's pot." His voice is high-pitched with a tone of surprise in it.

Stepping outside, I turn towards the plant pot Cian has been playing with all summer. In the middle of the pot is a single pink rose in full bloom.

29

The Impact Centre opens in September, without board funding or recognition. I am seven months pregnant.

It is 9.30 in the morning. Cian is getting breakfast and I am checking his new uniform for the fifth time.

"Tie, socks, jumper . . ."

"It's all there, Aileen, don't worry."

"I can't believe my course and Cian's class are starting on the same day at the same time."

"Look, you have dedicated yourself to Cian. Don't worry. All you need to know is he will be there at ten o'clock. I'll run you down first."

"Maybe I shouldn't go. It's only a writing class. It's not important. I probably will not be able to string two sentences together."

"Now, come on. This is the first time you have gone to anything that didn't have the 'A' word in the title. Besides, you can't pull out now. You will let the author down and it will not look too professional when you go to publish your bestseller." Eamonn sups his tea, smiling. I hit him with a tea towel.

"Don't be ridiculous. Oh God, what will I do? I don't want to walk in late. Look at the size of me. They will think I have joined the wrong class. It's antenatal exercises I should be going to."

Excited and sick with nerves, I allow Eamonn to drive me to a creative writing course. The course is eight weeks long and I know I probably will not get to the end of it before the birth, but I am desperate for distraction. It is four years since I left work and I have never been among adult company for any reason other than to discuss our children with autism.

Cian looks all shiny and new in his fresh uniform. His brow furrows with puzzlement. We have told him he is going to school and he is wearing a familiar uniform – the same as Christopher's – but neither of us knows if he fully understands. Still, he is eager to get on with it. He belts himself up and shouts, "Let's go."

"Eamonn, I really don't think I should go. I need to leave Cian –"

"That's right. You need to leave Cian be. He is going to be fine."

"Should I not wait and take Cian in to his class? He might need –"

" . . . A break from his Mum molly-coddling him. Cian is a big boy now. He is going to school. He doesn't need to be lugged around by the apron strings any more . . . don't you not, Cian? Tell your Mammy to give your head peace and go and do Mammy things."

I laugh, knowing that Eamonn is really proud that Cian has a "school" to go to. "Thanks, Eamonn. Gosh, this must be what it feels like for ordinary parents –"

Eamonn glances at me, ignoring the hint of sadness in my voice.

"Right you are, nearly there. Remember what you have to do. Switch off Mammy hat and put on writer's cap."

I wave him off and turn towards An Creagán Visitor's Centre. The tall conifers whisper way above me and I crunch across the cobbled stones with my heels. *I must be mad in the head. Over seven months pregnant and doing a course!* As I walk towards the charming round stone building, I know that I am glad to be distracted. I could not sit at home and wonder how Cian is doing. I need my mind busy without worry, but most of all I need to let go.

As I stand at the reception, a man approaches.

"The writing course?"

"Yes, they have just gone up. Let me show you the way." The man points me through the reception area and up towards a flight of stairs. "It's the first door on your left."

"Thank you."

My heels echo on the stone flags as I head towards the stairway. Cian seems so far away and yet so close. I reach the top of the stairs and see the green door. I wonder what the colour of the door Cian walked through was? Did he walk through? Did he panic, just like me? I look down the stairs again. If I go now, no one will know I have been. Then I remember that I have no car. I have no choice. Neither does Cian. Someone would have met him and opened the door. He would have spied the colourful toys and games. I bet he went straight to them.

"Hello, can I help you?"

I am standing in the door frame. Curious faces turn away from a lady standing at the top of the room. Her arms are folded about her petite frame and long auburn hair is spilling over her mottled green silk dress. She is looking at me.

"Yes, I am so sorry, am I late?"

"No . . . not at all, come in and take a seat. I am Martina Devlin."

I smile and nod at the faces nodding and smiling back, telling me that they are Carol and Deirdre, and Liz and Chris. I tell them I am Aileen and sit down, hoping I don't look too pregnant. A few people haven't showed up and they thought it better to make a start. I smile and say that is okay. Sitting back, I relax into an environment that doesn't have *Thomas the Tank Engine* in the background.

The morning slips by. I listen to the discussion on writers and writing. Most of it sails right over my head. From my seat with a view I watch the swans and ducks clean themselves down and swim idly in a pond at the side of the stone building. I think of my "lame duck" from time to time and wonder how he is doing, but mostly I think of how wonderful it is to be in a room with people I don't know, listening to their stories and experiences with no expectation to be mum or therapist or advocate or cook. For a little while, I can be me.

* * *

In the third week, we are given a "homework" task. We are asked to write about a time in our lives when our thinking changed, an event, an experience that had a long-lasting impact on our lives. I don't want to do it. I can't think of anything but the "A" word. How can I write about that? I am trying to escape it, for heaven's sake; but there is no way out. No matter how hard I try, no matter how many pieces of A4 I scribble on and crumple up, they all end up in an overflowing wastebasket. I can't come up with any other event or idea. I have nothing else to write about. So I write about my visit to the paediatrician – chapter three of this book – and dread the morning I am going to have to read it out. *Don't be ridiculous; it's only a story*, I tell myself. I try to detach myself from the fact that it is still my reality.

I keep my head low while others volunteer their offerings. Liz shares about her regimented school days; Carol's story – observations at a Catholic wake – is hilarious; Chris has written a beautiful, moving piece about correspondence with her mother when she lived in Brussels; and Deirdre tells us about the fear she experienced when she attacked her brother with knitting needles. We laugh and clap and encourage.

Then it is my turn. My voice croaks a little from time to time, but I try to detach from the emotional content, reminding myself that this is a writing group, not a bloody psychotherapy session. After I read my piece, there is a long pause before Martina speaks. "That's a very powerful piece, Aileen, a story that needs to be told. Did you ever consider writing a book?" Her comment is certainly not what I have been expecting but her gentle encouragement rekindles my interest in writing and diminishes my fear of addressing the "A" word.

30

The anaesthetist tells the midwife to remove my jewellery. She comes closer and lifts the delicate chain from about my neck, fingers the tiny heart-shaped medal and drops it again. "It's a miraculous medal, leave it," I hear her whisper behind my back.

My nails dig into Eamonn's flesh as the needle sinks deeper in my back. I can't for the life of me think why I opted for an epidural. There is a clatter of something tinny. Then we are on our own again. Eamonn doesn't know what to do with his hands. He asks me if I'm okay a thousand times. He keeps grinning at me like a Cheshire cat. He can hardly contain his excitement. Time lapses.

Voices drift in and out and fuse with the white hum of the fluorescent tubes. There is a sudden shift of energy. A door springs and flaps. Cool air wafts past me. White coats and muzzled faces mumble and hover. There is a commotion at the bottom of the bed. White light seems to illuminate around me. Someone tells me to push. I can hear another voice, a voice from the past – soft and reassuring, warm but firm. I do not mistake Granny's voice. She is telling me not to push.

"Tell the doctors the baby is not ready. It will be twenty minutes."

I can feel myself laughing and talking, but I can't hear what I am saying. I can see her and I can't see her. She fills my senses. I am not aware of anything else but the space between Granny and me. I want to get up and go to her but a weight is pressing down on my arm. Granny is telling me that everything will be okay as Eamonn's voice booms in my ear, "Are you okay?"

He sounds anxious and my hand finds his squeezing down on my arm. I release it and laugh up at him. His eyebrows wrinkle with curiosity, maybe amusement. I can't tell for sure. He is half-smiling. I tell him, "Granny is with me." I laugh out loud at the idea of it. "The baby will not be born for another twenty minutes. What time is it?"

"It's twenty-five to one." He fixes my hair and tells me I am wonderful and it will soon all be over. Eamonn turns to the midwife and says something. Shadows slip through the flapping doors again. All goes quiet except for the midwife, who comes and holds my hand in a strong warm grasp. She is full of life and chatting ten to the dozen, but I can hardly keep my eyes open. Her voice is loud and piercing and full of cackles. She tells Eamonn that anything can happen in a labour ward. She has seen it all. Engagements, separations, marriage proposals, divorce proceedings, even confessions. Talking to past loves ones is common enough too. She reassures him I could do worse and cackles again. Her plastic gown jiggles up and down against my arm. Below their voices, my eyelids rest against my face as my grandmother wipes my brow and places her arms around me, giving me strength, easing my anxiety, removing my fear.

The pains are coming closer and closer. I ask Eamonn the time.

"Ten to one. Fifteen minutes is up."

I ask Granny how long now and she says, "Tell the doctors to get ready. The baby will be born in five minutes."

At five minutes to one, Laura Marie enters our world, 8lb 3oz, healthy and well. I am blissfully happy but very weak. I need a blood transfusion.

Hours creep into days. I can't seem to shake the exhaustion. Bits of my body are not working properly. I want to see the boys and want them to meet their little sister, but I become ill first. Jacinta is visiting and marvelling over Laura's brand new features when I suddenly feel breathless and woozy. A sharp pain stabs me in the back. An x-ray confirms fluid on my lung. Jacinta, who happens to be a staff nurse off duty, teases, winking at her peers.

"A stint in maternity tethered to a catheter isn't enough for my sister . . . Nah, she has to check out the heart monitor in the medical ward too . . . two for the price of one, she is after." They all laugh and I doze. I hope I can continue nursing Laura Marie. After Cian's difficulties I am anxious that I build her immune system. She needs the nutrients from my milk. A week later, the wonderful staff, under-staffed and underpaid, have nursed me back to a weak but stable state. Wires and tubes are still connected to me but I beg Eamonn to take Christopher and Cian in to see Laura. I can't wait any longer.

Both of them are excited about the baby. Christopher's wish has come true and it shows on his face. He has wanted a baby sister for so long and marvels over her. Cian doesn't know who to concentrate on, the baby or me. It is obvious he has missed me. I hold little Laura in one arm and Cian under the other. He timidly touches Laura's tiny fingers, shouting "Baby, baby", making her jump. From the start he is calm and gentle and fascinated by her. He shows no signs of jealousy or upset. Around me he is hyper and loud. My little laughing angel is so heavy in my arms now.

* * *

Two weeks later, I am allowed home. Laura is a dream child, doing what little babies are supposed to do, feed and sleep. Cian makes up for her.

The diet has slipped and so have his behaviours. Little Mowgli is back doing his striptease act and jumping over furniture, climbing into the windows and swinging from the banisters again. Locked doors and keys are everywhere but he still manages to escape from the back garden, dragging tricycles, garden seats, anything that will give him a leg up over our high fence and help him climb on to our shed roof. Behaviours he has displayed many times before due to a food reaction have all returned – poor sleep, bouts of crying, lethargy, hyperactivity, biting and frustration. Old behaviours are returning and school reports note a change in his behaviour. He is increasingly unhappy and new disruptive behaviours manifest. They perceive it as something to do with Laura's arrival but I know in my heart that Cian is very happy about Laura's arrival. He seems to have a sense of her fragility and does not venture near her on his own. Cian's behaviour is a direct reaction to unresolved gut issues. His sugar cravings and screaming outbursts return sometimes out of the blue.

One Monday evening we are all in the kitchen. Cian is sitting next to Christopher, who is reading the latest *Harry Potter* book. Laura has just finished a feed and is gurgling sweet nothings in my ear. Eamonn is cooking tea and reading *The Irish News*. Juliet Turner is singing in the background. For once there is something normal about the moment. I am thinking how nice it is to have everyone safe and happy and okay. Suddenly Cian springs from his chair and roars out like someone possessed. Laura jumps in my arms and Christopher looks up. Cian rushes and butts his head off the wall, rams his body into the furniture and bites anything he can sink his teeth into.

In a curled ball on the floor he sobs and heaves, lashing out if we approach. From a distance, unable to hold him or comfort him we watch him sob until he lies moaning, like he is trying to say something. We strain to understand and become conscious of two faint utterances riding on Cian's outward breath, over and over.

"'Urt. Soa' p'ace."

The words are barely formed, barely audible, but confirm everything.

Cian is "hurt". Cian has a "sore place".

31

Fearing his screaming outbursts would be dismissed as part of his autism, I do not go back to the doctor's surgery but examine my notes of the conference I had attended in Dublin three years earlier. I study a note about DAN (Defeat Autism Now), a group of medics formed over eighteen years ago to pursue and plan a medical protocol for children with autism. When the children are tucked up in bed I boot up the PC and Google information on DAN doctors. There are no DAN doctors in the UK so I choose a doctor in America who comes highly recommended by other cyber parents. Dr John Green, a specialist in clinical ecology and nutritional medicine in Oregon, has been a medic for twenty-seven years and believes, after monitoring over 300 of his patients, that children with autism are physically sick.

On contacting his office, I am asked to complete all necessary documentation, including a month-by-month account of Cian's medical and developmental history. It takes me a whole day to gather facts and details, but the result of the timeline is full of telling signs that Cian's difficulties lie among the pages of his early medical records. Endless questions whiz around the inside of my head. Did Cian arrive in this world with a predisposition to a weakened immune system? Did an early toxic-laden vaccine compromise Cian's metabolic system? Was the measles virus and others still floating around his intestine, creating antibodies? And what of all the infections and antibiotics in between? What have they done to my baby?

* * *

A few weeks later, I have a consultation with Dr Green, who orders some tests. Unlike the tests that were done at the local health centre, these tests are more specific and confirm that Cian has a bad yeast overgrowth in his gut – just what I had suspected and queried three years earlier. Dr Green explains how high levels of Candida albicans may be a contributing factor to many behavioural problems. One scenario is that when a child develops a middle-ear infection, the antibiotics that help fight the infection destroy microbes that regulate the amount of yeast in the intestinal tract. As a result, the yeast grows rapidly and releases toxins in the blood; these toxins influence the functioning of the brain. Cian is ordered off all sugar and prescribed an anti-fungal drug called Nystatin to kill the yeast.

Nystatin and a specific carbohydrate diet gradually work some magic. Cian becomes a quiet, calm, peaceful child again. Some autistic behaviour disappears, as do the fiery red ears and the black rings under his eyes. He has a good bedtime routine and sleeps every night, all night long. His bowel movements improve and for the first time in his life he has what we call a full-formed, perfect "trophy". We celebrate with the *Jungle Book 2* movie.

Slowly but surely, bite-by-bite, Cian learns to eat real food again – carrots, spinach, cabbage, cauliflower, meat, salmon, stewed fruit and, eventually, raw fruit. Since his food habits changed around the age of three his abhorrence for fruit had been so strong he would refuse to walk past the fruit bowl.

I try to desensitise his abhorrence and pick a fruit that is attractive and sweet. I choose strawberries, leaving them around everywhere – on the table, at the sink, on the counter-top. Every time he looks in my direction, I take a bite of a strawberry and say "Yummy!" After a couple of weeks he tolerates them beside his plate, then on the side of his plate. Eventually, I cut one and encourage him to touch it. We make a game of it.

"Red Strawberry, Strawberry Red, Red Strawberry . . . I will eat your head."

I bite the top off the strawberry and Cian giggles. I pretend to put some on his lips but he pushes me away, laughing. I have to be very patient and careful not to step over the thin line between teasing and torture. A week later, he tolerates a tiny bit on his lips. I cut it even tinier and the next week he allows it to touch his tongue. I reward him with a little piece of food he wants to eat.

Three months later, Cian lifts a strawberry from the fruit bowl and eats it all by himself. We are delighted. After a little while I introduce another fruit. Just because he eats a strawberry doesn't mean he will eat a banana. We have to start the teaching process all over again.

After a summer of fundraising and street collections, Cian returns to the Impact Centre with a little fruit in his lunchbox. He looks happier and healthier. Unfortunately, our bank balance for the Impact Centre is not healthy at all. There is still no government funding or recognition of our centre and there is a huge threat that we as a charity can no longer sustain the facility. The jury is still out on the future of Cian's formal education. Worry and stress prevails.

* * *

Around this time I buy a book called *Children with Starving Brains* by Jaquelyn McCandless, a medical doctor from California whose granddaughter suffers from autism. When I contact her with some queries, she informs me of an autism conference that she, along with some other colleagues who support biomedical treatments for autism, will be speaking at in Edinburgh in November. I book online to attend and distribute details about the conference, with a copy of Dr McCandless's book, to a few health centres in the hope that someone from medical services will take an interest and hopefully attend the conference. As far as I know, no one took me up on the offer.

At the conference we meet Dr McCandless and many other physicians who lecture extensively on the most up-to-date medical advances on how to treat our children with autism. I also meet Jean Muscroft, a nutritionist, who implements the DAN protocol in the UK. I explain to her that Cian is getting some help from Dr Green but I would like to have supervision closer to home, to strengthen communication and access supplements locally. Jean agrees to take Cian on and shortly after I arrive home I complete the necessary paperwork, detailing a thorough family and child health history. I also include Cian's timeline. In correspondence with Jean, diagnostic lab tests are ordered and completed to determine what biomedical issues need to be addressed, including whether heavy-metal toxicity is present. A basic blood count, metabolic chemistry, urinalysis and thyroid panel is obtained. Other tests are obtained according to Cian's symptoms and history, which include tests for immune impairment; presence and levels of viruses and fungi, involving both urine and stool studies; and food sensitivity and amino acid panels, as well as essential mineral tests to direct proper nutrition.

The blood test results reveal that Cian's body is awash with heavy metals, chronic viral infections, a seriously impaired immune system and inflammation of the gut, with much bacterial overgrowth and pathogens. There are many abnormalities in his blood function test and he is deficient in a whole range of vital nutrients due to the lack of enzymes active in the gut, leaving him unable to digest food properly. A supplement programme is gradually introduced, including enzymes, minerals and vitamins and probiotics and once again emphasis is placed on a low-carb sugar-free GF/CF diet.

Over the next few months we see slow gradual improvements in Cian's physical demeanour and small progress in other behaviours. He still, however, gets irritable at times, with sudden outbursts. Jean considers gastrointestinal distress and suggests I seek a referral for an x-ray examination of his abdomen.

At the hospital it becomes clear to me that the paediatrician doesn't agree with my presumptions and suggests an ECG. I insist that there is nothing wrong with his head that would show up on an ECG and demand the flat panel X-ray to rule out chronic constipation. The paediatrician comes and goes and in between give me a pep talk. While I cry and Cian screams he assures me he understands my concerns. He is a father and he knows what it is like to become anxious at times about our children. He encourages me to try to understand the nature of Cian's condition, as many of Cian's behaviours are autism-related. Maybe I am still grieving and stressed and feeling depressed? I have to look after myself and not waste time searching for reasons in places where there are no answers. Feeling I have been diagnosed with borderline depression, stopping short of Munchausen's Syndrome, I remind the doctor that a diagnosis of autism should not exempt a child from a medical examination to rule out constipation. Pressure and patronising words from a doctor who concludes that I am crazy to think I can cure autism does not help, but I refuse to leave, confident that I know more about Cian's condition than he does.

Eventually, three hours later, we are granted an x-ray. As the results are held up against a white light, my hand involuntary clamps my mouth. A dark shadow representing the contents of his intestinal tract bulges and swells right up underneath Cian's rib cage. Leaving the hospital with a script for Lactalose and a fire burning in my belly, I sum up Cian's medical care in my head as borderline medical negligence.

Just as I arrive home, the phone rings again. It is Elizabeth, Cian's "music therapist". Once again she comes to my aid. She happens to have an enema kit, unused and unopened in her garage. Only a practical European lady would have such a thing ready and waiting. Feeling the power of angels fluttering around me once again, we treat Cian's constipation with liquid paraffin, natural herbals, homeopathy, pear and Noni juice and enemas. Elizabeth treats my shock with chamomile and vanilla herb tea and quiet company that smiles and reassures – until Pauline, a parent from IMPACT, rings me later that evening.

The Impact Centre is no longer sustainable. Despite fundraising tirelessly, we have only enough money to keep it open until the end of June.

* * *

Fearing Cian will have no educational facility come September, Eamonn and I visit a local special care school. During the visit it becomes clear to me that the principal's laudable vision stretches way beyond the budget he works under. We stand in a classroom and speak with a teacher who is responsible for ten children; all with varying needs, with only the help of one floating classroom assistant. It is Cian's potential classroom. It doesn't take long for us to conclude that it would not be a suitable placement for Cian. He would not receive one-to-one provision or autism-specific resources to meet his needs. There is no guarantee of speech or occupational therapy and sensory integration is non-existent.

The constant battle to meet Cian's medical and

educational needs while trying to cope with everyday life swallows me whole, leaving me wretched, frustrated and angry that I am unable to access basic needs for my child. Without support it just becomes grief, dipping and diving, a manic rollercoaster gone out of control, a rollercoaster that never seems to end, with my stomach constantly in my mouth.

* * *

Cian loves rollercoasters – the furiously fast ones; the faster the better. I love them too – not the ride itself but the way Cian grips my coat and the white of his knuckles tightens, holding on for dear life. Rolling up and down and around with adrenaline swirling through our veins, our bodies fuse and vibrate on the iron seat. But the best bit is when Cian turns his head and looks directly in my eyes and grins from ear to ear through my windswept hair as if to say, "Isn't this great?" I am giddy with happiness. There is an understanding between us. I don't want it to end, this moment. I want to stay that way forever and bottle the connection between us as we tumble and toss together, laughing in a perfect bubble of illusion, holding our breath before it bursts, before the rollercoaster slows to a stop. Cian is still smiling as he steps out into another rollercoaster, a manic rollercoaster of worry and anxiety that makes me sick to the pits of my stomach, a rollercoaster that I can't get off. The only way off is to jump.

32

It isn't premeditated. Leaving. Not like people who have harboured some half-baked idea for years and then one day gather up lock, stock and barrel to follow their dream, or folk who impulsively turn their back on contemporary living and wind up on some remote island to find themselves. No. I don't experience any of that. Leaving has never entered my mind. Running away has. Just for an hour or two so I can get a little headspace. Time on my own. After a particularly stressful day, I would head out the door as soon as Eamonn returned from work and go for a walk, maybe a drive to reflect and contemplate and move on.

The day I drive to Donegal is just another ordinary day. Ordinary for our household, that is. Overwhelming chaos prevails. It is the middle of the Easter holidays. The children are off school, demanding some much-needed attention. I am not having a good day. The phone hasn't stopped ringing. We are in the middle of organising another fundraiser, a last bid to keep the Impact Centre open. The Tyrone GAA football team is on the run for autism. Many of the GAA women's and men's football teams from all over Tyrone are joining them and the whole community is behind us, running the Belfast Marathon. I am making a last attempt to tidy up before I go to a funeral. The house is a mess. Cian is going through his "pouring water over everything" phase and has developed an obsession with our front-room rug. He will not allow anyone to walk on it or put anything on it or disturb his complex pattern of videotapes on the sofa.

Laura keeps crawling over the mat, pulling herself up on the sofa, knocking down Cian's creative display, sparking off Cian's meltdown. Cian goes berserk and attempts to push her off, screaming wildly. Choosing my battles, I take Laura away from the rug but she is having none of it. She ploughs right back over it again and I eventually have to lock her out of the room. She sits wailing at one side of the French doors and Cian wails at the other while Christopher, completely oblivious to the noise he is so accustomed to, wants to know if he can have a pet snake. Holding the Yellow Pages, he informs me that the best ones are in some pet shop near Belfast; when can we go? I make a last hurried attempt to tidy up the breakfast dishes while trying to persuade him to go for a goldfish instead. Ever since his puppy died, he has grieved sorely and seems to hanker after a pet that he can put in a glass box. I just couldn't cope with a snake's culinary delights and there is no way on God's earth I will be keeping dead mice in our freezer. As I rush around and Christopher moans, Eamonn comes into the kitchen and opens cupboards and drawers.

"What are you looking for?"

Christopher and Eamonn answer at the same time.

"A pet snake."

"The Yellow Pages. I can never find it when I need it."

"Christopher's reading it."

Christopher starts begging his daddy for a pet snake. Cian wants out of the living room and Laura wants in. I need to go and Eamonn needs to stay. He is scolding about nothing and everything, muttering a few choice words that are wrapped in matted tones of frustration, a reaction to the overwhelming stress that has ebbed its way into our daily lives. Like the onset of autism, it is a gradual realisation that casts ominous shadows on an ordinary life, forcing us to confront what we do not want to see.

Like most parents, Eamonn and I have had good days and bad days when the very seams securing the lining of our intrinsic virtues are tested. Stress rages underneath the surface, wearing tiny holes in the fabric that makes up family life. Autism doesn't happen in a vacuum. Families with disability still experience the same joys and tribulations of everyday life – keeping a roof over our heads, dealing with ill health and other forms of loss. Still, we all have to submit to some of life's many lessons. Our world has become small, made up of funerals and wakes, rushing there, rushing back. Shaking collection buckets on street corners, grocery shopping, attending meetings about meetings that fail to secure Cian's needs. To all intents and purposes, we are on our own, in our own little world.

When our front door closes, we only have each other to lean on, to carry the burden, to take turns at sitting up with Cian, to run after him before he reaches the middle of the road, to rescue him from our roof or a neighbour's house at some ungodly hour in the morning, to clean up mess after mess, to feed him, to change him, to rock him as he sobs uncontrollably. We can't sit down and have a cup of tea together without having to check on Cian every single minute. Year after year after year until we are running on empty, until we start to compete for time and argue about whose turn it is going to be.

Communication has unravelled to a defensive litany that is nothing short of a blame game. A collection of badly chosen words are now stacked up one on top of the other – words that are so throwaway it is difficult to measure the disastrous imprint they leave on an unconscious mind. We have become victims of our own distorted reasoning. Nerves are shattered through worry and lack of sleep and stress that never seems to pass on. Rows blow up over the silliest of things. Bursts of awareness and trying to support one another are short-lived. Like swapping a run-down engine for another run-down engine.

Standing in front of the kitchen window I watch an angry wind torture the leaves on the trees in our back garden. The leaves hold on for dear life before they are torn away from their life force towards a new purpose.

I could turn around and tear into Eamonn, defend everything I do. I could join him in the ring. Blame him for everything that isn't anyone's fault . . . but I don't. I just look into the trees. How did we get to here?

Events of the past five years flash and fray through my head, like data in a computer being deleted, shutting my body and mind down in slow motion. As I lift the car keys, everything is magnified. The sound of my heels on the hall tiles. The swish of the lining of my jacket. The front door feels heavy as I haul it open and climb into the car to go to the funeral. Eamonn follows me, staring into a face of a whole lot of hurt. I look at him but don't know who he is. I don't know who I am. The constant uphill battle for services while substituting the role of "mammy" and "wife" for "doctor", "nutritionist", "therapist", "Mary Poppins", "fundraiser", "advocate" and "crisis intervention specialist" has finally got too much.

33

The mourners at Isobel's funeral are cramped shoulder to shoulder in a small chapel on the outskirts of Omagh. I never knew Isobel. I only met her once. I was dropping Chris off at Isobel's when she invited me to come and meet her sister. It was out of the blue – an invitation into a private sacred space that concealed the pieces of a broken heart. I felt humbled – honoured to meet someone I felt I already knew, a lady who celebrated her life at every given opportunity. She was sitting in the kitchen with her friend. They were both laughing and eating chips.

"It's hard to beat the chip-shop chips," Chris mused.

"Especially with red sauce," Isobel added, waving a floppy red-tipped chip in the air.

Chris laughed, giving me permission to laugh too. I tried not to look sympathetic or sad and averted my eyes from the pretty multicoloured scarf that held her wig in place. Since the writing course, Chris had dedicated most of her time to caring for and nursing her sister. She rarely talked about it. She only talked about Isobel.

Family and friends celebrate her life now and the service is alive with her spirit as the priest shares the light, love and laughter that she emanated. As the service comes to an end everyone who held Isobel dear is laughing and crying. I am inconsolable. I do not cry for Isobel. Isobel does not need my tears. I grieve for my own abandoned life, the life that died when the "A" word rocked and ricocheted through my world, the life I still had, the life I was not living.

In the graveyard under a sombre sky, Chris thanks me for coming. I hug her close and hold her cold hands in mine for a moment. She is glad for Isobel. Isobel is at peace at last. It has been a long journey. Now another begins, another journey without Isobel. "Alas! Life goes on." Her sigh is low and weary.

When does life go on? I recall the countless times I opened Cian's little baby book only to realise I had nothing to declare. How diligently we waited for him to talk, to show excitement at his birthday, to ride a bike, holding on for the benchmarks that would normalise life again. When Cian learned to imitate, I reminded myself of the times he didn't react to anything around him. When he learned to name things, I saw progress. I saw progress as he developed each new skill. Signs of moving forward sprinkled me with stardust, but so many reminders reeled me right back to the place where life had changed in an instant – a family on bikes, a toddler doing things Cian still could not do, a silent child returning home with only a few scribbled lines in a diary to let me know if he had a good day or bad day, children playing happily with his toys in our back garden while Cian lay on the floor naked and severely autistic in an upstairs bedroom. Life has gone on but in a different gear.

* * *

I am driving into Ballyshannon before I become conscious that I have crossed the border into Donegal. Every now and then I stop and find myself standing in the solitude of churches, thinking.

Donegal. I have always loved Donegal. As a child, words like "beach", "holiday", "peace" and "Donegal" all belonged in one sentence. I had never heard of Florida then but if I had I would still have opted for Donegal. Maybe it was to do with living in the turbulent North, but when we crossed the border a sense of freedom fell about our shoulders and seeped into our bones. Donegal was a great escape. We could relax and forget for a while.

It rains in Donegal. On the highs and the lows of it, on the rocky hills and on the barren land that stretches to the Atlantic Ocean. It rains through the hunting ruins of derelict cottages perched among the mountains and glens and on the caravans behind the sand dunes until it eases and eventually stops.

Somewhere near Glencolmcille, I stop and get out and listen to the wild roar of the deep swelling and crashing against the cliffs. My mobile jingles – a text from Eamonn, asking me where I am. I snap the flip-phone shut, and retrieve an old coat of mine that I take for walks on really cold days. I will answer Eamonn's text later, when I know where I am in my mind. Eamonn will be fine. The children will be fine.

I immediately feel guilty. Wouldn't they just love to be here now? I sniff at the air and breathe in. *Stop this guilt thing.* They *will* cope without me for once. *Stop. Stop. Stop it.*

Inside my coat pocket I find a psychedelic green woolly hat and pull it over my ears. It was purchased by default one icy morning while doing a street collection for the Impact Centre. My ears were in danger of dropping off so I popped into a chic boutique. Any desirable hats were the price of a coat so I found my way to the bargain basket and begrudgingly handed over cash that would have paid a therapist to work with Cian for three hours. Still, I need my ears.

The thought of the Impact Centre brings me to a jarring halt and I stand, broken and perplexed. Cian will not have a school to go to in September. Holding my coat close, I suck in the Atlantic sea breeze and expel into the mist-covered landscape. Physically and mentally I know I can no longer fundraise and fight systems that refuse to acknowledge our child and his needs. I am worn out and all I ever wanted was to be a mum. What mum doesn't want the best for their child?

Over a blackened path amid long grass I trudge downward to a deserted stretch of sand. Salty tears unite with the mist from the sea, bathing me in the depth of a great sadness. I am sure of one thing. I can't do it anymore. I can't go on.

Back in the car, I follow roads that rise and fall. Driving into Glen, a chapel looms in the bushes. I impulsively park and inspect the moat and the elongated sloping roof. The jagged shape of the headstones, the names and the bits and pieces that loved ones had placed there. I wander around aimlessly as if I am looking for something. I survey the grey and silent bulk of it suspiciously – wondering why my head is full of churches, fearing it is a sign of desperation. That's what Catholics do. They cling to God when they have nothing else. They make connections with the past and hook up with a beardy man, our father, our creator who knows all things. I no longer saw God as a beardy man, I saw God in simple things, but if I did, if I had done, like when I was a child, I would have reached out. I would have clung to him.

I was raised Catholic. My faith was part of my upbringing. Prayer was part of every day; the rosary, part of every night. Before we owned a car, my parents walked a four-mile round trip to Sunday mass with my brothers, sisters and myself lagging behind. I was two at the time but Mum reassures me I walked most of the way. I never took their devout faith lightly. There was a message in it somewhere and as I grew older, went to university, mingled with other cultures and religions, I became fascinated, intrigued by the diversity of human belief systems. Some teachings nourished my own belief and learning about other Eastern religions such as Buddhism and Taoism only enriched my own exploration of it at a deeper and more personal level through meditation and other forms of knowing God. In recent years I could have become disillusioned by the appalling and criminal behaviour of representatives of the church I was born into, but I didn't. My own personal connection with God is much greater and I choose not to let the actions of others deflect me from my own personal journey. I continue to believe in the teachings of Christ: love, acceptance, compassion, trusting in the faith

I was brought up in, allowing it to comfort me like a well-worn blanket.

Since Cian was diagnosed I prayed often – sometimes in thanksgiving, more often in pleading and begging and bargaining when things have seemed hopeless. Today I am not doing so well. The familiar blanket is slipping off the shoulders a bit. My body and mind are numb and heavy. I can hardly string two thoughts together and prayer doesn't come easy among the trees and shrubs. I bow my head and lift it again. My eyes meet another pair of eyes staring out from a well-worn face. A woman with a purple coat and black hat is standing at a grave to the left of me, clutching her rosary beads, frantically praying, tight-lipped and frowning. There is no joy in her prayer. I look away and look back again. Her beady, half-closed eyes pretend not to be watching.

I decide to create distance between us in case I upset her or she upsets me. I am upset enough. I take refuge in the empty church and unhook a little rosary chain from my wrist. Deirdre had given it to me; a little keepsake when we all took Mammy to Fatima. I kneel down and think of Granny Drummond. She had great faith in Our Lady. I pray as Catholics do. I pray to Our Lady; I pray the rosary. I don't get the whole way through. My eyes roam around the inside of the chapel and I start to wander – examining the architecture, the Stations of the Cross, the pulpit.

Lost in my reverie, I am abruptly interrupted by a voice scraping through the air like a rooster in the eleventh hour, pinning me to the vestry door.

"He's not here. He's not in there. He's not here today. You'll not find him today."

"Who?" My voice echoes in the darkness, high-pitched and full of fear. It's a silly question.

"The father." Her answer is flat, without reverence.

"God." I gasp as my hand rises to my chest as though to slow down my heartbeat.

She grunts and looks about her, implying that she really is dealing with a complete and utter nutcase.

"No . . ." she breathes heavily. "The priest. The father. You better be on your way now. It's getting late."

Her sharp tone is full of impatience. I am a nuisance, an intruder. Through the dim light of the church, I study the lady in front of me and stifle a giggle. She has one hand on her bag and I have a vision of her pulling out a Colt 45, so in a very timid "please don't hurt me" voice, I tell her I am just going.

I trundle on through every narrow vein of County Donegal. When shadows start to creep over the landscape, I stop at a small general store filled with everything you could possibly want in the middle of nowhere. Walking back into the cold with a few essentials, I pull my coat about me, trying to keep out the damp, but it is the darkness I fear the most. I need to get myself to safety. Heavy rain pelts the windscreen. I have no idea where I am but soon I find an open road that leads me to the bright lights of a hotel and a bath that soothes my aching muscles.

* * *

Slipping below the surface, I hold my breath as the heat hums on my face and my lungs are about to burst. Pushing upwards again, water falls and splashes around me as I squeeze the corners of my eyes with my fingertips. As I look around at the shadows and the mirrors, it slowly dawns on me that I still don't know where I am.

Reluctantly I clamber out of the bath, swiftly dry myself and slip into the white t-shirt I bought in the general store – extra-large; it was the only size they had. I open the plastic of a black hairbrush and brush out my hair in front of the mirror. My t-shirt smiles back with a big sunshine face that says "Welcome to Donegal".

In a drawer by my bed I find a black leather-bound book wishing me a pleasant stay. Under the dim glow of a wall light I find out I am in Buncrana.

Bolting upright, I stare at the wall. Buncrana. I look back at the name again. Yes, that's what it says. I go to the window and peer out into the night, into a town resting in the shadows. Water shimmers and reflects in the moonlight. Buncrana. Granny came here once when I was sixteen with Uncle Brendan. I was away and came back to an empty home. Mammy and Jacinta and Áine were away with them. They had a wonderful time. The girls sang the whole way there and the whole way back, Mammy said. I was sad I missed it, a place in Donegal that was different from Downings or Bundoran. The name appealed to me. I had intended to go myself one day but I ended up going other places, overseas. I forgot about Buncrana until the fifteenth of August, the Feast of the Assumption, a day set aside to celebrate the belief that Our Lady had been taken straight to heaven – body and soul.

The fifteenth of August 1998; Omagh, Buncrana, Spain, united in grief. Blinking my eyes, I shake my head at the vividness of it all flashing around in my head still. None of it has faded. Nothing has become vague. It may as well have happened yesterday. I was late that day. I was meeting Paula at three but Eamonn had left tools behind him at his father's grave. He had to go back. I phoned Paula. She was late too. I told her I had to collect a wedding present in Nicholl and Shiels. I would do that first, then wait for her upstairs in the café next door. She couldn't wait to see the baby but when Eamonn arrived back, Cian was a bit unsettled.

"Best for you to go on yourself," Eamonn had said. I reluctantly left Cian behind. I had wanted to show him off. He was beautiful. It was a beautiful day. I was wearing short sleeves. I was happy and carefree, driving along to Eva Cassidy. Mum had bought the *Songbird* CD for my birthday. "Fields of Gold" was her favourite – mine too. I had just pressed the repeat button and turned it up full blast along with the air conditioning. I was crooning louder than Eva. "You'll remember me when the west winds moves . . ." I didn't hear a thing. " . . . Among the field of barley." Something shuddered. A flat tyre? No, the car seemed okay. ". . .When we walk in fields of gold . . ." I drove straight into it – hell on earth. ". . . So she took her love for to gaze a while . . ." The door handle releasing, . ". . . In her arms she fell . . ." standing, holding on to the car door, refocusing. Crazed expressions, absolute terror. ". . . Among the fields of gold . . ." Black bellowing smoke, the bleeding. ". . . Will you stay with me . . ." The utter devastation. ". . . You can tell the sun . . ." Water, running. ". . . I'll remember you . . ." Piercing screams. ". . . When we walked . . ." The filth. ". . . I never made promises lightly . . ." The smell of evil, the sight of an open-air asylum where Nicholl and Shiels had been – a shop full of pretty things. "We will walk . . ." The ugliness dawned slowly. ". . . in fields of gold." Faster and faster . . . "We will walk . . ." and faster until it filled me up . . . "in fields of gold . . ." to overflowing. "We will walk . . ." Wailing alarms, killing the song. Killing the music. Killing. I blanked.

I only remember the trembling – the terrible trembling, trying to stop it so I could drink the tea a young man had handed me in a small staff room at the back of a shop. Waiting in the hollow silence until I could drive home. I got home when others didn't. Hours later. I shouldn't have been on the road; my body and mind were in no fit state. The guilt of being glad for being spared ran down my face for days and weeks while three communities plunged into a bottomless pit of grief and wept in anguish. The wickedness, the futility of it all removed the need to dress or eat or sleep.

Buncrana. I watch orange lights glow and flicker in the distance. Everything else is still. Three little boys lived here once. I close my eyes against the unimaginable grief that belongs to others, the only comfort being that the bodies and souls of their loved ones went straight to heaven – to a better place, where the darkness of the human psyche can never touch them again. A tiny star twinkles defiantly through the mist and automatically I raise my hands and send healing light to all the families who lost loved ones that day. Faces form in my head, faces from photographs I had seen so many times on television. The names of the children from Buncrana roll off my tongue – Oran, Sean and James and their little Spanish friend Fernando – a bitter, poignant reminder that peace can't be won by bombs and tanks and guns. I send my thoughts to the star, I make a wish that from the brokenness, men's hearts will heal and turn good from evil with a desire to embrace and celebrate difference, to learn to live among people for the greater good. I want to believe, still, that if energy is channelled positively, man can do the decent thing and be a worthy human being.

I reflect on the lives lost, the young lives from Buncrana. I am not sure how old Fernando was but James and Sean were twelve and Oran was eight. Cian was three months. I left him behind. Now he is eight. I have left him behind again. I hope it is a good omen. Thoughts tumble and fuse. I think of a phone-call I made once to Donegal, to Doreen. She was liaising with a local school to develop services for autism. Maybe it was the school the little boys went to? Doreen was from Buncrana.

It is a long time before sleep takes me into a restless troubled place full of children's faces and people I don't know. In the night I am startled from my resting place. I lean into the wall. The room is empty but I sense I am not alone. I am not afraid. I climb into bed again and fall into a more settled sleep. I dream of flying.

* * *

The next morning I sit alone, picking at a breakfast I do not eat. It is Easter week. Mammies and daddies with bed hair and tired eyes walk to and from the breakfast buffet, feeding their young. Chairs around my table are empty and vacant. I try to imagine the children there. It is so easy. Laura would want to be down on the floor. Cian would have his two knees up to his chin, chewing a piece of bacon fat.

A face I do not know appears in front of me.

"Are you okay?"

Startled out of my reverie, I lift my bag. I am so choked up I only nod at the waitress and stumble blindly out into the sun-drenched April day. I do not want to weep. I have no reason; I have no right. My children are safe – they are barely awake, snuggled up in their own beds. I will see them again. Blinking away the sorrow and sunshine, I feel raw – cut open. The steering wheel is heavy and clumsy in my hand. I drive slowly down a one-way street but no one blows their horn or speeds up close behind me. I am in Donegal time now – a tick and a tock that is slower and better paced.

I feel the need to walk. I walk past the shorefront. The Lough is sleeping still – like a mirror reflecting the mountains beyond. People say hello and remark on the weather. I think I will like it here. I startle myself. Where did that thought come from? I laugh out loud – the thought of it – but calmness has settled around me, in me, on me. I can feel it, like I have come home.

I drive by a church, reverse and park. I wander in and out, discovering a little prayer room. The Blessed Sacrament is present in the tabernacle. I tiptoe into the silent sacred space. One other person is there, a man with his eyes closed, deep in prayer. I am relieved his eyes are closed. I sit for a long while, my thoughts bruised and battered, making no coherent sense. I remember why I am here – why I don't know why I am here. I wish the man would leave. I can feel the force of a dam. As though he can read my thoughts, he stands up, picks up his cap and does the decent thing. He bows reverently and walks quietly out the door. As the door shuts, the dam bursts and my body shakes and sobs with grief. *Why am I here?* I try to pray but my mind is blank, like a blackboard, everything rubbed off it but the little white bits at the edges that the duster didn't quiet reach. Closing my eyes, I still my mind. The peace and silence calm me. For a long time I hold on to my faith and meditate on hope – that hope will take hold of my heart again.

When I eventually leave the comfort of the prayer room, I stand for a moment and allow my eyes to adjust to the morning's brightness. There is a little heat in it. I turn and head towards the car, passing a little grotto tucked under the base of the chapel. I bless myself with holy water that has been mixed with water from Lourdes and at the same time notice a building that looks like a school. The door is slightly ajar. A smell of cleaning detergent fills my nostrils as my heels echo down a corridor. No one is about. On tiptoe, I wander around empty classrooms. Thinking, how little anyone can teach you about life; how much you need to teach yourself. Tons of chairs are stacked up against each other in the corridor. It looks so odd not to have teachers and pupils milling about.

Suddenly a small man carrying a jar of something appears from nowhere. He is wearing a cap and a grey t-shirt and a shocked expression on his face.

"Oh . . . How did you get in here?"

"The door was open."

"But the door is locked." He looks over his shoulder, puzzled.

"It was only open a little bit."

The man sets the jar down and retrieves a bunch of keys from his pocket. He doesn't believe me.

"It can't be open. I locked it. No one should be in here."

"Sorry, I didn't mean to –"

He fiddles with the bunch of keys and looks about him nervously. He doesn't know which one to deal with first, the door or me. "Are you looking . . . I need to check . . . excuse me . . . in case . . ." He sprints down the corridor I have just come up, disappears and reappears, looking surprised. "That's really odd. I locked that door and it is still locked." He is shaking his head.

"It must have locked when it closed behind me."

The man stares at me in disbelief, as if he is looking at a ghost. I am thinking of leaving when he asks me if I am looking for someone. I can feel my eyes welling up again.

"Are you all right?" The man shifts from foot to foot.

"No." I answer as the tears begin to drip.

He looks helpless, uncertain what to say or do next. For a moment I feel sorry for him, having to deal with a man's worst nightmare – a blubbering female. I must look a sight – a face cut out of candle-wax, puffy-eyed, wretched with untidy hair.

"Were you looking for somebody?" he asks again.

I am so choked up I can't speak.

"Listen, I am Malachy, the caretaker here." He tries not to look at me.

"Where is here?" I sob.

Malachy is taken aback. He folds his arms and turns his head sideways.

"Do you not know where you are? This is Scoil Íosagáin."

He looks about him, thinking of something to say to quell the noise I'm making. He starts to talk rapidly, as though silence will cost him money.

". . . And it's a great school. We teach all sorts of kids here. I have worked here for a long time . . . great school, great staff and the kids . . . all great kids . . . all sorts and sizes . . . they teach everybody here."

Malachy stops and remembers his manners.

"Ah . . . wait 'til I get you a chair."

The heap of chairs rattle and the caretaker heaves one out of the pile next to us, setting it near me, gesturing, folding his arms, looking about him, trying not to look at me weeping. It is not nice to watch someone weeping.

". . . It's a very big school and well run, the principal is second-to-none and the staff, you know. It's a great school and the children come from near and far, children that find it hard to learn, with difficulties. We even have classes for the wee ones with autism, you know."

I hold my breath; the trembling, the whimpering and the sobbing all stop. I look up and see Malachy, the caretaker, who loves his work, his job, his Scoil Íosagáin. He loves the kids. Warm twinkling eyes light up his whole face, even though he is not smiling. I am looking at him and he is looking back, wondering what he has said that stopped everything.

"Are you all right now?" He speaks more slowly, concerned, less nervous.

"Autism." It's the only word I can manage to pull from the wreckage inside me.

"Autism?"

A fresh stream of tears starts again.

Malachy bends forward a little and then bends back, running his hand over his head and pulling at his ears. His pep talk hasn't worked. He is nervous again, stepping forward, stepping back, and not knowing what to do. I howl uncontrollably. He holds up his hands as though to hold back the ocean. He tells me I need to talk to someone.

He is going to find someone. It's Easter week and the principal is away but he will try to find someone else.

"I have a little boy with –" I go to stand up.

"No, no, you stay here. I . . . I . . . I am going to phone someone." He puts his hands out and I sit down again. Sunshine spills into a yellow puddle about my feet and I breathe in and out, in and out. Malachy is behind the reception desk. He is phoning someone. I lean forward and try to catch the sunbeam. I know why I am here. My prayers have been answered.

34

When I get back home, I gather the children to me and take time to gather my thoughts, letting them simmer for a while. I tell Eamonn about Buncrana, about the school, about the facilities for children with autism. Communication doesn't flow freely. There is nothing easy about making a difficult decision, especially when it involves children, particularly a child who cannot express how he feels or contribute to the decision. On a wing and a prayer I can only hope we make the right one. For Cian every opportunity needs to be grasped with both hands to enable him to be the best he can be now and in the future. It is something I try not to think too much about. The future and the legacy of autism, which will begin another struggle for his siblings, another chapter that will echo many of the same struggles of their childhood. For that reason alone Cian needs to be encouraged and supported, to be the best he can be, to learn appropriate behaviours among his peers, to be accepted and understood by those classified as "normal".

In a way moving Cian out of his community goes against everything we have stood for. We wanted him to live and grow and be taught with his brother and cousins and neighbours. Without autism facilities, this is impossible. We have done everything in our power to keep him in his own community and the community has done everything in its power to support the Impact Centre, but without government support it was not sustainable. When Christopher learnt that the Impact Centre was closing he was upset. He liked the idea of Cian wearing the same uniform as him and getting to know his friends. In his own words he is "cool" about the move to a new school.

The secretary of Scoil Íosagáin calls to arrange an appointment time to meet the principal.

"Where are you going anyway?" Christopher has overheard my telephone conversation. Undoing his tie for the tenth time, he waits for an explanation. Reaching out for the tie ends, I pause for a moment. *Do I lie or tell the truth?* Christopher never was good with lies. They don't wash with him, ever. I decide to tell the truth.

"I am going to look at a school, Christopher. They might have a place for Cian…"

He pulls away, checks his tie in the kitchen door glass.

"Where is it?" He stuffs his hands in his pockets and turns towards me.

"It is far away. It is in Buncrana in Donegal."

"Is there a beach?"

"Yes."

Immediately he turns, rips the newly knotted tie from

his collar and takes the stairs two at a time, shaking himself out of his jumper and shirt as he goes.

"But Christopher, it's Tuesday. You have to go to school."

"No, I don't." he shouts over the banister in a sing-song voice.

"Yes, you do. I am only going up to look at the school."

He disappears into the bedroom with his uniform trousers at his knees and hops back out again as he struggles to get into a pair of tracksuit bottoms. Sailing down the banister, he lands in front of me naked from the waist up, with a Nike t-shirt under his chin.

"Will I be going to this school?" He struggles to turn the t-shirt outside in.

I absentmindedly take the t-shirt, straighten it and put it behind my back.

"Well, I would like to talk to you about it . . . but this is not the time, you have to go to school."

Christopher grabs the t-shirt and starts to lecture me.

"Look, Mammy, if there is a school to be looked at I'm going." His head disappears into the t-shirt and then pops up again. "After all, it will be my school too. Besides, you have no one to look after Laura when you're talking to . . . whoever it is you're going to be talking to." He rolls his eyes and turns his hands upwards. "And I know you'll take ages, so I will be able to entertain her."

His hands wave as he delivers his message. I resist a giggle. He turns, pops a slice of bread in the toaster and raises a full glass of breakfast juice to me. I shake my head at my mature happy nine-year-old who loves Donegal beaches and any excuse to get out of school. Even though he is showing no signs of anxiety I have no doubt he is fully aware of the implications of our journey. It is pointless arguing with him. Maybe it is best that he is informed from the outset. To him, it is all an adventure.

He takes a slug of his orange and slips his arm around my waist.

"So you're not going to school then?"

"Nope. I am going to a school in Buncrana."

* * *

The meeting is positive. After much talking I am advised that the school will be able to offer Cian a place. He will have his own personal workstation and a curriculum tailored to meet his needs. There will be opportunities for integration with his peers in mainstream classes. On various days of the week, Cian will go swimming, horse-riding and bowling and benefit from a variety of other therapeutic activities that are supported by iCARE (Inishowen Children's Autism Related Education), a local parent support group that provides additional resources and transport for the children with autism. Before we leave Christopher gets to visit a class full of boys and girls his age and when we walk back into the May sunshine Laura wants to go to the beach. On the side of a rock we munch on our "picnic" lunch while Christopher and Laura chat about crabs and seashells. Cian rests his head on my shoulder and gazes at the hazy purple of the horizon. I tell him it is the prettiest horizon I have ever seen.

35

It has been raining steadily all morning. Rain drums on the roof and runs down the drainpipes and windows, blotting out the breathtaking view of Lough Swilly. The children munch on their cereal as I peer into Christopher's schoolbag, checking everything for the fourth time.

"Right, Christopher. Copybooks, pencil case, ham sandwich, apple, yogurt, orange and pineapple drink . . . there you go."

Christopher tugs at the zip. "Thanks, Mammy."

"And now Cian's bag . . . welly boots, toothbrush, toothpaste, change of clothes, swimming kit, digestive enzymes, roasted chicken, vegetables, brown rice, banana, kiwi, strawberries, blueberries, hemp seed bar, bottle of mineral water in a glass bottle, *Thomas the Tank Engine* trains, *The Caterpillar* storybook, money and daily record diary."

Christopher giggles. "You would think Cian was going camping for a week, not starting school . . ."

"Well, he could be camping before the morning's out."

Both of us burst out laughing. Laura laughs too. I help Cian to finish up his breakfast. Christopher pulls his drink bottle from his bag and pretends to report for the RTÉ news.

"This is Christopher McCallan with some sweaty palm news here in the RTÉ newsroom. A young man broke free from a school in Donegal this morning, bypassing bewildered elderly people and sleepy dogs going to morning mass."

"Come on Chris . . ." I hand him his coat and scramble though a wicker basket for some hats and scarves. "We are going to be late."

"His teacher . . . er . . . Ena Flash lived up to her name and hounded after the young boy, past bus stops and beaches, towards the Donegal hills and they haven't been seen since. Staff at the school hope they will return soon but the pupils hope the teacher doesn't turn up at all. They consider the young boy a hero."

Laura tells Christopher he is very funny as she puts on her coat while I strain to do up Cian's zip.

"Mammy, what would happen if Cian did get away . . . if we really did lose him?" Christopher shakes himself into his coat.

"I would put on weight and you wouldn't get any daily exercise . . . Come on, let's go."

When we arrive at the school, the downpour is easing off. Christopher decides to make a dash for it.

"But I said I would walk you in."

"Everywhere's flooded; Cian and Laura will only get soaked."

"But I promised you . . . Are you sure? Do you know where you're going?"

"Mum, I'll be fine! Honest. Sure, I can watch out for Ms McLaughlin if I get lost. Bye, Cian. Bye, Laura. Bye, Mum. Love you . . . see you later."

The door slams before Laura answers.

"Bye, Christopher, love you too."

I watch him run through the school gates and disappear around a corner, his bag swaying from side to side on his back as if he has done it a hundred times before.

Turning my attention to Cian I notice he is shoeless and coatless. We have taught him many things, like putting on his coat and shoes. Teaching him to keep them on is another story. I tap his legs as he slowly unscrambles himself. "Okay, Cian, this is your new school."

Reaching out, he touches the window and tracks the raindrops with his fingers. Laura wriggles in her car seat as I pop open her safety belt.

"Come on, Cian, we need to put your shoes on again."

Cian moves as though his body is wading through mud, without a reason, without a purpose. He reaches for his shoes without looking at them, dazed by the trickles of water on the glass. I try to encourage him, but I have to choose my battles carefully. Heading into school isn't the time to insist on independence. I end up pushing his feet into both shoes and pulling him up to a standing position. Laura is itching to get going and climbs right over him, jigging up and down in front of me until I hoist her up on my hip. Cian steps out and immediately bends down to touch the wet tarmac. There are puddles everywhere. I help fix his schoolbag on his shoulders and clutch his hand.

"That's us, Cian, we're good to go now."

Grey and red uniforms block the front door as the pupils filter through with their pink satchels and Pokémon bags. Cian pushes and shoves; faces turn to look and I try to tell Cian to wait. "We have to line up." Cian pushes and pulls some more and I say "sorry" about twenty-five times as he drags me after him into the smells and the noise and the colour of the unfamiliar building. But Cian remembers. His eyes dart towards the colourful library with its array of interesting books and vibrant murals on the walls. He has made up his mind. He is going to the library and breaks free.

The crowd expands and Laura and I scurry after him. We find him on his knees looking at a book about a crocodile. I coax and cajole him and tell him the teacher will take him back later. Reluctantly, he trails after me, eyeing up the computers and another set of books on display by the door. He lets me steer him out as I breathe a sigh of relief. Laura totters after me, tripping over the umbrella, staring into legs and up into teachers' faces, all saying "hello" and telling her how cute she is. We walk slowly to Miss Friel's classroom – a classroom specifically for children with autism.

Cian wants to run but I hold one hand while he touches the walls with his other, feeling the coat-hooks and the felt on the notice-boards, bending down every now and then to run his hands along the cracks between the blue-grey tiles. I give him time. I don't want to rush him. Not today. He has waited eight years for this – to be part of something bigger than him, to wear a uniform that says he belongs, to avail of a basic education like everybody else. He examines the window ledges and feels the pale blue glossy paint, hesitating and peering in through the window of each classroom as he passes. He checks out a fire extinguisher and raps his knuckles against it. I move him on while he is looking back down the corridor, his curiosity getting the better of him. He would love to break free just like Christopher said and weave in and out of classrooms, checking the lie of the land, mapping it in his mind, exploring all the nooks and crannies, revisiting any classroom he has been to during his first visit, losing and finding himself again; but this is not the time.

A lady with long hair tied back in a ponytail is standing, patiently waiting at the end of the corridor just outside Cian's classroom. She is wearing glasses but something about her reminds me of Donna. As we approach, she smiles and introduces herself as Rosemary, Cian's assistant. Bending down, she says hello to Cian while she helps him hang up his coat. Cian is not hot on formalities. He pushes past her, edging the door open, keen to escape into the room. Rosemary says something I don't quite catch but it sounds reassuring. I place his little hand in hers and let him go. She smiles at me again, nods her head and leads Cian into his very first real classroom. He does not look back.

* * *

Spikes of sunshine poke out through clumps of dappled grey cloud. Laura wants her umbrella up but I tell her it's not raining any more.

"And if you put it up you will not get to see the rainbow."

"Oh." She looks up and follows the line of my finger, pointing towards the sky.

Delicate shades of red and indigo and purple lie side-by-side, smudged and seamless. The sight of it puts me in the mood for a walk.

On a path along the edge of Lough Swilly, Laura chatters about the flowers, every syllable like sweet music to my ears. Living by the shoreline has refreshed me. Inishowen and Cian's school has breathed new hope into my lungs.

It may sound harsh but, at the beginning, Cian's diagnosis bore the hallmark of a prison sentence. The psychiatrist delivered the verdict and one word, the "A" word, completed the sentence. We were taken down to the lowest depths of grief I have ever known and entered a hostile world without help or support while we clung to Cian, doing everything we could to pull him back from the brink. Despite our best efforts, autism took hold, behaviours became difficult and the remnants of our happy family life lay tattered and torn. We became an undiagnosed family at risk, living inside a pressure cooker. When the pressure blew, no one but the grace of God and divine intervention came to salvage us from the wreckage. We bear scars of that wreckage today. I trust time will heal the broken pieces and make them whole again. Hurt is fading but residues will remain stuck in the recesses of my memory, reminding me where I have been, how far I have travelled, how far I have come.

On a bench, Laura's head peeks out from under my arm as we sit. I have forgotten what it is like – to sit. My motor neurons keep telling me to get up, to run, to shout. The constant flow of adrenalin has left me a nervous wreck. Shattered. Burned out. Living it every day, you get so tired. Worn down like last year's underwear – jaded, off-white and not very sexy. You just get fed up with it all. Fighting.

It seems a century since the very first punch. The diagnosis. The black hole. Waiting in the wings for someone to do something. Accepting the invitation to a merry dance, running to and from appointments while the hands on the clock swing faster and faster until you fizz with frustration, faced with endless roadblocks; the "head in the sand" approach to autism, the inadequate provision compounded by worry and stress about the future; but the most unforgivable roadblock is the mindset – how autism is perceived, how the diagnosis is dished out with the poor prognosis and a "no help, no hope" dressing. The way in which parents are judged is also unforgivable – wrong for having too high an expectation, wrong for chasing interventions with no scientific proof that it will help.

Laura points at a large black hump appearing and disappearing from view. She thinks it's a whale, but I reassure her that it's a rock. As in life, things are not all as they seem.

The perfect key to autism doesn't exist, but what do exist are viable treatment options that could make a difference no matter how big or how small to a child and their family. They just haven't been recognised or made accessible. We should be celebrating the fact that there are treatments out there, treatments that each child should be able to avail of, a chance to develop and grow. To bash a treatment because it doesn't have a sealed stamp of approval as best practice to suit everyone's needs or because it doesn't lead to full recovery is not a good enough reason to reject a parent's wish to help his or her child. No loving parent will put scientific research before the welfare of their own child.

The steps that a child with autism takes are tiny in a day, a week, a month, but in the year of a family they are huge. Being able to cope with crowds in a public place without fear means the difference between a family going shopping and not going shopping. Learning to know the difference between morning and afternoon and evening gives a child order to their day. Being toilet-trained brings independence and as a child grows older could mean the difference between being housebound and not being housebound. It doesn't matter what the therapy is called, as long as procedures are put in place to support progress. If it takes a couple of years of ABA therapy or Son-rise or Sensory Integration Training to teach a child any of the above examples, try telling a family it's not worth it.

All children respond differently to therapies, even in the same family, but to prevent families from availing of such therapies and maximising the potential of each individual is unacceptable. Therapy and treatment often require out-of-pocket expenses and limit the possibilities for children and for thousands of families who can't afford private fees, families who by right are entitled to educational and healthcare provision. Yet government departments duck and dive as we crumble and crack under the strain. Here in the twenty-first century, they can put a man on the moon and take biotechnology to the point of human cloning, yet in one of the wealthiest nations in Europe we can't work together to establish specific educational and basic health provision for children with autism at a time when the number of children diagnosed with autism is soaring.

Nationally the debate rages about "cause" and "best practice" for autism, a debate that grinds on my eardrums while children with autism put up with less than adequate support services. Children who have not known life without anxiety, confusion or pain. Each behaviour is a coping strategy to manage one overwhelming moment after another. They do what is necessary to get by. True understanding of autistic behaviours is found through compassion.

Laura wriggles out from under my arm and hops down onto the tarred path. She picks a flower and hands it to me; a daisy, as common as grass but simple and beautiful in its own way. I look up and meet Laura's eyes, staring intensely at the blur of my eyes. I wrap her up in my arms and give her a hug. We find a café and bond over an orange juice and a sausage.

A jacket hanging on a wall near the counter starts to rap. A young girl with red streaky hair and a ring in her nose retrieves a mobile from the jacket pocket. The rapping stops. "Hiya." Her voice is excited. She is smiling and teasing while she examines her black nail polish. She is laughing out loud. I can see the stud in her tongue. She can't wait to see whoever she is talking to. When she brings our order, I can't help but notice that she has five earrings in one ear and three in the other. I find myself wondering why on earth any young girl would deliberately want to fill herself up with holes.

Laura stares after her for ages before turning to tell me that when she is a big girl she is going to be a princess. I tell her she already is one.

* * *

In the afternoon Christopher splits company with two boys smiling and waving back at him running through the school grounds. He waves until they disappear behind the school gates, then turns, says "hello" to Laura and hugs my neck.

"*Dia duit, mo mhamaí.*"

"Hello to you too! Wow . . . you are speaking in Irish?"

"Yes. I had a great day and only for Cian I wouldn't have met a whole bunch of new friends."

His face is shining and I breathe a sigh of relief. Christopher's happiness is the benchmark I need to reassure me I have made a positive decision. So far, so good.

Rosemary walks Cian out to the car. Cian has had a good day too.

36

Eighteen months later, Cian's teacher, Mrs Giri, is very pleased with his progress.

"Cian is a very clever little boy. He is intelligent. We just need to tap into it and keep him motivated and interested."

I smile at her and savour the moment. Nine years I have waited for someone to concentrate on what my son can do rather than what he can't. Nine years I waited for someone to see what I only got glimpses of over the years – an underlying intelligence that I am unable to describe in words, an intelligence I could not ignore despite the severe disabling autistic behaviours. Still, Mrs Giri makes it sound so simple, but it is not.

Like most children with autism, Cian needs to be taught *everything*. Well, almost everything. We never had to teach Cian how to work a DVD player, or how to unlock a double lock and scale a six foot wall. We did not have to show him how to alter the system files on a computer and he seems to have a fair idea what money is for. Some of these "skills" may be beneficial through time but it is vital to understand that children like Cian need help to make it in life, a life full of complicated and confusing rules and regulations that are constantly changing.

Scoil Íosagáin works tirelessly with a number of determined parents to secure autism-specific provision, promoting diversity and inclusion, but like all schools, their efforts have been burdened with a constant battle to secure essential funding and whole school training, specialised resources and therapy space. Furthermore, necessary support services to allow them to access education – special needs assistants, speech and language therapists, psychologists, occupational therapists, sensory integration specialists, music therapists and educational nurses – for the most part are either not guaranteed, missing or inadequate. Children in need of these services all over Ireland and the UK are faced with long waiting lists and inexcusable inconsistencies, depriving them of essential therapists and therapies. It is a constant struggle, fighting for vital educational services and therapies necessary to provide free and inclusive education. How can education be free and inclusive if you don't have the services to enable children to communicate and engage with others?

Instead of being able to access autism-specific education, viable treatment interventions, family-centred support and respite services, parents find themselves in front of tribunals and on street corners holding collection buckets, working hammer-and-tongs trying to fundraise and organise vital facilities through parent-led groups that should effectively be provided by the government. The current situation is crying out for urgent autism-specific funding and services from government departments, most notably the Departments of Education and Health. The reality – that parents feel the need to set up their own local groups to support and pursue respite facilities and therapies – highlights that their needs are clearly not being met by statutory and non-statutory partnerships and funding that is available, if not regulated and subject to quality assurance, may not be effective in addressing the needs of our children and families affected by autism.

Current provision of second-level education is another worry. The Education for Persons with Special Educational Needs (EPSEN) Act has a cut-off point of eighteen years of age, which is absurd. People with autism need lifelong learning and vocational training. Therefore we face every day knowing that there is no long-term education or health provision in place as our children become teenagers and young adults, which is aggravated by a lack of collaboration between the health and education sectors. Autistic children represent a percentage of the most vulnerable members in our society. Society is judged on how well we take care of our most vulnerable members. If policy-makers are going to make a dent at all in the tsunami wave of autism, the mindset must change and the epidemic of denial must change. For children like Cian, who are presenting with undiagnosed conditions on the inside, something else must change: Medical services.

* * *

It is the last Saturday in June, when families are thinking

315

about holidays and picnics and icecream. It is a dry sunny morning, a morning for hanging out the washing and tending the garden. Instead, a larger number of parents spill into a lecture theatre in Manchester to attend a "parent2parent" conference run by Treating Autism, an organisation born of both hope and frustration. Hope, that biomedical treatment protocols may help our children, and frustration that the information required to learn is so disparate, particularly when looking for UK- and European-specific resources.

While I queue for my delegate's pack, I survey the scene. It occurs to me that none of us would be here, not even the organisers, if our children were not suffering physically due to undiagnosed problems. Had we access to medical treatments and care that our children are entitled to, we would have better things to be doing. If our children didn't have compromised immune systems and hadn't been pushed over the toxic threshold, we could spend our money and time on more pleasurable things than paying carers to nurse our responsibilities at home while we go hunting for knowledge and information on how to treat our children diagnosed with autism and undiagnosed with immune dysfunction, heavy metal toxicity, gastrointestinal problems, bowel loading and multiple allergies.

There is a quiet lull as we are welcomed to the conference. Delegates dive into bags to switch off their mobiles phones as Jean Muscroft, a mum, a nutritionist and Cian's DAN doctor, takes the stand. When the deafening applause dies down, she delivers a PowerPoint presentation that begins and ends with a healthy gastrointestinal tract. She makes Gillian McKeith look like an amateur, sharing studies that have found that severe constipation is a frequent finding in children with gastrointestinal symptoms and autism. She discusses the effects of heavy metal toxicity and weakened immune systems and how we might improve our children's elimination systems. Other parents report that their child's seizure disorders and reflux episodes go undiagnosed. And what of the chronic viruses and yeast and bacteria and parasites that are the norm in the autism population?

When Paul Shattock takes the stand he gives a highly entertaining account of the reasons behind the gluten/casein-free diet, multiple food allergies and intolerances that children with autism suffer from, but despite his light-hearted presentation skills, keeping us alert after lunch, this is no laughing matter. His finger clicks on the computer mouse and a number of images of different children in the same peculiar positions flash across the projection screen. Only within the last few years have parents and doctors come to realise that these children, crouched and bent in two, are trying to relieve the awful pain in their bellies.

In every image I see Cian, hanging over the arm of our sofa or lying over a therapy ball for ages. The images are a disturbing reminder of the suffering he endured in silence while I trailed and cajoled my wilting toddler along to developmental reviews and therapy appointments, holding up his floppy body through treatment sessions. Memories flood my mind of therapists finishing up fifteen minutes early, declaring Cian to be distracted and disengaged. He was not motivated. He was inconsistent. He seemed irritable. All the while I was thinking, *how the hell could he be anything else?* He had been up all night, suffered from severe constipation and hadn't eaten anything but foam out of a teddy bear in days. What child wants to play when they are in pain? I did try to tell them but my attempts were constantly dismissed and comments such as "it is all part and parcel of the autism" just wore me down. Yet we continued to address strange noises, head-banging and bizarre behaviours with behavioural interventions. Bleeding eczema and bums that burn with thrush and nappy rash, night terrors and food intolerances are not even questioned.

Parents who have had much success in recovering their children through biomedical treatments give presentations, backed up with video footage, sharing their knowledge in the hope that they might help someone else. Children who could not speak now smile at us through video lenses, telling us about their gluten/casein-free diet and their favourite toys. Five-year-old Lee is sitting in the front row watching his mammy and daddy relay their experiences of helping Lee make his way back home again, home from autismland. They too show a video, a younger version of Lee walking aimlessly back and forth, back and forth, along the perimeter of the garden, like a rodent in a maze, jogging my memory, my memory of Cian lost to autism. While they explain and encourage, he calls up to them, "Hey! Mummy, what you doing up there?"

It feels like *déjà vu*, when I sat in another lecture theatre watching American children laugh and smile again. Now recovery is happening with the help and support of our American counterparts. There are still a very small number of DAN doctors in the UK but an ever-increasing number of parents are healing their children, only to find the autism diagnosis no longer applies. This time I have more energy, a DAN doctor and hope. This time I am listening.

* * *

There is some good news. Bowel problems, a poor immune system, food allergies, intolerances and an impaired detoxification system are treatable. By treating such conditions, tantrums, hand-flapping, repetitive sounds, yelling out and obsessive behaviour can be effectively eliminated. It can also increase speech, eye contact and social skills that just about eradicate the autism characteristics.

There is no talk of cures or quick fixes. Healing the body takes time, patience and loads of loving, with the dogged determination and mental state of a growling lion protecting the cubs. What works for one child may not work for another child. An individual's biological make-up plays a large role in any breakthrough. Children with compromised immune systems present differently. There is a huge acceptance that our children have all managed to reach autismland via different routes. They are all affected differently. We may not get rid of all the symptoms, but healthy children will have a better chance to recover old skills and learn new skills. We can nourish their bodies and minds towards a healthier, happier demeanour. They can become aware that they are part of our family and feel loved and accepted.

Some children do recover completely. Others are still travelling on the road to recovery while others may gain a little benefit. A little benefit can mean a huge difference to a child and family coping with autism. Parents who are concerned about their child's internal health should have, at least, access to tests and opportunity to receive biomedical treatments for their child. There is no promise, no guarantee, but much to celebrate. Jean's daughter is going to boarding school. Children *are* getting better. One must appreciate that recoveries and significant cognitive improvements could not happen if these children were truly born "defective" – thankfully, they are not.

The conference is a success. We have regrouped, listened and learned from each other. The organisers have only made one mistake. They haven't included packets of tissues in the delegates' packs for the many tears that have fallen. These are not the same tears that fell in diagnostic clinics but tears of joy watching another child escape across the autism border to live a pain-free life again.

A bunch of parents hug me on the way out, wishing me luck. The take-home message is: *I am not alone and autism is treatable.*

* * *

In the grand scheme of things, however, I believe there is a much greater message that is not only relevant to my son's autism. The message is simple. We live in an ever-increasingly toxic world. Nature has been weakened at the hands of man. We have underestimated the intelligence of a single bacterium.

There is a need to go back to basics, to nature's medicine chest and unprocessed whole foods to nourish our very own intricate healing systems. We need to open our minds and re-evaluate our excessive obsessions with quick fixes, ready meals and the use of chemicals, pesticides, fluoride, electromagnetic fields and genetically modified foods. Increased awareness at a personal and parental level is essential to protecting our health and to lobby governments to re-evaluate the connection between environmental toxins, excessive antibiotics, toxic-laden vaccinations and impaired immunity, most of which have not been fully addressed by government. No stone should be left unturned to quell the currently unprecedented tragedy that is having a devastating and detrimental long-term effect on the bodies, minds and spirits of our children diagnosed with autistic spectrum disorder. We have to investigate all environmental triggers fully, which include everything we breathe, everything we eat and drink and everything we absorb through our skin.

While tragedy continues to strike individuals and their families by the thousands, we must not continue to work as adversaries, fighting to defend principles which in the end we all believe in. Not all children's conditions are the same, but it is clear that many children have medical problems that need prompt attention. When I started out on this journey, the onset of autism was around eighteen months. Now it has conveniently crawled up to three years as it accommodates a never-ending array of conditions pouring in and out of our diagnostic clinics and schools.

Thankfully there are a number of medics and health professionals, the "Dr Quacks" of the autism world, working relentlessly hard to advance our understanding and to help us treat our children suffering from toxic bodies and impaired immune systems. Many have been touched by autism through relatives, friends and clients, and in many cases their own children. It is the children who have had a deep resounding impact on their work. Autism has increased tenfold since 1989. A child with autism is already in a street near you, in our shopping centres, in our schools, in our back yards. Will autism have to become "passé" before the medical community is shamed into doing something about it? Will autism become part of who we are until we acknowledge our own autism and wake up to the deeds we have done, which have unravelled the whole human process of having healthy, happy children?

Causes still remain speculative and puzzling. To date no single gene or combination of genes has been identified as a cause and if genes alone cause autism, scientists would have a huge conundrum to solve, given the exploding number of autism cases. Genetics can't change that quickly over a period of thirty-odd years. But slowly, steadily, many myths about autism are falling away, as researchers and scientists uncover new information on what is happening in the bodies and brains of people with autism. Current research indicates that autism may arise from a combination of genetic vulnerabilities and environmental triggers. It is also indicated that Alzheimer's, Lupus, Ulcerative Colitis, Rheumatoid Disease, ME, Chronic Fatigue Syndrome, Multiple Sclerosis and a number of other diagnostically puzzling illnesses are all considered to be toxic-related conditions and immune-connected. What are our bodies trying to tell us?

For Cian, dietary changes, biomedical treatments and homeopathy have all played a significant part in alleviating many autistic symptoms and his body is healing slowly and purposefully from the assault he suffered on his immune system.

Sadly, mainstream medicine still views regressive autism as a hopeless, lifelong disability. I long for a day when there is a paradigm shift among government agencies and health and educational authorities and a new precedence obliterates the dire prognosis. Autism is treatable. We need our doctors to help us. We need those who have advanced the causes and treatments of autism to be recognised, acknowledged and supported. We need medical groups and government agencies to join together and deliver healthy solutions for the sake of our children's future.

37

There are those who are quick to remind me that autism *is* a neurological disorder, that there is no cure and that, instead of searching, I should find joy in autism. I should accept Cian's autism as part of him and not try to change his true autistic state. When Cian was bent in two, clutching his sides and banging his head off the fireplace, I failed to experience joy and disregarded this opinion as purely sadistic. Having to endure opinions from many who did not understand my motives or appreciate how we struggled to comprehend the complexities of Cian's difficulties did not help.

With hindsight, however, I have realised that children with autism do not all present the same and that it is possible that individuals with such opinions may not have experienced what we experienced with Cian. I have now come to respect this point of view, so long as it does not interfere with progress. Had I been of this opinion, had we not pursued the interventions that we did, had I not been driven to find answers, I would have failed Cian and would never have experienced the joy of celebrating every step he takes towards a better quality of life, a life free from pain and anxiety. ABA therapy taught him all that he knows and continues to teach him appropriate everyday behaviours in the home and in the community. His autism-specific education, delivered in a holistic and committed environment, continues to challenge his mind and nurture his confidence and self-esteem. A healthy nutritional diet, homeopathy and biomedical treatment bring Cian closer to wellness.

Now we experience sheer joy, joy that is reciprocated – like when he clambers to claim his place at our family table and hangs out of the shopping bags to see what we have bought him, when he asks me "Where's Christopher?" and tells me "Lawa's quing", when he runs out a door and then opens it again to wait for me, when he welcomes Colin and Kathy home from Australia with open arms. Joy is the essence of him.

Cian has not recovered from autism, but he has recovered from where he was two, three, five, seven years ago.

So have I. Little pieces of me have recovered too, bits I had forgotten about; little details that matter – the colour in my cheek, the smile on my face, the dreams in my head. Many of them for Cian. Many that have come true already.

The child who could not walk through the door of a supermarket without going into meltdown can go into a shop and buy a magazine after raiding my purse. He has modelled in fashion shows for an iCARE fundraising event and has taken part and dressed up for St Patrick's Day parades and Halloween. He has revisited Africa, and has taken a trip down the Zambezi River and flown over the Victoria Falls in a helicopter. He likes to Google on the computer, and swim and watch football and jump on a trampoline and go to the cinema – pretty much what any ten-year-old wants to do. He goes horse-riding and takes music lessons. He loves to strum the guitar and listen to his music, the louder the better.

Still, there are many challenges ahead. Difficult behaviours appear. Things happen in Cian's life that he is unable to question, protest or understand. The computer loads too slowly or crashes. His moneybox has been moved from where he wants it to be. A man comes and puts a cupboard where his train set used to sit.

One day his *Jungle Book* DVD works. The next day it doesn't. It is scored. He goes into meltdown. The DVD refuses to play and Cian cries for an hour, dragging me again and again to the DVD player. I try to tell him again and again that it is scored. I try to tell him it is "broke". He understands broke. "Broke, Cian, broke." He studies it and throws himself on the floor. Another meltdown. How could it be broke? It looks the same as when it played yesterday. Things are only broke when they are in two halves or if they are in pieces on the floor. The meltdown lasts the rest of the evening.

Even small changes that seems like nothing to us can rock Cian's world. Using a different door into a building; furniture being moved around; being misunderstood; driving past somewhere he thinks he is going, even if I have told him he is going somewhere else; a reaction to a certain food. Frustration comes easily – a painful reminder of Cian's deficits. What starts out as a fun family outing can spiral quickly into tears and screaming if Cian is bothered by something. We don't always know what that is. Tears on his face frustrate him more as he tries to stop them streaming down his eyes. He hates crying, his face wet and sticky. He puts his head back, trying to hold his tears in.

We cannot plan for every eventuality. We have taught Cian many things. We can teach him to run a bath, we can teach him hot and cold, but how do we teach him that hot water will eventually run cold and that there is not enough hot water in the hot press for a bath? How can I teach him that neither the lights nor his television work because there is storm damage down the road and it has knocked off the electricity? How do I explain to him that a man will not have it fixed until tomorrow? Abstract grey areas are difficult for Cian to comprehend, yet they make up the fabric of daily living in a complex world.

I still find it difficult to explain the "A" word to Christopher and Laura. Thankfully, I don't really have to. Our wee Mowgli is just our Cian to them – drop-dead gorgeous, loving, funny, quirky, often frustrated, always forgiving Cian. Their unequivocal acceptance astounds me. They do not stand and measure the distance he is from normal but there are times it is difficult for them to accept he is different.

Christopher scribbles down this poem one night. His thoughts pour onto the page. I am glad he has a way to express how he feels, what he feels.

Without Cian
Without Cian
I wouldn't have a brother
He is different
I know
From the rest
But I wouldn't have another.

Without Cian
I wouldn't have to hide
My books, my food, my things
I wouldn't have to wait around
To see what each day brings
For planning isn't easy
Not when you have a brother
Who runs away
And shouts out loud
But I wouldn't have another.

Without Cian
I would never have met
Daniel, Ger or Donna
Or visited Fran in Africa
Or met Sean in cool Buncrana.
Without Cian
I would not understand
What it's like to have a brother
A brother like mine
Who is doing fine
But I wouldn't have another.
When I'm with Cian

It sometimes makes me sad
Because Cian
Could have been
The brother I never had.
I don't really understand
Why he does the things he does
But when he cries
I know he's not crying
Just because.

When I'm with Cian
I take his hand
I'm proud to be his brother
No one knows him
The way I do
I wouldn't have another.

Christopher McCallan

From early on we included Christopher in our decisions about Cian and the reasons why certain things happened. We answered his questions carefully and he was part of the planning process behind much of our decision-making. Quite often there was a pay-off by default. Christopher got to enjoy all the new toys and trips and fun therapies too. Therapists fussed over him and bought him little gifts when they were giving something to Cian. Despite the chaotic madness, he thought it was cool to have a garden like a playground and opportunities to do a lot of fun stuff. In a safari truck in Africa, bungee jumping in Covent Garden, in Waterworld outside Alberfo, in the playground of Scoil

Íosagáin, he thanked God for Cian's autism. It is his way of seeing the glass half-full rather than half-empty.

The "A" word that once threatened us, keeping us at arm's length, grieving and sore for what might have been, often defines us now, but we are happy to let autism define our lives if it means it does not have to define Cian's.

I am not sure if Cian knows he is different. When he bursts into tears sometimes, for no apparent reason, when he comes to me staring silently into the gulf between his world and mine, I bleed inwardly. When he looks about him and looks back with only the ability to express himself with one word – "sad" – I want to sink my teeth in the thing that took him away from us and left him in such a compromised state. I want to claw out the eyes of those who prefer to turn the other way and refuse to acknowledge that treatments for autism do exist. Yes, I can accept my child. Yes, I can live with autism. But to live with the silence? The lack of accountability? The lack of urgency to secure autism-specific services? I struggle to live with that.

I still mourn, at times – when Cian is having a bad day, when I can't figure out the reason; when I see a boy about his age kicking ball and hanging out with his mates as I drive past a youth club; when Christopher goes for a ride on his bike on his own and Cian stares out the window after him; when I see yet another child like mine and a mother trying to cope.

Sometimes it is mothers and fathers like me who have helped me to cope. The resilience, the generosity, the perseverance and sense of humour of parents I have met and corresponded with on this journey have never ceased to amaze me, buoying me up when my own coping skills are

AILEEN McCALLAN

waning. Each of them is doing whatever they have to do to ensure that their child gets everything they need to live the best life possible. The best information, resources, ideas, support and encouragement I have received have come from other parents. If we could be relieved from our twenty-four/seven caring duties, I think we could take over the world. We would make a great government. Our children would come first.

As well as parents, many "angels" have fluttered in and out of our lives, with that natural ability to take Cian as they find him, from the health visitor I christened Halle Berry to Donna and her family – thank God she still flutters in and out with two other little angels, Luan and Mia, crawling behind her, for now she is a mother – and, yes, Cian sensed her unborn baby from early on and has been a little cool with her ever since. Some new "angels" have dropped in: Eleanor, who patiently teaches Cian piano; Patricia, Cian's swimming coach, who would shrivel up like a prune in the water just to give him a few extra strokes. Then there are the teachers and assistants who go above and beyond, like Cian's assistant Geraldine, who offers to take him home one day when I have to be somewhere else. The old twinge in my throat flares up. This is so much more than minding Cian. This is a little peace of mind. . . .

I still don't know what the future holds for Cian but I'm pretty sure that there will always be people out there who will care for and love him, even when it's not part of their job description. Even when it's not easy. And even when I'm no longer around.

* * *

332

One day I bumped into "Postman Pat", who told me that Matthew's parents, with the help of their church, had set up a local youth club for special needs children. I thought how Matthew's memory lives on, inspiring and achieving in an area where governing bodies fail, as such a service is practically non-existent in many communities.

It is a refining process, trying to makes sense of sorrow, grief and hard lessons in life that are supposed to make us more of whom we should be. Though some things have gnawed away at our strength and faith in better things . . . we must not end up in life bitter. It is easy to do. I need to enjoy where I am today because where I am today is a place I dreamed about two years ago. I have learned that inner peace comes from knowing you have done the best you can do, given the circumstances and the coping skills you have at the time. I have made peace with autism. I have made peace with myself.

A diet of hope and lots of faith gets me through these days. I live with a degree of uncertainty, caught up in the little furrowed crease between my eyebrows and a quickening of my breath sometimes. I still suffer a few gut-wrenching moments and my purse has developed leaky gut, but all of it comes out of love for our champion Cian, for he has the greatest battle to face every day, trying to exist in a mostly hostile and uncaring world that does not understand. Yes, we have invested much, but dividends are rolling in now – like this morning when he wrapped his arms around me. A sleepy head rested on my shoulder and I could feel the softness of his lips whisper "Mammy". It is the sweetest joy.

Even though he remains aloof, he is no longer

disconnected. He can now participate in family get-togethers, even a noisy New Year's Eve party. His uncles Terry and Phelim remark the change in him. He spends most of his time with his granny and granddad while his cousins play PSPs and Nintendos and text on mobile phones, leaving me wondering why I worry about Cian's social skills. When he gets tired, he goes to his Uncle Sean and looks up at him.

"I want go bed."

Sean is taken unawares. "Good man, Cian, you know whose house you're in and you know to ask permission too. I think you are the only one." He throws a snide glance at the other thirty-five cousins spilling out from the sitting room in the kitchen. Everyone laughs. Sean shows him up to his bedroom and later he reappears just in time for "Auld Lang Syne". I kiss him and wish him a Happy New Year, glad that he has been able to join the party at last.

Sometimes he takes people by surprise, mostly elderly folk who don't quite know what to make of him. If there is a connection, it is simply the power of love. If there is an awakening, it is the human spirit transcending the imperfection of the human body.

EPILOGUE

My en suite door creaks. A lid rattles, water trickles and a toilet flushes. The lid rattles and the door creaks again. A sleepy smile curls around my lips. My son only has to wee to make my day, and I am not even up yet. The duck-down duvet is tugged back and a little torso wraps itself around me. A small hand explores the back of my neck, my face, feeling if my eyes are open or closed. Giggling and playful, he hums a tune, pulling my half-wakened body close. There is no denying. Cian loves his mammy.

Eddy Dee starts talking. Cian sits up abruptly and stares at my radio alarm clock, tuned to ICRfm. Cian leans across me, "Press the button," and pushes OFF.

"Ah, Cian, Eddy Dee will not be too happy with you . . . he'll come back to haunt you in ten minutes, you know . . ."

I turn on my back and reach out to hold him and wish him a happy birthday. He shows immediate delight that I am awake, leaps on top of my tummy, jockey-style, and laughs into my eyes.

Throwing himself down again, he starts to play with my hair. As we stretch out side by side, Laura stirs in her bedroom. Slowly, gradually, I become aware of Cian's endless chatter and mutterings.

"Lawa's quing . . . sad . . . what happened . . . okay. Press the button . . . I want mote."

I hold my breath and strain to listen. The pronunciations are distorted, the tone is flat, but there is no doubt about it: *Cian is talking to me.* I can interpret every one of his mumblings.

"Laura's crying, sad. What happened? That's okay. Press the button . . . I want the remote."

A fizz of excitement builds up inside me. He thinks Laura is crying. He is telling her it is okay, that he doesn't want the radio on. He wants the television. I lift myself up on one elbow and turn towards him. He gazes at me, his eyes connecting beautifully with mine . . .

"Cian, Laura is not crying . . . Laura is not sad. Laura is waking up."

Cian suddenly stops verbalising and looks at me. A full smile spreads across his face. *He knows I understand him.* Excited and playful, he pushes in against me.

"Tickles."

I tickle him until Christopher and Laura appear with birthday presents and want to know what time the party is at.

We are going to The Carlton Redcastle Hotel for Cian's birthday. It is only thirty minutes from us. It boasts a wonderful spa pool and a very kind manager called Michelle has agreed to allow us to use their leisure facilities for the day. Cian's school friends and teachers and helpers are coming. We buy *Thomas the Tank Engine* balloons and cups and plates and a tablecloth to decorate the table. It is going to be a real party. Cian has never had a real birthday party, not with friends and candles and balloons. I bake a cake and buy some candles. Maybe this time he will blow out his own candles.

Cian has a brilliant birthday party. The children love the pool and Cian is in awe of his *Thomas the Tank Engine* table, covered in streamers and balloons and birthday cake. We sing "Happy Birthday" as Cian clambers on a chair to lean forward in the middle of all of us to blow out his own candles. I point at a banner and ask Cian his age. He shouts "Ten" and everyone claps and sings "Happy Birthday" again.

* * *

Later the children want to go to the beach.

They undress quickly along with Cian, who rips off his clothes and runs, arms outstretched, down the shore.

"AREEBAREEBAAAAAAAAAA."

Christopher and Laura disappear behind the rocks.

An elderly lady walks down the path dressed for a walk. Her pale navy scarf covers her head and is tucked in under the lapels of her coat. She nods and smiles.

Cian, son of Dian Cecht, God of Healing of the Tuatha Dé Danann, is running, naked and swirling, his arms outstretched in the late afternoon sunlight. How vulnerable he is. That is what I am thinking as the sky, the Swilly and little Mowgli are mottled together in a shimmering silvery light surrounded by the sultry purple blue hue of the Donegal hills. Free as a butterfly. A freedom to be envied.

Without lifting her eyes off Little Mowgli, she pulls her scarf a little tighter and nods her head at the great beauty that surrounds us.

"You know what?" Her voice is shy of a whisper. "Next stop's heaven."

Christopher and Laura reappear, look up and wave. Immediately we wave back. Cian is running back along the water again, free and full of birthday cake. Suddenly he turns and looks up. Two hundred yards of rock and sand stretch between us as he strains to focus. Very slowly, the right hand moves and points upwards, shaking to the left and right. A ray of sunshine splits through a torn cloud and streams down on him – beaming him up. I can't be sure but I think he is smiling. So am I, and I can't help thinking a little piece of heaven is already here.

RESOURCES

All about Autism

Irish Autism Action
National Office
41 Newlands, Mullingar, Co. Westmeath
Phone: +353 (0)44 9331609
Email: kevin@autismireland.ie
Web: www.autismireland.ie
Charity Number: 14656
Patron: Keith Duffy

Diagnostic and Assessment Centre
Solas Centre, St Gabriel's Road, Dollymount, Dublin 3
Phone: +353(0)1 8531572 Fax: +353 (0)1 8531577
Email: solas@autismireland.ie

Opening hours for both offices are 9am to 5pm,
Monday to Friday.

Irish Society for Autism: www.iol.ie/~isa1
National Autistic Society (UK): www.nas.org.uk
Autism Society of America: www.autism-society.org

Educational Support Services
www.saoirsesupportservice.com
www.senac.co.uk

A Variety of Educational and Therapeutic Programmes
Parents Education as Autism Therapists:
www.peatni.org
The Son-Rise Program: www.son-rise.org
Relationship Development Intervention: www.rdi.com
Verbal Behaviour: www.verbalbehaviornetwork.com
Coping and Dealing with Sensory Issues:
www.out-of-sync-child.org

Biomedical/Dietary Interventions

UK and Europe
www.treatingautism.com

USA
www.talkaboutcuringautism.org
www.generationrescue.org

Magazine
The Autism File – a quarterly support journal for parents of autistic children: www.autismfile.com